# THE COFFEE DIARY

a novel by Caroline Kellems

# THE COFFEE DIARY

a novel by Caroline Kellems

MACADAM CAGE

MacAdam/Cage
155 Sansome Street, Suite 550
San Francisco, CA 94104
www.MacAdamCage.com

Library of Congress Cataloging-in-Publication Data

Kellems, Caroline.
The coffee diary / Caroline Kellems.
    p. cm.
ISBN 978-1-59692-363-8
1. Americans—Guatemala—Fiction. 2. Inheritance and succession—Fiction.
3. Coffee plantations—Guatemala—Fiction. 4. Guatemala—Fiction. I. Title.
PS3611.E4235C64 2009
813'.6—dc22

                                                                    200902891

Manufactured in the United States of America.
10  9  8  7  6  5  4  3  2  1

Book and jacket design by Dorothy Carico Smith.

*This book is dedicated to my two beautiful daughters,*
*Caroline and Andrea, who were the inspiration for the story.*

# CHAPTER ONE

WHEN VIOLENCE TAKES A LOVED ONE, WE ARE NEVER PREPARED. I THOUGHT my father would always be there, that I had time to make up for the rebellion that drove me from home. But my apology would never be heard.

It was two years ago when I received the phone call. "Veronica, you'd better catch the first flight home. I hate to be the one to tell you, but your mother is in no condition to talk. Your Uncle Carlos has her on tranquilizers."

"What did you say? Who is this? What's happened?"

"Your father refused to pay the extortionists, and the bastards killed him. The whole town is up in arms."

At first the information refused to register. Then it slowly began to sink in.

The voice belonged to Guillermo, a family friend and owner of the funeral business in Moyuta, my hometown in Guatemala.

I hung up the phone, collapsed on the nearest piece of furniture, a living room chair, and stared blankly out the window. An hour, maybe two, passed before I overcame my initial shock and made the necessary arrangements to return.

I was like an observer at the funeral, disconnected from the events around me. I kept my stay in Moyuta brief, wasting no time in getting back to my life in San Francisco, back to my reality. In his will, among other things, my father left me his two coffee farms. I couldn't bring myself to think about them, so I entrusted both properties to my great-uncle Carlos who lived nearby.

Back in California, I immersed myself in work, buried my memories and thoughts of home beneath day-to-day activities. I knew I'd have to deal with the property eventually, but put it off until the day another unanticipated phone call summoned me. Moyuta's mayor wanted to buy *Las Marías,* one of the coffee farms, and build a low-income housing project on it.

Was it for sale? I didn't know.

I had to return.

"Welcome to Guatemala," the flight attendant said when we touched down. Passengers gripped their arm rests, brakes screeched, engines roared. Excitement filled the cabin as the plane taxied to the terminal. Applause broke out. Faithful Catholics crossed themselves. I smiled—a typical arrival. Had things changed? So far it didn't seem like it.

I glanced out the window. Behind the private hangars and the tree-lined runway loomed a rambling metropolis of four million—beyond the city a land dotted with volcanoes, native customs, and centuries-old traditions.

This was where I was born and spent my childhood: where people open their doors wide to friends, family, and neighbors, where faithful towns-people and villagers throng to white steepled churches. But even here, in this seemingly idyllic land, criminals extort and murder, justice rarely plays out, and guns are the final court of law.

In this country, two percent of the population owns more than ninety percent of the land. The Spanish *conquistadores* dominated the native population and forced them into servitude, creating a deeply entrenched class system which continues to this day. The poor struggle their entire lives, yet barely scrape together enough to eat. My family ranked toward the top of the social scale—not ultra-rich, but well off, wealthy by Moyuta standards. Like most Guatemalans who grow up here, I took the class system for granted and didn't discern the injustice of it until I moved to the United States.

The U.S. legal system was also surprising. Known criminals are assumed innocent until proven guilty. That's not the way of things in Guatemala.

With discontent rife in these fertile lands, young men search for work in *El Norte,* looking for the American dream, or become involved in politics or organized crime, the only tangible means of acquiring wealth. A civil war ravaged the country for thirty-five years; the Peace Agreements were finally signed in 1996. Left over was a penchant for weapons and a distrust of authority.

I glanced toward the edge of the runway, where men and boys crouched in the branches of trees, looking out toward the airport, watching planes taking off and landing. Though I couldn't see them, I knew they were there; they were always there, wishing, hoping, longing for a flight away from here, to somewhere, anywhere.

I disembarked the aircraft, my Birkenstocks clanking on the metal stairs and my daypack hanging from one shoulder. Business travelers carried laptops. I left mine at my San Francisco apartment. I had taken a leave of absence so work wouldn't interfere with the decisions I had to make.

I stepped into the warm night and followed the other passengers to an open door. An airline attendant, clipboard in hand, turned to me. "Is this your final destination, ma'am?"

"I'm not sure." Then I caught myself. "Oh, yes. Yes, it is."

Buffed granite floors shone. Indigenous children smiled from posters hung on the gray walls of the long hallway leading to the immigration counters. I waited my turn in the line of passengers.

"*Buenas noches*," I said to the woman behind the counter after she motioned me forward.

I fumbled with both passports, then handed her my Guatemalan one.

"*Ah, usted es Guatemalteca*. Welcome home."

I swung my daypack over my shoulder and headed to the carousel. Dogs barked on the other side of the curtain as they sniffed the luggage for drugs. Guatemala is a major stopover for cocaine and other prohibited substances smuggled between South and North America.

A uniformed officer eyed the crowd. I resisted the urge to pet the on-duty German shepherd beside him.

When my brown duffle bag came into view, I pulled it off the conveyor. The customs official waved me on. Outside, I pushed my way through the waiting crowd.

"*Con permiso, con permiso*."

I searched for my half-brother, who had agreed to meet me at the airport. Distinguishing anyone in the confusion was close to impossible. Relatives shouted to arriving loved ones. Children raced to and fro, slipping underneath the metal railing that held back the waiting crowd. Peasant women wearing sandals and clad in hand-loomed traditional costumes jostled women in high heels. Men in suits and ties pressed against humble villagers wearing cowboy hats and smelling like campfires. Tattooed young men skulked around the edges. I kept my hands firmly on my bags.

"Miss, would you like to go to Antigua?" a driver offered, thinking I was a tourist with my light hair and jeans.

"*No, gracias,*" I said.

"Veronica! Veronica!" I turned toward a familiar voice. Juan José rushed over with his young wife, Ita. "There you are! We wondered if you'd ever get here." I smiled wryly, admonishing myself. I knew I'd put it off far too long. Not counting the trip home for the funeral, I'd been gone ten years. I left when I was eighteen, never looking back.

We hugged for a moment. Juan José was my size, five-seven. He felt wiry in my embrace. I stepped back to look at him. His dark hair was short, slicked down. His glasses emphasized his large brown eyes. We shared little family resemblance.

"You look great, Juan-Jo. Married life has agreed with you." Glancing at the young woman next to him, I introduced myself. Her dark eyes smiled at me. I recognized her from photos—glossy shoulder-length black hair and a slight figure. We hugged and gave each other the traditional kiss on the cheek. "I can see you've been taking good care of my *hermanito.*"

"Oh, Veronica, I try my best, but you know Juan José, he doesn't let me do much. We've been so anxious for your visit." Juan José grabbed my bag and carried my things to the waiting car. We talked about the flight, about the weather. We talked about my work, but not about why I'd returned.

"Guatemala has changed a lot since you were living here," Juan José said as we raced down the silent *Avenida de las Americas* to his home.

"Is that a good thing, or bad?" I asked. "I hadn't expected any change at all."

"It's been a long time."

We drove onto the main street of the gated neighborhood where they lived.

"Thanks so much for picking me up and letting me stay with you tonight," I said.

He glanced at me, his expression puzzled. "Vero, you're my sister. What's mine is yours. After all, family is family."

"Thanks, Juan-Jo." Tears filled my eyes. I'd been a rotten sister, never visiting and hardly writing.

"What are your plans?" Ita asked, changing the subject. "Will you be with us tomorrow or are you headed out to the farm right away?"

"I need to get to Moyuta as soon as I can. I have my first meeting with the mayor the day after tomorrow and I need to get settled in."

The car slowed and Juan José announced, "Here we are. Home at last."

He grabbed my bags before I could say anything and took them into the spare bedroom.

"I have something for you, Veronica." He left for a moment and returned with keys and a cellular phone. It was an extra one of his, which he urged me to take so I could stay in touch. He had to be at the hospital early and said he probably wouldn't see me in the morning.

I looked at the familiar set of keys hanging on Mom's favorite chain— keys to the gates of our farms and to our family home. The keys to my past.

I protested when he handed me the keys to his SUV.

"This is the car Mom left two years ago. I've been using it, but it's as much yours as mine. So consider it yours now."

I nodded. "I'll call in a few days."

"If you need anything, just let us know."

"Thank you, *hermanito*. Goodnight."

I slept fitfully, my mind full of doubts and conflict. Did I have the strength to go through with this? Should I have even come?

How could I think that? I couldn't give up my home and heritage so easily. Would the money be worth losing the property? In the end, what would Dad have wanted?

Sunlight filtered through the curtains. I took my bags out and set them by the front door, ready at last to make the journey home. Home to the family estate, home to my father entombed in his family vault, home to the coffee trees nurtured under the partial shade of taller, flowering trees.

Juan José had left a note on the kitchen counter. It read: "Vero, there is fresh coffee in the thermos. Take it with you. Good luck."

Ita slept soundly. I stowed my bags and the thermos in the back of the car and left.

I drove slowly, unsure of the way. Guatemala City had grown; new overpasses and roadways had sprouted in my absence. Somehow I managed to find my way onto the highway toward Moyuta.

The closer I drew to the small mountain town, the more conflicted my feelings became. I had anticipated the guilt over my abrupt departure as a teen, the anxiety about returning to the scene of my father's murder, but the excitement to be home again was unexpected.

Soon the familiar landscape came into view. Pine trees brushed the sky. They rose on the distant hills, dark green sentinels against the lighter open pastures. The fields were silent and empty. Our family home lay beyond the shaded coffee trees at the top of the hill.

A tree-lined boundary hid the barbed wire that surrounded the farm. Ours was one of many such fences where workers had strung wire over live posts that took root and grew into trees.

I stopped the car and hesitated before the padlocked metal gate, my heart pounding. I wiped my wet palms on my jeans. What would I find inside?

A cracked wooden sign reading *Las Marías* hung crookedly on the post. Fumbling with the keys, I gazed past the gate at my inheritance. The serene pine forest alive with a light breeze calmed me. I unlocked the gate and drove in. The car slowly bumped along the gravel road. As it became steeper, I switched to four-wheel drive. I parked a short distance from the house, got out, and paused. As I approached the front door, my eyes were drawn to one side.

*It was here.*

Two years had passed since my father's murder. I gazed at the four large pines, witnesses to our family's tragedy, half expecting to see pools of blood beneath the trees. Instead, birds sang and trees swayed and creaked in the breeze. Wooden planks, some riddled with holes, still hung on the trees. My father had nailed them together as he prepared for his attackers. New bark grew where bullets had blasted the trunks.

*Why, Dad? Why didn't you run? You didn't have to confront them.*

After the murder, the townspeople said my father was brave to stand up to the extortionists—eight against one—refusing to give in or run. He killed two before they captured him. The remaining six retaliated viciously.

My jaw tightened and stomach churned as I thought of what they put my father through. I had tried not to think about it since his murder. If he'd chosen to take the easy way out, he might still be here today. But I knew he couldn't do that. My father didn't crack under pressure; he was a man of principle and honor.

Hand-rolled cigarette butts and shell casings from automatic weapons had dotted the area where he had been found. His murderers probably mocked and taunted while they tortured him—just another evening's work. That was the Guatemala I didn't want to face.

I shuddered and forced my gaze back to my family home. My father built this house for his American bride when they returned to Guatemala after graduating from college. He used pine, cypress, cedar, and mahogany, mostly from trees on the farm. A local quarry provided slate rock for the base and first three feet of the walls. The upper half was wood with exposed beams. Large bay windows, a source of amazement to the villagers, provided sweeping views of the Pacific Ocean to the south and El Salvador's green valleys to the east.

Soon after the murder, my mother locked the doors to our family home. She left Guatemala and moved to California to be near my aging grandparents, and far from reminders of my father's violent end.

I unlocked the front door and peered in. The sour smells of mildew and dust assailed me. My eyes adjusted to the dim light as I entered quietly, afraid of disturbing any sleeping ghosts.

A recliner and a sofa huddled under dirty sheets, gray phantoms of our past. A broken dining room chair rested on its side in the front room. An old telephone directory lay on the floor, its binding at an angle and the pages folded inward.

Through the dirt-streaked bay windows, the town of Moyuta was visible in the distance, just below the crest of the volcano. Sunlight reflected on the church's silver-domed roof. In 1976, the year before I was born, and the year my father began construction on our home, a disastrous earthquake shook Guatemala, killing twenty-five thousand people and toppling towns all over the country. Reinforced concrete block houses topped with corrugated metal replaced the adobe structures and their quaint tile roofs. Even the original church was rebuilt in this fashion—not as pretty, but definitely safer in a place that sways and rocks to its own seismic rhythms.

Only shadows remained on the walls where photographs once paid tribute to our happy lives. The hinges squeaked as I pushed open my old bedroom door. The room was empty except for dust and trash. The open closet door revealed a box in the back. I rummaged through the papers scattered on top of it—loose letters from high school friends I'd made during the brief time we lived in San Diego, old quizzes from the Colonial School in Guatemala City.

Underneath them, I discovered *The Coffee Diary*. My mother had given me this journal on my fourteenth birthday, the year so much happened in my life. Though my solace as a teen, I had completely forgotten about it. My interest aroused, I picked up the book and an envelope dropped out, falling behind the box. I ignored it, transfixed by the diary. I shook dust from the cover, and it fell open to a well-worn page in the center, the ink stained and smudged from tears of frustration.

> *June 26th, 1991*
> *Dear Diary,*
> *I hate Dad. Why did he do this? Today a boy showed up at our doorstep—to stay. My apparent half-brother. He's nine-years-old! That means Dad was fooling around when I was a kid. Was Mom not enough for him? Was I not enough for him? Will more "mistakes" show up? You'd think we would have known about him before. It's not like Moyuta's a big city.*
> *I hate Dad. He's ruined my life!*
> *Mom totally freaked. We left last night for California. She says she can't forgive him. What about me? I was happy at home. Now I've got to make a new start in a strange place. Do they have any idea how hard it is to be new in high school?*
> *I hate him for messing up our family. Things will never be the same.*

Five months after we left, my father arrived in San Diego to bring us back home. By that time Mom and I were glad to return.

I swallowed back the emotion that welled up around the old words, echoes of my earlier unhappiness. My relationship with my father had never totally recovered. I slipped the diary into my shoulder bag to scan through later.

I wandered outside, sat on the steps, and gazed down on the fields and trees. The sounds of the forest lulled me.

My home. I love the quiet beauty of this place.

Gravel crunched. I turned toward the sound. A man wearing black rubber boots and carrying a woven bag approached. His hand rested on a sheathed machete hanging from his belt.

"*Buenas tardes,*" he called.

"*Sí?*" I answered, feeling vulnerable alone on the hillside. "*Quién es usted?*"

The man wore ragged clothes and a respectful smile. In the manner of humble villagers, he didn't look straight at me, but beyond me to avoid confrontation. Though the man looked harmless enough, in spite of his machete, I tensed as he approached. I hadn't expected anyone to be here.

"Are you *señorita Vero*?"

I nodded. "And you are?"

"Juan Bautista, at your service."

"What's your business here?"

"*El doctor Carlos* sent me to invite you to his house for lunch." He unsheathed his machete and stabbed it carelessly into the ground.

I jerked my head up, startled.

He shifted his feet and stared at the ground. "Is there anything in particular you need me to do? I'll be working here all week."

"I don't know," I said, relieved. "I've only just arrived."

I admonished myself for being so jumpy. *Veronica, he's only a worker.*

"I'll start by repairing those fences." He pointed to some areas where barbed wire had come apart and posts were missing.

The fences weren't the only things that needed work; no maintenance had been done since my father's murder.

In the empty garden, plastic bags and trash littered the ground where flowers once grew. The rockwork, my mother's pride and joy, was in disarray. Fallen stones had not been replaced. Though I knew I'd love to have the rockwork looking as it had years before, fences took priority over gardens.

I hadn't expected my great-uncle Carlos to send anyone to work at *Las Marías*. I had told him over the telephone I'd take care of the repairs myself—if I decided to stay.

The mention of lunch brought hunger to the forefront of my mind. I hadn't eaten anything since I left the city. My watch indicated that it was half past noon. Lunch sounded wonderful, so I took a deep breath, and took a last look at my home.

I bade Juan Bautista goodbye and drove down the steep, tree-lined driveway, avoiding the branches and rocks scattered over the road. Moments later, I parked my car in front of my great-grandparents' old house and stepped out onto the cement block street in the town's center. A sign hung over the sidewalk: *CLÍNICA MÉDICA: DR. CARLOS VILLAGRÁN*. I peered into the dim interior.

"*Buenas tardes*," I called. "Is anyone here?"

My palms felt damp again and my head light from hunger.

"Who is it?" a female voice asked.

"It's me, Veronica. *Está mi tio en casa?*"

"Carlos, your niece is here."

"Vero! *Pasá adelante!* Come in, come in!"

"*Con permiso,*" I called out.

"Vero, this is your home. Please don't be shy."

Encouraged by his words, I entered. I walked toward the light streaming through a doorway that opened onto a courtyard. Tio Carlos, a little rounder and quite a bit grayer than the last time I'd seen him, sat at an outdoor table with a plate of food in front of him. A small, thin, energetic woman about ten years his junior fussed around him. I vaguely remembered her as one of my uncle's many admirers and a friend of my mother's.

"Vero! *Mija!*" Tio Carlos said. "I was hoping you would come today. Did you get a late start?"

"No, I've been at the farm looking over the house."

"I sent Juan Bautista over there in case you arrived. Did you see him?" I nodded.

"He was supposed to call me and let me know when you got there. Of course he forgot. You just can't trust anyone to do the simplest things these days."

Tio Carlos labored to his feet to greet me. I leaned over and gave him a big hug. He felt solid in his roundness. "I'm glad you're staying with us, Vero. I've missed you."

"Thanks. I know I've been awful about not visiting. I appreciate your help with the farms."

"It's nothing. I've driven to *Las Marías,* but *Ojo de Agua* isn't as accessible. *El caporál* takes care of it." Concern creased his face. "Too bad both production and prices have dropped. I guess you've been disappointed with the income."

"No, Tio. I trust you completely. I understand what the coffee business is like. Some crop years are better than others. If the coffee hasn't done so well, it's because no one was here to supervise."

He sighed, seemingly relieved. "I was worried. I tried to keep the accounts updated, in case you had questions, but I'm afraid they're a mess. Do you want to see the books?"

"Not now—another time."

He sat back down and gazed at me. "It's been a long while since you've spent time here. We all expected you to come home after you finished at the university."

I hung my head. "I screwed up. I should have done things differently, said goodbye to my relatives, come to visit occasionally. I hope you can forgive me."

He waved his hand to indicate my apology was unnecessary. "That was a long time ago. We shouldn't have to be forever responsible for what we do as teenagers. The most important thing is that you're back. You flew in last night?"

I nodded. "I got in late and stayed with Juan José and Ita."

The woman behind him coughed.

He turned to her and said, "Oh, I'm sorry, *mi amor*. Do you remember María Celia, Vero?"

"Yes, I do. Nice to see you again."

We embraced.

"Likewise," she said. "We've been looking forward to your visit."

"It's good to be here. The farm looks beautiful. I guess my worries about returning were for nothing."

Her forehead wrinkled in concern. "I don't know. The mayor has been telling everyone in town that *Las Marías* will soon be his. Is that true?"

"Why would he say that? I'm not at all sure I want to sell. I told him I needed to return before making that decision." I paused, glancing first at Tío Carlos then at María Celia. "I really don't know what I'll do. But if I do decide to sell, at least I'll still have *Ojo de Agua*."

Tío Carlos' head jerked up, a question in his eyes.

"It sure has had us wondering," María Celia said. "You told Carlos last week you were unsure about what to do, so when the mayor told us you were coming to sign the papers, we didn't know what to think."

"Have you spoken to him about it?" I asked.

Tío Carlos' expression smoothed over. "He called a few days ago. You told him you'd be staying with us and he wanted us to remind you of your appointment tomorrow."

"As if I could forget."

"Did he offer you a good price?"

"Two million dollars—cash."

Tío Carlos whistled under his breath. He cleared his throat.

"I have two pieces of advice for you. Think long and hard about giving up the farm. It's a tie to your family and past. Second, in this country you must be very careful in your business dealings. You've been away a long time. You don't know how things are here anymore, but the fact he has all that cash should make you suspicious. You can't deposit that much cash in any bank and I don't need to tell you how dangerous it would be for you to have it in your possession. If you decide to sell, insist on a bank check or money transfer to a trustworthy bank. Better, a bank outside Guatemala."

"Carlos," María Celia interrupted, "where are our manners? Let the poor girl have some food before she faints from hunger. Veronica must be starved." She turned to me. "Please have a seat."

I took a chair across from Tio Carlos. My stomach rumbled and my mouth watered as she brought out a steaming dish of stewed chicken with rice.

"Remember, Veronica," Tio Carlos said. "This is your home and we are family."

I finished eating in silence. I had a lot to think about.

María Celia sat down next to me. "How's your mother?"

"She's doing well. Thanks."

"I got a card from her last Christmas, but it didn't say much. Is she still teaching?"

"Yes, she earned her certification last year and has been teaching at a school near San Diego. She loves it."

"She always enjoyed homeschooling you. She said you were an ideal student."

"I don't know about that. She's a gifted teacher." I remembered my things outside. "Tio, where can I put my car?"

"Celia, open the gate for Vero so she can bring her car in."

Outside, I maneuvered the car through the gate into the compound. High cinderblock walls muffled the noise from town and protected the house from thieves. I took my duffle bag and daypack to the room that María Celia had prepared.

When I returned to the patio, I found the hammock sagging with Tio Carlos' weight.

He heard me approach and said, "Come over here, Vero. I haven't finished lecturing yet."

I dragged over a nearby patio chair.

He spoke softly. "You must be discreet with the information I am about to give you. These things are known, but talking about them does no one any good. The mayor of Moyuta has strong ties to organized crime.

I raised my eyebrows and didn't say anything. He'd alluded to it earlier when he warned me about business dealings with cash.

"He's a dangerous man. Rumors link him to theft and murder. People who cross his path often disappear. Mayor Jaime is ambitious. His political power gives him access to illegal activities. He's able to move around without attracting suspicion and takes a cut on drug shipments coming across the border from El Salvador. He's made a lot of money that way."

"What about the authorities?"

Tio Carlos snorted in disgust. "You've been away too long. Around here, he is the authority. Government officials are the most corrupt. That's why people go into politics, or law enforcement, for that matter."

"How did a man like that get elected?"

"He employs a lot of people, many of them thugs. They threatened the villagers just before the election."

"Threatened?"

"They said a vote for an opponent would bring trouble. People thought their village might be torched at night, or the water source poisoned. No one wanted to take the risk. You know how naïve villagers are. Most of them decided they'd better vote for Mayor Jaime. The rest just didn't vote."

"So he preyed on their fear to get into office?"

"Don't most politicians do that?"

"I don't know. I would hate to think so. I expected things to be better now."

"I agree, dear. The entire town thought things would improve after your father's murderers were dealt with." He lowered his voice even more. "I have to tell you there are people who believe it wasn't just eight men that night at the farm. I've heard there might have been one or two who got away." He waved his hand. "It's all just rumor. Anyway, it really doesn't make much difference. For every culprit gone, several take his place. It's a plague, but unfortunately it's reality in Guatemala. Things quieted down for a while, but now kidnappings and extortion are rampant again, along with murders and other crimes."

"Do you feel safe here?"

"I'm the town doctor. I take care of the sick, including Mayor Jaime and his henchmen. They need me. I worry about you, my dear. If you decide to sell, I'll be so disappointed. If you don't, I'll be afraid for your life."

"No one back in California knows about my discussions with the mayor, not even Mom. I told my friends and people from work I was coming to Guatemala, but not why. I didn't tell Mom beforehand because I thought she would try to stop me. She's still bitter."

"Bitter? You mean about Quique's death?"

"That, of course. Then there were all the things leading up to it: the phone calls, the threats, the extortion attempts. Someone targeted Dad."

"He was the wealthiest man in town. That's reason enough."

"I guess."

"So, Liz doesn't know you're here?"

I shook my head. "She has a chip on her shoulder about Guatemala, especially Moyuta. But I'll call her after I've met with the mayor. That way I'll know where I stand."

"Veronica, there is something I want you to have while you are here." Struggling out of the hammock, Tio Carlos went into the back bedroom. He came out with a small .22 caliber handgun.

"Take this and keep it in your bag. Have it with you at all times. You may need it."

He held the weapon out to me, handle first. I stared at the silver semi-automatic.

I wavered with indecision. Then I took it.

# CHAPTER TWO

I SAT IN THE MAYOR'S OFFICE WHERE I'D BEEN INSTRUCTED TO WAIT. MY purse, heavy with the gun, lay on the desk in front of me. My heart pounded. Fear? Apprehension? I wasn't sure. All the things I'd heard about the mayor swirled in my thoughts.

The secretary poked her head into the room. "*Un momentito, por favor.* Mayor Jaime will be right with you."

No windows broke the monotony. The four thick walls, plastered and chipped, exposed adobe brick beneath the yellow paint. A faded blue and white national flag stood in the corner. Among certificates and honorary plaques on the wall—the kind the government hands out like coins to beggars—hung a high school diploma, probably a fake.

A few minutes later, a large man entered, took off his Ray-Bans and put them into a case hung on his belt. He paused, allowing his squinty eyes to adjust. I took a deep breath and prepared myself.

"*Buenos días, Señorita Villagrán,*" his voice boomed. He leaned over the mahogany desk, hands supporting his weight, and stared at me. "We finally meet face to face. I've been looking forward to this. More than you know."

I instinctively drew back. After everything I'd heard, I certainly hadn't been looking forward to meeting him. He looked like a villain in a low-budget Western, his skin swarthy, his face pocked with acne scars. He was massive for a Guatemalan, probably weighing close to two hundred and ten pounds. His piglike eyes were his most unusual feature and his invasive stare made me uneasy.

Gathering myself, I held out my hand. "Mayor Jaime, I'm glad to make your acquaintance."

He crushed it in his gorilla-like grip.

I cringed.

He laughed, then let go and swung his heavy body into the swivel chair behind the desk.

My eyes narrowed. "Do we know each other from before? I've been gone for many years, but you look familiar."

His head cocked to one side. "How old are you, Veronica? Twenty-eight? Twenty-nine?"

"Twenty-eight."

"You moved to the city when you were young, correct? Like fifteen?"

"I was still fourteen when we moved to the city so I could attend high school, but I came here on school vacations until I left for the university in California."

"This is not a very big place. We saw each other. I remember you. I remember your whole family. How could I not? Your family was like royalty here. Besides, how many young blondes lived in Moyuta? Only you."

"I guess."

The feeling stayed with me. Maybe the mayor was right. I must have seen him around town in my youth. As he'd said, it was a small place.

"Let's get down to business," he said abruptly. "I'm not one for beating around the bush. I'm sure you've heard all about me. I know. People talk. Especially in a small town." He appeared pleased that people might have warned me about him. "Have we come to an agreement yet?"

"I—I only got here yesterday. I still need time to think about it." I avoided meeting his eyes by studying the cracks in the wall, noting every discoloration, then staring at the papers littering his desk.

"I thought you came back to sign these papers." He nudged a folder toward me. "Do you need a pen?"

"I told you, what I need is time. After all, it's my family home."

"It's a good cause. People need housing. All the homes will be cement block with poured concrete floors and indoor bathrooms. The architect has just finished the plans for the project. Would you like to see them?" He reached for a three-ring binder lying on a shelf behind him.

"No, thanks. I need to make the decision to sell before I buy into your project. Besides, why *Las Marías*?"

"Water, electricity, access, and location. It's an ideal place. Really, Veronica, why is it so hard to decide? Surely that place holds painful memories for you. It's been abandoned for several years. Besides, you no longer even live in Guatemala. I thought I'd be doing you a favor. Why would you want to keep this property?"

"With all due respect, Mayor Jaime, both of my farms have been in our family for generations. My uncle's been taking care of them for me."

He raised his eyebrows and seemed to be laughing at some secret joke. Then he continued, "I'm only asking for *Las Marías*, at least for now. You can keep *Ojo de Agua*. By the way, I'm sorry for what happened to your father. He was a very good man. A very *brave* one."

What kind of dealings had my father had with him? I fidgeted in my chair.

"This news doesn't make me happy. You're a smart young woman and I'm sure you understand the importance of not angering me. Every wasted day costs me money. I have people on my payroll waiting for this housing project to begin. And the workers aren't the only ones getting impatient. We're already drawing up papers for the people who will buy the homes."

I looked at him, horrified. "You're already selling the property?"

"No. Not just yet. But people are interested."

"I'm not sure what I want to do. Give me time."

"You have two weeks. Take it or leave it."

"Fine."

"I want to see you in a week. Perhaps you will have come to a decision by then."

"We can meet. But I doubt I'll have my decision made." I got up to leave.

"If I need to see you sooner, I'll be in touch. And Veronica," he continued, his beady eyes boring into me, "before you go, I want you to know I expect *yes* for an answer."

I breathed a sigh of relief as I left the *municipalidad*. I had been nervous when I had entered the mayor's office, but I was leaving it in indignation.

*How dare he?* Who did he think he was? How could he think putting on a little pressure could make me give up the farm and my family home? I felt less inclined to sell now than when I had first arrived.

My heart still pounded as I arrived at Tío Carlos' house. The coolness of the adobe-walled interior helped me compose myself. I unpacked, arranged my clothes neatly in the standup cedar armoire, and emptied my purse, keeping busy so my thoughts could settle. As I slipped the gun into my daypack, my father came to mind. He had always carried a gun. Several times when he needed it, he hadn't hesitated to use it. As I fumbled in the bag, my hand touched the journal.

I took it out and placed it on my lap. My finger traced the embossed letters, *The Coffee Diary 1991*. Opening it, I studied my handwriting—hesitant and less mature, but essentially the same.

We were comfortable that year. The business was expanding; the later traumas hadn't yet begun. We had recently built a wet mill on the farm to process the coffee cherries. Each deep red, ripe cherry has two beans inside covered by a parchment-like outer shell. After depulping, the coffee is fermented and washed in its thin, papery covering and set out on patios to dry in the sun. Organic certification required having our own processing facility and it was also necessary for producing the best coffee. This was the year when Dad began teaching me about coffee. He'd hoped I would eventually take over the farms.

After the wet mill became operational, my father's next project was a large storage building, or *bodega*, for the sacks of coffee in their dry parchment casing. Construction took four months and was finished just after my fourteenth birthday.

Monday through Friday, a team of fifteen to twenty laborers, mostly bricklayers and their assistants, came at seven in the morning and left at four. Saturday they were supposed to work half a day, but less than half ever did.

Each morning, a local woman and her daughter prepared food for the men at an outdoor kitchen. They set out bread and snacks for breakfast and brewed coffee in large pots. Broths were the general fare for the midday meal, along with thick, hand-patted tortillas cooked on a large clay *comal* over a wood fire.

Villagers survive on tortillas with black beans when times are good and tortillas seasoned with salt when they're not. Since the men could count on at least one good meal a day with us, we never had a problem finding workers.

Much to my mother's annoyance, Dad and I occasionally joined them for lunch. "Quique, why didn't you tell me you weren't eating with me?"

she would later say. "I had the table set and food steaming on the stove. I hate eating alone. I wouldn't have prepared so much."

Dad would respond, "I'm sorry, Liz. I should have told you. Serve it to us for dinner. Vero and I show the men our appreciation and respect by sharing an occasional meal with them. You know I like to do that."

"You're always busy making a good impression on everyone. What about me?"

He nuzzled her neck until she smiled and forgot her annoyance. "Stop!" she giggled. "Vero's going to get the wrong idea."

I enjoyed spending time with my father and the men, most of them simple, hard-working farmers. I didn't mind being around them as long as we kept our distance.

"Dad, let's sit over here," I once suggested, choosing a spot upwind from the workers.

"Why? The whole point is to eat with them."

"The men," I said, my eyes flitting over to them, "they smell."

"You have to learn tolerance. You know there isn't much water available in the villages for bathing."

"I know that, Dad. But can't you at least ask them to use deodorant?"

"It's not my place. Besides, they probably can't afford it."

I spent a lot of time working outdoors with Dad and sharing meals with the workers. I got to know most of them. I particularly remember don Chon as one of my favorites: a bricklayer's helper, a small man with a big heart, humble, polite and kind. Poor vision ensured he would never graduate to master bricklayer. Thick glasses magnified his dark eyes and he moved by shuffling along, taking small steps, his feet cautiously checking the ground. He did much of his work by feel, "seeing" with his hands. He always had a smile for me and a treat from his house.

"*Buenos días, don Chon,*" I greeted him every morning.

"*Buenos días, señorita Vero. Mi señora le mando este.*" He would hold out a small plastic bag with sweet honey candies his wife made. Sometimes he brought me mangos or other fruit from trees in his garden. On days when he had nothing to bring me, he lowered his gaze and his shoulders sagged. He would feel around in his pockets, turn them inside out, and show me his empty hands. "The dog must have taken it today." He'd shake his head. "I'll show him. I won't let him outsmart me tomorrow."

It seemed at first the project would go on forever, but all too soon we were saying goodbye to the last of the workers.

"*Señorita Vero,* don Chon told me, "*cuídese mucho.*"

"Thank you," I told him. "You take care, as well."

We patted each other's shoulders in the customary way of the peasants.

When Dad and I arrived home later that afternoon, Mom was waiting at the door, bursting with excitement. "I've got a great idea. We've put so much energy and effort into the *bodega* that I think we should celebrate its completion. I talked to Father Octaviano and he agreed to come over Saturday to bless the building. And of course we'll invite guests as well."

"This Saturday, Liz? A party so soon?" my father said in astonishment. He thought about it for a few minutes then decided it was a good idea. "Okay, you deal with the menu. I'll take care of the beverages."

A blessing celebration seemed strange to me at first, since Mom and Dad weren't religious. But what Mom really wanted was to host a party, to acknowledge and be part of all the effort and work that had gone into the project.

The next few days were spent organizing and making preparations; then out went the invitations and in came the food and drinks.

# CHAPTER THREE

*February 16, 1991*
*Dear Diary,*
*We had a party today. The blessing of the bodega. Hundreds of*
*people came. Music blasted, people ate, drank, and danced.*
*Dad flirted with women from town again. Why does he do that?*
*Tio Carlos got smashed. He told Dad one of our farms should be*
*his. What did he mean?*
*Tio asked me to dance. I didn't. What a jerk he is when he drinks.*
*He danced anyway. He fell and broke his leg. Serves him right.*

I closed the book; my scrawled words brought me back to that moment.

The bustle of activity began at five that morning. Roosters cleared their
throats and prepared to give their morning wake-up calls. Dawn glim-
mered over Chingo Volcano. From north to south, women streamed down
the highway—hefty, middle-aged women with grey-streaked hair dragging
a child or two with them; thin, angular, malnourished-looking women;
even pregnant women pushing toddlers ahead of them. They made their
way through the gate and into the farm carrying hens bound in newspaper and tied up with string. Feathered heads stuck out of these cylindrical
tubes, turning left and right, bright eyed, seeming to have no inkling they
would be tossed into cooking vats that morning.

As women set their pots over open fires, the sun peeked over the mountains, bathing the sky in the colors of dawn. The big meal to be served was the traditional *caldo de gallina* or old hen soup as my mother called it. The cooks started early; these tough old birds needed four or five hours of stewing to achieve a measure of tenderness. *Subanic*, a Mayan delicacy, also was on the menu. Like many traditional Guatemalan dishes, it contains meat in a heavy sauce seasoned with roasted and ground squash seeds, allspice, cinnamon, and native dried chilies. Preparing the food would take hours; eating it, minutes.

My parents had invited nearly a hundred people from town, relatives from Guatemala City, and villagers who helped in the construction. We knew this meant up to three hundred guests could arrive. After all, when the Villagráns had a party, all the townsfolk wanted to be there. Guatemalans love a party, and the bigger, the better. Each invitation might bring a family, their neighbors, and friends.

The harvest was over, the parchment coffee sacked up and stored in the new warehouse, but the area for the party adjoining the *bodega* still reeked of fermented coffee. Where the machinery had been, the ground was black and sticky from dried pulp.

Dad and his workers hosed down, scrubbed, and repaired the coffee patios for the event. They covered the empty tanks used for fermentation of the coffee beans after the depulping, and they painted the low cement wall bordering the patios, which was to serve as seating since we only found a hundred plastic chairs.

I helped one of Dad's workers set the white chairs in semi-circular rows under a green-and-white striped awning. We put a chair behind a table in the middle to serve as an altar. The communion wine would be a foretaste of the full blown party to follow.

No party is complete without liquor; Dad made sure there was plenty of that. Several kegs of Gallo beer, cases of Johnny Walker whisky, and plenty of soda waited in a corner of the patio where my father could keep an eye on them. He didn't want anyone getting sloshed before the party began. Large chests of ice were brought from Jutiapa, a town about an hour away, as there weren't enough freezers in town to produce the ice we'd need.

A dozen women chopped onions, potatoes, carrots, and *guisquíl*, a local variety of squash. Other women washed dishes and vegetables at the *pila,* a large cement sink. Nearby, an elderly lady with thick, strong hands wrung hens' necks while three others plucked and cleaned the slaughtered birds.

I turned away in disgust.

Padre Octaviano Bartolini was expected at ten thirty, with the blessing ceremony to begin a half-hour later. Ten thirty came and went. Mom's eyes kept returning to the gate. Eleven o'clock passed. I could see my mother getting anxious.

"Don't worry, Liz," my father told her. "You know how Guatemalans are. It's poor manners to arrive earlier than an hour after the party is supposed to start."

"I never arrive anywhere late."

"You aren't Guatemalan. Don't you remember arriving at that dinner party last year and finding our hosts not yet showered?"

Mom pursed her lips and didn't say anything.

At half past eleven, a few relatives from the city arrived. A little while later the elderly priest hobbled through the gate, carrying a traveling bag with the holy cloths, the silver chalice, wine, and wafers. He was unabashed at the meager crowd and set up his altar. About that time, I went up to the house and glanced down toward town. People jammed the road.

I raced down the hill. "Mom! They're coming!"

They came all right: friends and friends of friends, family and distant relatives. People of all sizes—fat, thin, tall, short, some dressed in lacy gowns and party clothes, others in blue jeans and cowboy boots. Most arrived on foot, many on horses, and a few in cars.

I ran to the gate to welcome everyone.

"*Pasen adelante! Bienvenidos!*" I said over and over as waves of people surged by.

When the flow of guests began to ebb, Dad stood on a chair and called for attention. "*Buenas tardes,*" he shouted several times to no avail. Then he gave an incisive whistle that cut through the air like a sharpened machete. Heads turned and voices stopped mid-sentence.

"*Muchas gracias por venir,*" he called out to the multitude. "Thank you for joining us. We are honored that you have come to witness as we ask God's blessing on our processing plant, our warehouse, and our farm. We thank God for our abundance and also ask his blessing on all of you—our family, friends, and neighbors."

The priest began his service under the rented canopy with much genuflection and gesturing. There were no microphones or sermon pamphlets to follow, but his audience knew their lines and said them at appropriate times. Hundreds of people lined up to receive a communion wafer dipped in wine.

The main distraction was the slap, slap, slap as the tortillas were patted, reminding the crowd of the coming feast. When the service ended, the priest sprinkled holy water on the *bodega* wall and blessed it in the name of the Father, the Son and the Holy Spirit. Amen.

As soon as the priest said "Amen," people dashed to find seats as if the melody had stopped during a game of musical chairs.

My father, along with my cousins Antonio and Mario, stood behind a large table pouring drinks, laughing and joking with friends. Dad was a handsome man, tall and slim, his dark hair peppered with silver. He radiated vitality. People were attracted to him like bees to coffee blossoms. His eyes sparkled as he joked and chatted with several single women who gathered around the table, enthralled by his attention.

"...and that's why don Fulano never went out again." Dad's joke ended and he waited for the ladies to respond.

"Oh, Quique, you're so funny," one of them laughed.

The other smiled coyly at him. "I didn't know you were such a comedian."

"I bet there's a lot about me you don't know."

"Maybe you can share your secrets."

Dad appraised her like a piece of livestock. "Maybe."

I glanced over at my tall, slender mother. With her platinum hair and milky complexion, she stood out like an alabaster pearl among so many darker shades, varying from coffee with cream to espresso. Mom was talking to Aunt Antonia, who had come in from the city, but her eyes flitted back and forth to Dad, her mouth set tight.

Mom wasn't the only one watching my father. A husky young man with small, intense eyes watched the scene. He walked over to the petite woman and pulled her by the arm. "Get your butt home, Claudia. Didn't you learn your lesson when he got Silvia pregnant? One sister with a child of his is too many."

"Leave me alone. You're not my boss!"

"These people think they're too good for us. He would only use you."

"You're just like our father. It's no wonder *Mami* left him. Mind your own business."

Dad was about to protest the boy's rough behavior when Tio Carlos approached the bar. "Quique, my favorite nephew," he slurred loudly. The women moved off to the side, avoiding him.

"Tio, it looks as though you've had enough to drink."

"I just want to congratulate you. You know, I used to be envious of you—a beautiful family, lovely home, and two coffee farms, one of which should be mine. You've done well, although I really think you should share with me. But perhaps you really do deserve to have it all, while I just struggle along in my small clinic."

People inched closer, listening for gossip. My father took Tio Carlos by the arm and steered him away, talking to him quietly.

"Why? Is the truth so hard to hear?" I heard him say to Dad.

By mid-afternoon, the party was in full swing with close to four hundred people enjoying our hospitality. Amazingly, there was enough food for everyone. Some even took food home to those who, for one reason or another, hadn't been able to come.

Salsa and merengue music blared from speakers, and people shouted to make themselves heard. Several tottered on their feet from too many drinks and about thirty couples danced. Dad began putting the liquor away, thinking the party might never end if he didn't.

Tio Carlos, grinning with glee, danced with one young lady after another. Between rounds of dancing, he prescribed medicine to the afflicted. He wore a stethoscope around his neck to impress the women. His love of alcohol had turned his large hooked nose bulbous and purple. Being five feet tall and weighing about two hundred and fifty pounds, most of it hanging over his belt, didn't seem to hurt him with the ladies. I watched him, disgusted by his lecherous behavior.

"Vero, will you dance with me?" he asked at one point in the afternoon, swaying on his feet.

"No, thanks," I said. "You have enough dancing partners."

As I watched him doing the side-step, he staggered, tripped, and his legs buckled under him. Smack. He landed hard and loud.

Immediately the music stopped and people crowded around. Dad left his spot behind the bar and raced over. "Give him room! Let him breathe," he ordered.

Eduardo, the veterinarian from a neighboring town, pushed his way through. "Let me take a look at him. Give him another drink; this might hurt." He rolled up Tio Carlos' pants and began checking the bones. "I think it's broken," he announced.

The audience watched, enthralled, as Eduardo temporarily splinted the leg with duct tape and pieces of wood.

"I don't think it's broken," Tio Carlos slurred. "It doesn't hurt."

"Because you're already anesthetized." Dad and four other men carried the inebriated cripple to a waiting car that would take him to the regional hospital in Cuilapa, an hour away.

"Doctor! Doctor!" people shouted as the car pulled away. Tio Carlos, enjoying the attention, waved at the people with a smile on his face.

As the life of the party left, things quieted down and the cleanup began. Evening was descending when we finally returned to the house.

That young man at the party. Had his sister, Silvia, been pregnant with Juan José, and did my father have other seed spread around town? I wondered how my mother, an American, had been able to put up with it. Her parents had never trusted Dad; they despised him for spiriting Mom away to Guatemala to live her life so far from them. His easy-going ways seemed to them a sign that he would stray. Though Dad was attractive and a big flirt, Mom had refused to believe that of him. It was easy to turn a blind eye until the evidence showed up on our doorstep.

I put my thoughts aside. It was time to call Mom. I looked at my watch and decided she was probably home from work.

"Hello?"

"Hi, Mom! It's me."

"Veronica, where are you? I've been calling your apartment and no one answers."

"I'm in Moyuta, at Tio Carlos' house."

"What? Why? How come you didn't let me know you were going? I can't believe you left the country without telling me."

"I'm sorry. I left in a rush and I didn't want to worry you. I had an offer for *Las Marías*. I couldn't just sell it without coming back."

"Are you seriously thinking of selling?

"It's a tempting offer."

"How much?"

"Two million dollars."

The line went silent for a moment. I imagined my mother speechless.

"How much did you say?"

"Two million dollars—cash."

"That offer sounds too good to be true. Has the price of property in Moyuta gone up that much? Seriously, Veronica, think about it carefully. But if you decide to sell, don't accept cash, it's too dangerous. How did he come up with that figure, anyway? Where's the offer from?"

"The town mayor, Jaime Ramírez. He's planning on putting in low-income housing. From what I hear, it might be about laundering drug money."

"Jaime Ramírez? Where have I heard that name before?" She paused. "Oh, never mind. There are lots of Ramírez families in Moyuta." Her voice faded.

"Are you still there, Mom?"

"Sorry, I just got lost in thought. Be really careful, Vero. Moyuta can be dangerous, but I don't need to tell you that."

"I know. But it's beautiful. I didn't realize how much I missed it."

She hesitated. "I wish I could tell you what to do. But if I did, you'd probably do the opposite." She sighed.

"What do you think, Mom?"

"I think you have a great life in California. You love your job. Personally, I don't see you wasting your life in a small town in Guatemala. But you have to decide for yourself. I know how your father felt. He would have done anything to have you stay. Anything, that is, but have you put yourself at risk."

"I have a lot of thinking to do," I admitted.

"Maybe you should just take the money and get out. How trustworthy is this mayor? I remember few honest politicians down there."

"I haven't heard many good things about him, but I'll be careful and keep in touch."

"How can I get hold of you?"

"I have Juan José's old cell phone."

"How is everyone, Vero?"

"Tio Carlos is still sober. María Celia is living with him and they seem happy."

"Oh, tell both of them 'hello' for me. Celia must be thrilled. She always had a crush on Tio Carlos."

"I will. She asked about you. Oh, Mom, I have a question."

"Yes?"

"Remember at the party, the blessing ceremony for the *bodega*, when Tio Carlos told Dad one of the farms should be his? I've wondered about that from time to time over the years. Do you know what he meant?"

"It's a long story. Are you sure you want me to tell it?"

"Of course. I'm dying of curiosity."

"Your great-uncle Carlos was a late child, closer in age to your father and his siblings. Because he came to your grandparents so late in life, they were lenient and spoiled him, treating him almost like a grandchild. He had few responsibilities and spent his time drinking and partying. From what your father told me, one morning he staggered home after a night of gambling. He had no money, no horse, no shoes, and only the clothes on his back. His father was furious and disinherited him."

"Disinherited?"

"The idea was that when Carlos settled down and got his university degree, his father would reinstate him in the will."

"So why didn't he?"

"His parents, your great-grandparents, died before that happened. That's why your grandfather inherited both *Las Marías* and *Ojo de Agua* farms as well as the family home."

"That seems so unfair," I said. "But the house in town belongs to Tio Carlos, doesn't it?"

"It does now. As compensation, your grandfather deeded it to him after he graduated. Everyone in town knows Tio Carlos got a raw deal, but it was a long time ago."

# CHAPTER FOUR

"Veronica, are you there?" a voice called.

Where had I heard that voice before?

I stood next to the pump station at Las Marías. In front of me tractors and bulldozers leveled the land. Everywhere I looked, men worked on construction projects, a manmade forest of steel rebar planted in concrete foundations.

"You are in agreement with this, aren't you?" boomed the voice. "You signed the papers."

Over the buzz of chainsaws, I heard trees crash as they fell in the forest, silencing the doves and the songbirds. *Las Marías* was no longer the home I remembered.

"Stop!" I ordered, but no one heard me.

"No," I cried.

Pain lanced my heart. "No, no, no!"

"It's no longer for you to decide, Veronica," the voice continued. "It's out of your hands."

When I turned to look for the man behind the voice, I saw guns pointed at me.

Wait! I reached for the handgun in my purse.

The guns exploded simultaneously in a flash of light.

I awoke in a cold sweat, my heart racing. Firecrackers were exploding on a nearby street.

In the bathroom, I leaned over the sink and splashed water on my face. Shiny new tile floors and soft towels soothed me. Tio Carlos had done a lot of work on the house. Everything was modern and sparkling. In years past, everything had been old and falling apart. The improvements must have been María Celia's doing; luxury was never Tio Carlos' concern. I figured she must be living with him as his wife, though I knew they hadn't married. He was nobody's fool and wouldn't "ruin" a relationship with marriage. Entrenched in bachelorhood, he was too old to change.

On the patio, Tio Carlos weighed down the hammock, invisible in the colorful cotton strings that enveloped him. "Did you have a good rest, Vero?" asked his disembodied voice.

"A nightmare, actually."

"How was your meeting with the mayor?"

"As expected—very unpleasant."

"What exactly did he say?"

"He gave me two weeks to decide and made it pretty clear I'd better sell. He wants to meet with me next week to see if I've made up my mind. What do you think I should do?"

"Consider selling. I'd love to have you near, but your life is more important to me. The best advice I can give you is not to cross the mayor."

"If I decide to sell, I don't want to sell to him."

"Be practical. Look at it this way: You'll be walking away with a lot of money, more than you could hope to get from anyone else."

"That's probably true, but I don't know." I remembered my dream. "I'd hate to see them cut down the forest and ruin the land."

"You have time. Go to the farms and think about it. Perhaps you'll be able to reach a decision before your next appointment. You're on vacation. Do some relaxing."

I nodded. "It's hard to relax when I have this hanging over me, but I'll try. By the way, the house looks great. You've done a lot of work."

"Thanks, the clinic is doing well. María Celia's been a big inspiration. Perhaps I've finally found the right woman."

I smiled in approval. "I'm going out for a while."

"Where are you going? I'd like to know where you are—just in case."

"Walking through town. I might go to the cemetery later."

I stepped into the street. Moyuta looked the same as before: the same stores, the same dusty streets, and even the same people. I took a second look. A shining Commerce Bank stood on the corner where a neighbor-hood *tienda* once sold dry goods.

There had been no banks in town when I left ten years ago. I recalled how my grandparents hid their money around the house. After they passed away, Dad went through their belongings and found bundles of money wrapped in newspaper under mattresses.

Mom was appalled at the moldy odor when Dad handed her the cash to deposit.

"What did you expect, Liz?" Dad said defensively. "It's not like Moyuta has banks conveniently located on every corner."

"Where did this come from?" the bank teller in Guatemala City asked, not disguising his distaste at the stench.

"I'm so sorry. My in-laws had it hidden under their mattress for years." We waited an embarrassing thirty minutes while the teller counted and recounted the bundles of limp bills, which kept sticking to each other.

Past the bank, people cleaned streets, picking up litter and garbage from yesterday's market. I remembered a visit to the market, long ago.

The market that first Sunday in March had been much larger than normal. The coffee harvest had ended a few weeks earlier, and people had more spare cash than usual.

Mid-morning, Mom called to me, "Veronica, today is market day and I need to get some things. Can you come with me?"

Reluctantly, I agreed. We drove into town and parked. Even two blocks away we heard speakers blasting *ranchera* music and men with microphones competing for the crowd's attention, shouting their political agendas or urging people to buy their products.

"Come on, Vero," she urged.

"Do I have to go? Can't I stay at Ana's house while you shop?"

"You said you'd keep me company. You know I dislike shopping here."

Once inside the market, my reluctance vanished. Villagers and towns-folk filled the streets, dressed in their Sunday finery. The air of excitement was contagious. Children gazed in awe at all the tempting things to eat and buy. Peasant farmers greeted one another, laughing at jokes with snaggle-tooth grins.

Traditionally, villagers come to town on Sunday for Mass, a meal at a market stand, and to look over the wares, hoping to buy what they need and want but settling for what they can afford.

Vendors hawked goods out of old pickups or tent-like structures made from blue or orange plastic tarps, selling watermelons, cantaloupes, and pineapples. "Get your melons here. Two melons for ten quetzals."

Lacy dresses for toddlers hung from the wooden frames of makeshift shops. Bras and underwear dangled from ropes, tempting women from the remote villages, who could never afford to buy undergarments in a store. I saw several women eyeing the lingerie.

"Don't stare, Vero," Mom scolded. "Just because we have money to buy nice things in the city doesn't mean you can ridicule others."

"I didn't say anything," I said.

"You didn't have to."

Aluminum pots and pans hung in a neighboring stall. The salesman tapped on them with a stick, presumably to show their high quality or perhaps just to get attention. Spatulas, tableware, serving spoons, and other kitchen utensils were laid out on a table.

"*Qué le ofrezco, gringa?*" asked the salesman when we glanced at his wares. Annoyed, Mom turned away.

Other peddlers sold combs, brushes, and hair adornments. Nearby, an enterprising fellow with scissors had set up a portable barbershop, charging one quetzal for a haircut. When I looked at him, he smiled and motioned to his empty chair. "*Canchita*, let me trim your lovely hair." I shook my head and kept walking.

Standing on a wooden crate at the far end of the street, a middle-aged man dressed in a rumpled, shabby suit sold medicine guaranteed to cure everything from diabetes and dysentery to female problems and male dysfunction. "If you have insomnia, the flu, the runs, weak kidneys, or any other disease, this miracle medicine can help. It is a secret formula, brought out from the Amazon jungle." He gestured to the bottle in his hands and passed it among his listeners. "Yes, folks, the common cold, fevers, and chills, no more. For only fifteen quetzals a bottle, don't miss this chance to cure what ails you!"

I followed Mom deeper into the festive crowd, jostling against people here and there. I stopped for a moment to marvel at the caged parakeets, canaries and finches, reputed to be fortune tellers.

"Need to know your destiny?" asked an old man with baggy clothes on his scarecrow frame. "These birds can reveal secrets and change your life."

I watched, fascinated, as people lined up to question these winged prophets.

"Vero, come on," Mom urged.

"I'll catch up in a minute. I want to watch."

Children of all ages pushed their way through the crowd to see these feathered visionaries. A young woman stepped up to the cages and I heard her softly ask, "Should I marry Pedro?" The clairvoyant canary picked a slip of paper from one of several stacks and gave it to his master. The crowd stilled, waiting for the answer. When the old man whispered to the girl, a flush of pleasure spread over her face. It was clearly the answer she wanted. A middle-aged farmer went next. I didn't catch his question but the answer apparently wasn't what he'd hoped for. He left slowly, eyes lowered, dejected.

The old man gestured for me to ask a question. "Just remember, miss. It must be answerable by a 'yes' or a 'no.'"

I couldn't think of anything better, so I asked, "Will this be a good year for me?" I watched the little finch as he hopped down from his perch, picked a paper from the stack, and passed it to his master.

The man leaned in towards me, and with garlicky breath he whispered, "No."

Startled, I left quickly. I knew better than to believe the bird's guessing game, but the answer left me feeling uneasy.

Nearby, a man hawked pirated video and cassette tapes. "*Musica ranchera*, take your pick. Three cassettes for twenty quetzals, a real deal, folks." Two boom boxes blasted out music while village teenagers pawed through the tapes. "Miss, can I interest you in some music?" the man asked in heavily accented English over the microphone.

I shook my head in embarrassment. Three young men in their late teens looked at me from a neighboring stall. "*La gringita* has money. She can buy something. Maybe she can buy something for all of us?" they taunted, then laughed.

Two of them were dark and husky, similar looking, except one had acne. Both wore sunglasses. The third was thin, fair-skinned, and wore cowboy boots and a bandana around his neck.

The guy with the pimples moved closer. "You and your father, you think you're too good for us, don't you? You think we're trash. You just wait. One of these days I'll teach you both a lesson. We'll see who has the last laugh then." He was so close I could almost feel his breath on me.

"What do you mean? Why are you saying that?" I turned, pushing my way through the crowds to find my mother.

I heard him call out as I left. "Hey, where are you going? I wasn't finished."

Why would he say such things to me? My heart pounded with fright. I didn't look back for fear they might be following.

I caught up with Mom where she was bargaining for produce at a stand. When I had her in sight, my world felt safer.

"Vero, there you are. What do you think of this eggplant?" she asked, holding up the lush purple vegetable. "Isn't it a beauty? And she only wants two quetzals for it." She glanced at me. "Are you okay? You look shaken."

"Yes, I'm fine." It was silly of me to ask the bird and I'd overreacted. Did that guy really say those things to me? My heart settled down and things began to look ordinary again.

I looked over the vegetables: tomatoes, onions, carrots and peppers. There were baskets of herbs and spices, and smells of basil, thyme, rosemary, and oregano filled the air. Colorful tropical fruit spilled out from other baskets, tempting passersby: melons, oranges, pineapples, mangos, nancies, jocotes, papayas, and limes. Mom added two pineapples to her basket and paid the woman.

"I'm through here, Vero. Let's go."

We stepped over an unconscious drunk sprawled on the sidewalk as we picked our way through the morning's accumulation of garbage. We passed a tent that smelled like a still, where over-painted women served *Venado Especial,* a cheap cane alcohol, by the pint and by the liter.

Several men strode in; others staggered out, grasping for something to hold onto, trying to keep their balance. Raucous laughter floated from the entrance.

A tipsy villager eyed me. "*Señorita bonita,*" he slurred.

Already nervous, the unwanted attention made me more jittery.

"Don't pay any attention to them. They're harmless enough," Mom told me. I walked closer to her and tried to ignore the drinking men.

Sunday market was the community's weekly entertainment and excitement. But it was never the same for me as for the villagers. I stood out with my honey-colored hair and fair skin. I was Guatemalan and American, yet neither.

# CHAPTER FIVE

I WANDERED TOWARD THE PARK, WHERE BAREFOOT BOYS IN DIRTY T-SHIRTS kicked around an old plastic ball. "*Aquí, Pedro!*" yelled one of them, waving his arms in the air and running backwards.

I quickly moved aside to keep from colliding with him. "*Perdón, señorita,*" he said when he saw me.

"*Te gusta la gringa, Chepito?*" the other boys teased.

Not far from the church, an elderly woman asked if I wanted tamales, pointing to a large aluminum pot on top of her head that swayed slightly from side to side as she kept the load balanced.

"*No, gracias,*" I said.

In the central park, dry season ruled and the flowers and shrubs drooped from lack of water. A layer of brown dust covered them, dulling their usually vibrant colors. Soon the rainy season would turn everything green and lush.

"Shoeshine?" a waif asked. He appeared to be about four, but was probably older.

I looked down at my sandals. "I don't think these can be polished."

I reached into my bag and gave him some coins. It wasn't much, but probably more than he would make in several days.

"*Muchas gracias!*" He grabbed his shoeshine box and raced to the woman selling tamales. I glanced over and she smiled. Probably the boy's grandmother, raising the child while his single mother worked as a house servant in Guatemala City—a common story.

The Catholic church faced the park, its heavy wooden door open. I climbed the cement stairs and stepped over the threshold into the vestibule. I genuflected and made the sign of the cross. *In the name of the Father, the Son, and the Holy Spirit. Amen.*

Even more than the town, the church had remained the same. Framed pictures of the Virgin Mary and different saints lined the walls. Glass cabinets contained doll-like images representing the baby Jesus, the Virgin Mary, and San Juan, the patron saint of Moyuta. A large crucifix hung on the front wall behind an iron railing. My footfalls echoed on the granite floor as I walked down the aisle. I slid into a high-backed wooden bench and bowed my head.

My father had insisted I be raised in the faith. Like many, for him religion was more tradition than conviction. He considered himself a Catholic, just not a practicing one. His great-grandfather, a Jesuit priest, had founded this church. I was baptized and had my first communion in its sanctuary. My family had attended countless weddings and funerals here throughout the years. Two years ago, in a front pew, tears stained my cheeks, my heart wrenched in grief when I attended my father's funeral.

*My father's murder. How could God have allowed that to happen? What went so wrong that they killed him so violently and remorselessly?*

A handful of people lingered in the church. Two boys placed flowers around the altar for the next day's service. An older woman sat in the front row, head bowed in prayer. Was she praying for a soul taken from this earth by violence?

A peasant woman, scarf covering her hair, lit candles off to the side. She touched her forehead, chest and shoulders in the sign of the cross, then brought her fingers to her mouth and bowed her head in prayer. Hundreds of candles, in all colors and sizes, decorated the wooden table; dried wax coated the area, dripping down to the floor. There was so much need and so many prayers, each with its own candle.

With no candles of my own, I lit several already there after the woman left. I dropped to my knees and prayed silently. *Heavenly Father, I beg you. Please have mercy on my earthly father's soul. He was taken before his time. He was a good man. An honorable man. He was my father and I loved him. Amen.*

I got up, crossed myself once more, and left the church, hoping to buy flowers for my father's grave.

I stepped down onto the street. To my right was a funeral business, *Funeraria Godoy*. The owner's daughter, Ana, and I had lost touch years ago. She and her brother, Santiago, had surely settled elsewhere. In the capital city, perhaps.

I looked through the barred metal door of the business. The place seemed deserted, yet at *siesta* time, people might be resting inside.

"*Buenas tardes*," I called loudly. My voice echoed in the silent rooms. Inside, caskets ranging from infant to adult size lined the walls from floor to ceiling. I cringed at the sight of the tiny caskets. So many small children died unnecessarily in the rural areas from lack of the most basic needs— clean water, food, and medicines.

Candleholders and candles stood in a corner. Plastic wreaths and vases gave me hope I might find flowers here.

A boy of about eleven came through a door leading to the living quarters on the other side of a courtyard. He remained behind the locked grill of the entrance.

"*Si?*" he asked.

"Do you have flowers for sale?"

"*No creo*," he replied. "But I'll check."

A few minutes later, a young woman came into view. "Vero?" she said. "Vero Villagrán?"

She put a key into the front lock and turned it. The bolt clicked twice and she opened the door.

"Ana?" I exclaimed, not having dared to think she might be here. We embraced.

"Vero, I can't believe it's you! *Cómo has estado?* Come in, come in!"

"Ana, you haven't changed a bit." She was still petite and had a sprinkling of freckles across her up-tilted nose. Her smooth dark hair was tied back in a ponytail.

We walked across the courtyard and into the dining room. "Sit down, Vero. We have a lot of catching up to do."

She poured two cups of coffee from a thermos on the table and sat down across from me. It seemed like forever since I'd seen my friend. All of her family came to Dad's funeral, but I was dazed and remembered nothing but the pain of his death.

"Ana, I was sure you'd moved away."

"*Si, lo hice, Vero*. I haven't lived here since I started high school. I got married after I graduated from college. Oscar and I live in the city. We're here visiting my parents. *Papá* has some health problems and hasn't been well. Oscar and I took time off work to come and stay a few days."

"Don Guillermo's ill? What's wrong?"

"It's his lungs. Remember, he used to be a chain smoker."

"I'm sorry about your father. I'm also sorry about not keeping in touch. I've thought about you over the years and asked my parents about you."

"I missed you, too. I always hoped you'd come back to Guatemala. I was so happy when I heard you might be visiting. Are you still single?"

I nodded. "I haven't found the right guy. I was in a relationship for a while, but it didn't work out. Do you have any children?"

She patted her tummy. "In another five months we'll have our first."

"Congratulations!" I said, looking down at her slightly rounded belly. "Tell me about this lucky guy."

"*Se llama Oscar Santizo.* We've been married three years. He's an architect in the city. He's out right now with Santiago. They're doing the guy thing." She rolled her eyes. "They went to look at a mare my brother wants to buy."

"Oh, yes, I'd forgotten. The men around here are all about guns and horses."

"Some things never change. It's still just like the Wild West." Ana laughed. "We're leaving for the capital tomorrow after lunch. Why don't you come by before noon and I'll introduce you."

"So Santiago is around, too?"

"Are you still interested in my brother?" She studied me, then continued, "He's here today and every weekend. He comes on Thursday and leaves Monday. He teaches agriculture several days a week at *la Universidad de Rafael Landivar*. Since our father's illness, Santiago has taken over care of our coffee farm."

"What's he been doing all these years?"

"He was in California until two years ago. He left Guatemala in…" She looked at the ceiling, as if it held the answer. "Oh, 1999, I think, and got his Master's in Agriculture at U.C. Davis. While he was there, he fell in love. He was engaged to a girl from Sacramento, a fellow graduate student. A few weeks before their wedding date, she was riding her bike to work and was killed by a drunk driver."

"Oh, no. That's terrible."

"Santiago was devastated. He stayed another year, and then decided to come home."

It was strange and ironic. Santiago had lived only a few hours from me and I hadn't known.

"He was very depressed for a while, but he's recovered," Ana said. "He doesn't go out much, though. We're glad to have him back in Guatemala amidst family and friends."

I glanced at my watch. "I need to go now. I'll come by tomorrow. I'd love to meet Oscar and see Santiago again. Remember how I used to have a big crush on him?"

"Of course, I remember. I also remember he had a crush on you as well. And just think…you're both still single."

Ana, the matchmaker. Things hadn't changed.

I got up to leave. "I've got to get to the cemetery, Ana. I want to be back before nightfall."

"I'm sorry we don't have any flowers for you, Vero." Ana looked down at the roses on the table, and impulsively removed them from the vase and wrapped them in newspaper. "Here, take these."

"No, Ana," I protested. "I'll buy flowers at a store. You don't need to do that."

"I insist. Besides, you won't find any in town. I brought these with me yesterday from the city. I'll be honored if you take them."

I thanked her again and left.

The sun had lost some strength and it was a comfortable ten-minute walk to the miniature city housing the town's dead. I enjoyed the solitude and the cool breeze.

I passed under the aqua-colored archway into the citadel, the sacred ground protected by metal gates and high cement walls. The Villagrán family owned the most majestic home here, at the top of the hill, with a view facing the Pacific. I opened the metal-latticed gateway and entered. This stifling room housed my dead ancestors.

Two years ago, my family entombed my father here in a marble-lined vault. When the bricklayer finished sealing the opening, my mother cried out in anguish, "Quique, why did you leave us?" I put my arm around her and led her away through the crowds.

The heat accentuated the odor of dried flowers and dust. I put the fresh flowers in the metal vase on the small granite table in the center of the mausoleum. Using a tissue from my pocket, I dusted the table's smooth surface and looked down at the marble plate, my father's place in the vault.

Enrique "Quique" Villagrán
Nacido 2 de Mayo, 1951,
Fallecido 8 de Agosto, 2003

Underneath his slab were my grandparents' stone markers, and beside them, my great-grandparents. Other relatives flanked them: cousins, great aunts, and uncles.

"These are for you, Dad," I said aloud. "I wish you were still here with us." A tear slid down my cheek. "This should never have happened."

I knelt in front of the small altar, closed my eyes, and prayed. "Protect me from danger. Allow me strength to stand up for what is right and knowledge to back down when necessary. In Jesus' holy name. Amen."

I opened my eyes and gazed at the marble plate. "Dad, did you do the right thing, or was it in vain?"

The quiet filled me with peace. I lingered a few minutes, hoping for some kind of sign. Not receiving any, I said another prayer and stood.

As I left the mausoleum, I sensed someone watching me. No one was around when I'd arrived. A moment later, I thought I heard footsteps nearby. I turned. Untended brush and grass rustled. Something had dislodged a rock. Had it been kicked? Alarmed, I reached for the gun in my shoulder bag.

"*Hay alguién allí?*" My hand was on the gun, but still inside the bag. No one answered. Why would someone be spying on me? Maybe the gun was making me paranoid.

I sat down on a platform where coffins had been cemented into tomb-like drawers. While I rested, a dog appeared and limped slowly and uncertainly in my direction. It looked like the dog I'd had when I lived on the farm, but was flea-ridden, filthy, and not as old as mine would have been. Anyway, I recalled Mom saying he had died about four years back, while my parents were still living here. This dog was grey, mottled with brown and black spots. I thought white might have been the original color of his fur under the layers of dirt and dust. A *campo* dog, obviously bred and born from strays and mutts.

"Cacique?" I called. "Is that you?"

His ears perked up. His tail moved slightly, but warily, not enough to be mistaken for a wag.

"Hi, there," I said as he approached slowly. I breathed easier. "What are you doing here? Were you the one making all that noise?"

"Come here," I coaxed, and put my hand out, but he kept his distance. He seemed to hear something and turned his head, ears up, listening. "Is someone out there, boy? Did you come here with your master?" He turned towards where I heard the noise earlier, his hackles raised, his lip curled back. No owner appeared to claim him.

"Hello? Are you there?"

Silence. My mind was playing tricks on me, I thought. Perhaps it was a squirrel or a raccoon.

I picked my way through gravestones and weeds toward the entrance. The dog limped after me, keeping his distance. He stopped when I went through the cemetery gate and crossed the road towards town. I turned and saw him watching me.

The breeze strengthened and fog began to blow up from the coast. My damp, sweaty clothing now chilled me and I hurried back.

I welcomed the cool darkness of Tio Carlos' house and, without meeting anyone, went to the bathroom to shower off the dust and cleanse myself of grief.

In the kitchen, María Celia prepared the traditional evening meal of black beans, rice, and hand-patted tortillas. By the time I was out of the shower, supper was served. I sat down at the table across from Tio Carlos.

"*Mija*, how was your day?" he asked.

"Tio, I am so tired. I went to church, then to the cemetery."

He nodded. "Emotional exhaustion?"

"I've been feeling a little nervous. I thought I heard something at the cemetery, but didn't see anyone. No one would be following me, would they? Should I be afraid?"

"Let me give you some Valium. That will calm you."

"Thanks, but no thanks." My uncle loved prescribing drugs. I didn't need to be tranquilized; I needed to be alert. "By the way, I saw a stray mutt while I was there."

"That's your father's old dog. He lives at the cemetery. He was at the farm the night Quique was murdered. The killers shot him and left him for dead, but the dog survived. Liz found him and brought him to me. I worked on him for several hours. He still has a bullet in his back leg I wasn't able to remove."

I listened, enthralled by the story. No one had told me about this.

"People in town have tried to adopt him, but he's unfriendly to everyone. You know how superstitious folks are around here. They leave food for him and call him a protector spirit. He mourns your father and stays close to the family mausoleum."

"His name isn't Cacique, is it?"

"No, but he's one of Cacique's pups. I think your dad called him Centinela, one who stands guard."

I remembered Cacique, the puppy my father bought from one of his workers for fifteen quetzals. He was a pitiful little bundle when he arrived, flea-bitten and hungry, fur sparse and stomach distended with parasites. Within a week under our care, and after a series of baths, medicines, and good food, he was as adorable as any puppy.

"Call him Cacique, Vero," Dad had said. "He thinks he's the leader of our family. A Guatemalan thoroughbred mutt is just the kind of dog we need. Forget about the fancy breeds. These are specially bred for survival and viciousness."

He sure hadn't looked vicious to me then, but the dog at the cemetery was a different story. He was pitiful, but he also looked like he could be dangerous.

*Dad's dog? Was he protecting me from someone?*

# CHAPTER SIX

*February 13, 1991*
*Dear Diary,*
*I was doing my world history homework today when Tio Carlos*
*asked if I would go to the Ash Wednesday Mass with him...*

I closed the diary and held it against my chest as the long ago memory of that day rushed into my thoughts.

The phone rang. "Vero, would you come to church with me today? Your old uncle doesn't feel like he can do much on his own. You know...with crutches and all."

"Sure, Tio. I'll go with you. But it's Wednesday. What's the occasion?"

"It's Ash Wednesday, dear. The beginning of Lent. Didn't you realize yesterday was *Carnaval*?"

"I missed it! We didn't go into town yesterday and I forgot. I guess I'm getting too old for it anyway." *Carnaval* or Fat Tuesday was such a fun time for younger kids, the last day before the austere days of Lent. In Guatemala, women saved eggshells all year, carefully removing the contents in order to leave as small an opening as possible, then filled them with confetti and glued on tissue paper to close them. The local police blocked off the streets in town so children could run wild, smashing *cascarones* on each other's heads. Confetti scattered in the breeze, colors floating in the air before becoming litter on the ground.

I hung up the phone and went in to my mother's office. "Mom, yesterday was *Carnaval*. Why didn't you tell me or get me any *cascarones*?"

"You know I never keep track of those things. Besides, they make a huge mess." She saw my disappointment and caught herself. "I'm sorry, sweetheart. I really didn't remember."

Ana's mother did something special for every holiday. Sometimes I wished my mother was more like her.

"What exactly is Lent?" I asked.

"I'm no expert," she said, "but I believe it's a time of purification. A time for people to turn their thoughts to Jesus and the sacrifice he made for us by dying on the cross. Catholics make sacrifices in their own lives during this time. Haven't you been paying attention in catechism?"

Ana and I passed notes during class and made faces at each other, but I didn't want my mother to scold me. "Father Octaviano is getting old. Half the classes are cancelled. Besides, it's really hard to pay attention to him. I barely understand him."

"He's Italian," she said, as if that explained everything. "Why do you ask?"

"Today is Ash Wednesday," I said.

"Is it?" she asked absently.

"Mom, if yesterday was *Carnaval*, today is *Miercoles de Ceniza*." I was getting impatient.

"Whatever you say."

I could see I was losing her attention. "Can I go to Mass today with Tio Carlos? He just called and asked me."

She looked at her watch. "If you plan to go, you better leave the house in a few minutes. Church starts in a half hour."

The walk didn't take long. I took a path across the back of the farm and cut through the public school grounds. Several boys kicked a ball in a dusty field. They didn't look up as I went by.

Tio Carlos waited for me at the door. "*Mija*, let's go." He locked the door behind him. "It takes me a while, walking with these crutches." He waved them in the air as he balanced himself on his good leg.

I listened attentively as Father Octaviano exhorted his flock to give up something they enjoyed, or something that meant a lot to them, to parallel God's ultimate sacrifice.

What kinds of things could I give up?

When it came time for communion, we waited in line as Father Octaviano gave a wine-dipped wafer to everyone in succession. When my turn came, he looked at me and hesitated, then dipped his finger in the ash from last year's palm fronds. "Veronica Villagrán, I bless you in the name of the Father, the Son, and the Holy Spirit."

He made a cross on my forehead with the ash. Then he gave me my communion wafer and I returned to my seat.

"What was that all about?" Tio Carlos asked.

"I don't know," I said. But I felt special. Father Octaviano had a direct line with God, didn't he?

After helping my uncle home, I walked over to visit Ana. The streets around the park were filled with people making religious carpets, using dyed rice, coffee parchment, flowers, and pine needles to create artistic designs on the cement paving-stones. Ana examined a newly made carpet just outside her house. With a spray bottle, she sprinkled a light layer of water to keep the carpet from blowing away.

"Hi, Vero," she called when she saw me. "Look what our family has been working on since yesterday."

I walked around the carpet to admire it.

Crosses surrounded by flowers decorated four corners. Angels with spread wings looked toward the center where two hearts flanked the face of Jesus Christ.

"Why don't you stay here with us to watch? The procession will be coming soon."

We went into her house. Doña Alba was in the kitchen preparing beverages. "*Hola,* Vero. How do you like our work of art?"

"It's pretty. Too bad it won't be around very long."

We sat down at the table and she served us *rosa de Jamaica,* a crimson iced tea. Ana's forehead creased and she tilted her head. "Hey Mom, why do we make these rugs anyway? We put in all that work just to have them destroyed."

"It's our tradition." Alba said. "Their purpose is to remind us of Palm Sunday when Christ passed over the palm fronds and triumphantly entered Jerusalem. We are supposed to be reminded of the importance of sacrifice, that beauty and life are temporary. The parade itself is what matters. We pay homage to the procession with our carpets, just as the people did back then with palm fronds for our Lord. It doesn't matter that the beautiful creations disappear moments later."

Ana and I exchanged looks, still unsure of the significance.

She saw our puzzled faces and continued, "Okay, let me explain it like this. We must live our lives from day to day, rejoicing in each moment. Tomorrow may or may not ever arrive. Happiness can disappear in an instant."

I listened carefully to doña Alba. My mother had a much different outlook. She always told me to plan ahead. Her motto was, "The present is only a steppingstone to the future."

Ana interrupted my thoughts. "Vero, listen!"

The first cadences of church music drifted in from the street. We raced out to watch. Ana's father, Guillermo, took the last few photos of the carpet to show it with the procession approaching in the background. "I want Santiago to see these," he said, puffing on his ever-present cigarette. "This is the first year he hasn't been here to help."

"*Papi*, I thought you were going to quit smoking for Lent."

"Yes, dear. I'm quitting tomorrow."

The religious parade began at the church and advanced slowly. The carpet in front of Ana's house was the first one trampled. Twelve neighbors, dressed as Roman soldiers, took on an otherworldly appearance in their purple robes as they swayed to the music and labored under the weight of a polished mahogany platform carrying life-size images of Christ and the Virgin Mary. Men swung incense burners both ahead of and behind the platform, smoking out evil spirits lingering in the streets.

It was somber, yet thrilling. Ana grabbed my arm. "Oh, Veronica, here they come!" We each held our breath as they marched over the carefully constructed carpet, the remnants of the original design now an indistinguishable blur. The words of doña Alba echoed in my thoughts. *Live our lives rejoicing in each moment.*

A young man, holding one corner of the platform, caught my eye. He glared at me. I shivered under his stare. He was the one who had taunted me in the market, his black, close-set eyes filled with resentment.

"What is it, Vero?" Ana asked me. "Are you okay?"

"Do you know who that guy is?"

"Which one?"

"The one on the corner, in the front of the procession."

"No, I didn't get a good look at him. They all look the same in those purple robes."

The procession swayed on toward the next carpet, leaving bits of color in its wake. As it wound through all the streets of town, many joined it and others came out of their houses to watch.

I headed home after saying goodbye to Ana and her family.

My parents were in the living room when I arrived. Mom looked up from her reading. "Hi, Vero. You took a long time. I was beginning to worry."

"I was at Ana's house watching the procession. Sorry I didn't call."

"Is Santiago home yet? Did they mention how he's doing in high school?"

"No, and I forgot to ask. He hardly ever comes home." I remembered something else. "Ana and her family invited me to come every Sunday during Lent to watch the processions. I can, can't I?"

Mom didn't say anything, but consent showed on her face.

"Why don't we go to church more often?" I asked. "We hardly ever go as a family."

"I wasn't raised Catholic. And your Dad won't go to any of the Protestant churches. He considers them all too evangelical."

"What does that mean?"

"Your father's family is very Catholic. He wouldn't be comfortable worshipping God in a Protestant Church."

"Dad isn't comfortable worshipping at all."

My mother shrugged.

I waited for Dad to say something. When he didn't, I pressed him. "You used to go every Sunday. You told me you'd been an altar boy."

"I was."

"Why did you stop?"

"I became a very big sinner."

I wondered if he was teasing. "But, Dad, that's more reason for you to go."

"God and I have a special kind of relationship. We each mind our own business."

# CHAPTER SEVEN

I AWOKE UNDER HEAVY WOOLEN BLANKETS. MY GAZE WANDERED ABOUT the sparsely furnished room: a pine chair with a neatly folded extra blanket, a desk by the window, a cedar bureau with a closet area and mirror.

Outside, clouds covered the entire mountain, an eerie whiteness glowing in the first light of dawn. The cool damp air reminded me of Golden Gate Park in San Francisco, where I often jogged in foggy weather.

I dressed in a T-shirt, jeans, and sweatshirt, then went to the kitchen to fix some coffee. While rummaging around looking for matches to light the stove and get water boiling, María Celia came in. She was a different person without her makeup, pale and drawn. A colorful scarf covered her hair and pink rollers peeked out from beneath the splashes of red, purple, and blue.

"*Buenos dias, Vero,*" she said, sleepy-eyed. "Are you looking for matches?" She opened a drawer and handed me a matchbook. "The coffee is in this jar." She pointed to a nearby container.

As I prepared coffee, I turned to her. "I hope I didn't wake you. I'm usually up with the sun."

She shook her head. "*No tenga pena.*"

When the coffee was ready, I poured a cup, took it to the courtyard, and sat down in one of the low wooden chairs facing the garden. Roosters, the town's alarm clocks, crowed from all directions. In the backyards of several homes, turkeys gobbled with impatience and hunger; hens announced the arrival of fresh eggs. Several caged parrots squawked, protesting the cool air. This choir of fowl awoke the town each morning.

The first bus to the city arrived, engine roaring and black smoke bellowing from the exhaust pipe. The bus driver's assistant shouted through the streets its imminent departure to the capital. "*Guate! Guatemala!*"

Firecrackers popped like machine-gun fire nearby, no doubt celebrating someone's birthday. Seconds later, dogs in neighboring houses barked in response. Anyone who had been sleeping would be awake now.

As I listened to the sounds of Moyuta awakening, I thought about the day ahead. I wanted to visit the original coffee farm near the volcano's cone where the bulk of our coffee grew. *Ojo de Agua* was separate from *Las Marías* and not in danger from the mayor. I planned to leave early, before it got hot. I wanted to be back in time to see Ana before noon.

As I finished my coffee, Tio Carlos came out of his room. "*Buenos días, mija.* I didn't expect you to be up so soon."

"How can anyone sleep with this racket?"

He chuckled. "You're right, Vero. I never thought much about it, but townspeople never sleep late. What are your plans for the day?"

"I want to visit *Ojo de Agua* this morning."

"Take food and something to drink. It's a half-hour walk from here."

"Have you been lately? How's the road?"

"*Mija*," he said, patting his gut, "I just don't have the energy anymore. I haven't been out there for years. Juan Bautista takes care of any needed work."

María Celia brought over a breakfast tray. "Have some pastries and more coffee."

After eating, I filled a water bottle and put it in my daypack along with the gun, bug repellent, and sunscreen.

María Celia handed me several bananas and a mango. "Take these as well."

"And take a machete," Tio Carlos said, indicating one that stood in a corner of the hall. "The weeds and grass will be tall."

I couldn't see myself walking around with a machete hanging from my belt. "No thanks, I'll manage."

The street was still vacant, though morning activity had begun. I passed houses painted aqua, fuchsia, and mint green. To a visitor, it might seem as though a local paint store had run a special on gaudy hues. But these colors brightened up the town's drabness. No yards or gardens with flowers were visible, only houses built wall-to-wall, courtyards in their central areas.

Most homes in the middle of town had storefronts for the family's business. If the family didn't run a business, they rented the space out. Pictures in windows and on walls displayed the stores' wares to illiterate townsfolk and villagers.

Clapping sounds from women patting breakfast tortillas came from all directions. Smells of black beans and cooking eggs wafted into the street.

The town's daily hour of running water began at the crack of dawn. As I walked, it began to flow. Pipes groaned and creaked, burping out air trapped in corners. From faucets left permanently open, water sprayed, splashed, dripped, and splattered into sinks all over town. People scurried to fill containers and catch the precious liquid for later use. Only a few affluent households had large reservoirs that pumped water up for use as needed.

We never had shortages. *Las Marías* possessed a deep well in the lower part of the farm with water stored in tanks just above the house. As part of the agreement for the town's use of our property to drill the well, we had our own tank and as much water as we needed.

Every morning, a man from city hall came and opened the valve releasing water to the town. Gravity carried it to various neighborhoods in Moyuta and other nearby villages. He returned an hour or two later to close and seal the controls.

I remembered when the city officials came for the well drilling—the former mayor of Moyuta had sent a delegation. Word got out to townspeople. The possibility of a new source stirred up excitement and dozens showed up to watch.

Mom was surprised to see the crowds. "Quique, what in the world are all those people doing down there?"

"You must remember, in a town as dry as this one, a new well is a celebration."

A few people brought food for a picnic and others sold snacks. When the drill hit water, the crowd clapped and cheered. A twelve-inch-wide stream of warm water gushed out, showering everyone who stood under it. It was a baptism of hope in this thirsty land. It gushed for three days before the pressure eased.

"If you listen carefully at the well, Veronica, you can hear the roaring of the underground river below," my father told me. I spent many afternoons there quietly listening.

—

The two years following Dad's funeral seemed like a dream. I lived in and loved San Francisco with its winding streets, Victorian homes, and eclectic mix of people. I worked at a computer company in Silicon Valley, a short commute. I was happy with my job and my coworkers. People knew me for who I was, not for whom my parents were, or for my past.

But when I thought about my future, doubts beset me. Did I want to spend my life in the Bay Area? Could I make a home and raise a family so far away from my roots? Would it be so terrible to live in Guatemala among people who had known my family for generations?

I thought back to the first call from Moyuta. "Is this Veronica Villagrán?" a man with a heavy accent asked.

"Yes, it is. What can I do for you?"

"This is Jaime Ramírez, mayor of the town of Moyuta."

"Yes?"

"I am interested in buying *Las Marías*."

"It's not for sale."

"Think about it. It might be in your best interest."

I was about to reply when the phone went dead. I looked down at the receiver. He had hung up on me.

A week later he called again, "Miss Villagrán, have you considered it?"

"Mayor Ramírez?"

"Please, that sounds so formal. Call me Jaime. And can I call you Veronica?"

"Okay, Mayor Jaime."

During the second call, he tried to convince me that it was the right thing to do, that the low-income housing project he planned for the farm property would benefit many. He also told me how much he would pay me.

After his call I looked at his offer scribbled on a notepad sitting on my glass-covered oak desk. It stood out among other jotted notes in bold red letters: TWO MILLION DOLLARS underlined three times. What a lot of money. Could *Las Marías* really be worth that? I knew I couldn't sell it without returning to take a last look at the house where I'd grown up, but the thought of returning and facing my memories, along with the circumstances surrounding my father's murder, was abhorrent to me.

Still, I couldn't just let the farm go. It was a link to my past, my family home.

When he called a third time, I couldn't put it off any longer. I knew I had to return to Guatemala.

"When shall I expect you?" he asked.

"I'll make the arrangements soon."

"Until then, Veronica…I'll be waiting." He hung up.

At work the following day, I popped my head into my supervisor's office. "Hi, Bob, have you got a minute?"

"Veronica. What can I do for you?"

"I need to take time off. I was thinking about a month."

"How about two weeks vacation and two weeks unpaid leave of absence?" he said. "When do you need it?"

"As soon as possible."

The last call came the night before I left. "Veronica, what day do you arrive?"

"I'll be in Moyuta on Sunday."

"Where will you be staying?"

I thought it strange he would ask. "With my uncle Carlos."

"Come to my office at the *municipalidad* in town Monday morning at nine."

"I'll be there."

"Disappointing me would be a very bad idea. Don't think I don't know everything about your family. Surely you wouldn't do anything stupid. You're a smart young woman. And I'm making you a very generous offer."


My heart beat a little faster as I thought about that last conversation.

I left the paving-stone streets of town. The road narrowed into a dirt path, the edges littered with the trash of poverty: empty plastic bags, a broken plastic container, banana peels. I smelled smoke from a cooking fire. In the distance, church bells chimed, summoning the faithful to early Mass. The fog lifted, and the morning chill disappeared from the air.

*Ojo de Agua* was named for the nearby community spring. Men strode past on their way into town, machetes hanging from their belts. Women gracefully picked their way down the path with plastic jugs on their heads to fill with water. Boys carried bundles of firewood home on their backs. Close to the waterhole, several women washed clothes on large rocks. Wet clothing was hung on fence wires, stretched out over low shrubs, and draped on boulders. Children darted along the path, playing tag while their mothers worked.

The farm's entrance was a short hike around the bend. When I arrived, I found the gate sagging to one side in need of repair, the barbed wire fence opened in several places by trespassers.

I shook my head at its rundown state. My uncle was misinformed; Juan Bautista hadn't been out here.

The oldest coffee trees in the region were planted in the rich black volcanic soil of *Ojo de Agua*. Dad's great-grandfather, the Jesuit priest, planted these trees after Jesuit monks first brought coffee to Guatemala. He and his two brothers came over from Spain, all men of the cloth, to help Latinize the native populations. After arriving on the continent, the brothers split up, and my great-great-grandfather ended up in Moyuta, an area originally populated by Mayan-descended Pipíl Indians. Once settled, he began changing both the region's culture and gene pool, starting his own colony of fair-haired, fair-skinned people. So much for the celibate priesthood.

I opened the lock on the sagging gate with the key Juan José had given me. Inside, the guard's house stood in ruins with few boards still on the framework and the tin roof gone—all probably part of someone else's home now. Ashes and cinder littered the cement foundation.

High weeds made walking difficult as I started toward the coffee field. Branches and brush blocked the path. I wished now I'd brought that machete, as the farm was a dense jungle of growth. Spiderwebs entangled me as I tried to get through and low, prickly branches scratched me. The disturbance brought out swarms of gnats. I went a short distance into the coffee field, but soon gave up and looked for a place where I could observe the rest of the farm.

I climbed up on a large rock. Great *amate* trees, their trunks up to five feet in diameter, towered over and shaded the coffee. The shade trees needed major pruning as did the coffee. I realized I was checking off things to do. Did that mean I wanted to stay?

Acres and acres of two-tiered forest spread out before me, leguminous shade trees above and coffee bushes below—a scene of spectacular color and beauty. *Cuernavaca, pito,* and *cuje* were all in bloom, bursts of lavender, flaming orange, and cream-colored blossoms interspersed on a green background.

The coffee looked healthy, although overgrown with weeds. The branches showed buds ready to open after the first rains, which would be here soon. I looked forward to the coffee blooming, to that one-day event when white blossoms covered the fields like a blanket of freshly fallen snow. The over-powering sweet scent would signal bees and other flying insects to engage in a mad dash to pollinate the flowers before they wilted and faded the following day.

I hadn't realized how much I missed this connection with the coffee farm. I owned two *caballerias* of land, of which forty-five *manzanas* were planted in coffee. After living in the U.S. for so long, I had to stop and think through the measurements. In Guatemala, land is measured in *tareas, manzanas,* and *caballerias*. A *tarea* is twelve *brazadas* by twelve *brazadas*. A *brazada* is the arm span of an average Guatemalan man, so to measure a *tarea* it takes twelve men standing arm span to arm span. One *manzana* consists of sixteen *tareas* or about 1.7 acres. Sixty-four *manzanas* is a *caballeria*. A *caballeria* is nearly 100 acres. I calculated my land to be 200 acres with about seventy acres of coffee.

It's no wonder people always have disputes over property boundaries, I thought. Things will be easier when Guatemala adopts the metric system.

I gazed out on the land, remembering the time I rode my horse to *Ojo de Agua,* where Dad and his men were planting.

"Saddle up Estrellita, Vero. Come visit me at *Ojo de Agua* later today and bring lunch," Dad said. "It's a gorgeous day. Spider webs are up all along the pathway."

My mare carried me through town and into the countryside. The wet, musty smell of earth and rotting leaves rose around me. The fine silken threads along the road sparkled like stars in a darkened sky, giving a surreal look to the landscape. When the rains begin, beautiful brown-and-cream spiders, their bodies up to an inch and a half long, spin strong sticky webs that stretch twelve to fifteen feet across. I cut a passage through them with a machete I kept attached to my saddle. By evening, I knew they would be repaired.

It rained for at least an hour every afternoon. Occasionally there was a morning shower as well. Since the rains were now constant, Dad's workers set out coffee seedlings, planting new sections and replanting areas where the coffee trees were damaged or dying.

*Las Marías* housed a nursery where palm fronds shaded nearly eight-thousand seedlings planted near a faucet for watering. Every year during and after the harvest, the best coffee beans were selected, processed, dried in the shade and later planted in black plastic bags in the nursery, awaiting their final destination in the ground the following year.

When I got to the farm, Dad put down his shovel and smiled. "Hey, Princess!" he called.

I dismounted and greeted him with a kiss on the cheek.

A few minutes later, he put down his machete and turned to the men. "*Bueno, señores. Paramos aquí.* Let's break for lunch."

The workers' meals hung from tree branches in woven bags. The men grabbed their food and gathered around a small bricked-off area. One lit a fire to make coffee and heat tortillas. Dad sat next to me and opened the lunch container I'd brought. "Here, Vero." He pulled out a sandwich. "Would you like to share this?"

"Thanks, Dad." We ate our sandwiches in silence, listening to the birds in the trees and the men talking quietly among themselves.

It didn't take long for the mosquitoes and black biting flies to find us. I swiped at them when they landed on me.

"Did you know that Moyuta means 'land of flies' in the Pipíl language," Dad said.

I shook my head.

"Have you noticed that many pickers smoke homemade cigars during coffee harvest? It's to keep the insects at bay."

When we finished our lunch, Dad gave me a sweaty hug. I got back on my horse and headed for home.

I spent a lot of time with my father that year while he worked on the farm. He taught me about coffee and always told me the farms would one day be mine. Much later, I decided to go my own way, but he gave them to me anyway. Had leaving been a mistake?

I scrambled off the boulder toward the gate and started back to town, contemplating the beauty of the area, content to be here again. The deserted road was quiet, and I breathed deeply of the fresh mountain air.

I heard noises behind me and glanced back. Two men wearing jeans and cowboy boots approached, seeming to appear out of nowhere. They were larger than the villagers, definitely from town. Dark Ray-Ban glasses shaded their eyes, reflective mirrors on their faces. One was large and swarthy and, except for his moustache, could have been the mayor's double.

The other was fair-skinned and gangly.

I felt vulnerable and suddenly afraid. It hadn't occurred to me a walk to the farm could be dangerous. I slipped the daypack off one shoulder just as they reached me.

"Veronica, Veronica Villagrán?" the one to my left growled.

My heart beat quickly. These men weren't friendly. "Yes?"

"I have a message for you."

"A message? From who?"

"Mayor Jaime needs to meet with you on Thursday." The man on my right bumped me intentionally. Then I felt the other man's hip against mine. I felt the cold hardness of the weapon tucked in his belt. I wished my gun were handier, not in the recesses of my daypack.

"I thought I was meeting with him next week."

"Be there Thursday at ten."

"One more thing." He turned toward me again. His breath smelled like he'd never owned a toothbrush. "Show up alone."

The men crowded, bumping me on either side, matching their speed to mine. I stepped up my pace and glanced at them. They were unpleasantly familiar.

"You're Chico, aren't you?" I asked, and turned slightly to the other one. "And you're Mickey."

"Chico Negro," the swarthy one replied, showing a glint from a gold tooth. "I'm flattered that you remember me. We still have unfinished business." His eyes took me in from top to bottom. He flicked his head toward his companion. "This here's Mickey Montaña. We call him Montaña Ocho." My eyes must have questioned the name, because he clarified a second later. "The eighth son of twelve."

I recognized them from my past, and remembered what they were capable of. A few minutes later, much to my relief, they dropped back, leaving me alone. My palms were clammy and my heart racing as I hurried to Tio Carlos' house.

# CHAPTER EIGHT

I RAN A BRUSH THROUGH MY HAIR AND PINNED IT BACK IN A SIMPLE BUN, glanced in the mirror, then tucked my tank top into my black capris. As I left the house, I thought about Santiago and wondered what it would be like to see him after all these years.

The street was deserted. Women were home, fixing the midday meal. When I reached the house, the wooden door behind the metal bars was closed. I rang the bell and peered in the window. Ana came through the courtyard in jeans, tennis shoes, and a pink T-shirt, her glossy black hair tied back. The door clicked when she unlatched and then opened it.

"Veronica, I was just thinking about you."

"Hi, Ana." I hugged her.

She realized we were still standing in the doorway and backed up quickly. We went through the courtyard and into the kitchen.

"Have a seat. I'll get you some coffee."

A wooden dining table sat in the center of the small kitchen, each chair brightened by a colorful cushion. The aroma of freshly brewed coffee filled the room. Family photographs crowded one wall, reminders of memorable events. Ana and I smiled out as children in a few of them.

The back door of the kitchen was open and a village woman in a tattered dress worked at a *pila* in the patio area, plucking feathers from a freshly slaughtered hen. "*Buenas tardes.*" I said when she looked at me.

"Doña María, this is my childhood friend, Veronica."

"*Mucho gusto.*" She smiled. Her lips curled in where her front teeth were missing.

Ana brought two mugs of coffee to the table, then sat down across from me. "Would you like *pan dulce*?" She rummaged through a basket of sweet breads. "Look! We have *champurradas.*"

"You know I never pass up a *champurrada.*"

She took out several large, flat crumbly cookies sprinkled with sesame seeds and put them on a plate in front of me. "I can't eat these without thinking of you. *Mami* always made a special trip to the bakery for them when she knew you were visiting." She thought for a moment. "Do you suppose she knew you were coming today?"

"Only if you told her." I smiled at my friend. She was as sweet as I remembered. "What are you doing in the city now, Ana? Working?"

"Teaching literature at the Colonial School. You went there, didn't you?"

"A lifetime ago." I gazed out toward the garden. "Do you remember *The Coffee Diary*? The journal Mom gave me on my fourteenth birthday."

She thought for a moment. "I do remember that book. You were so disappointed not to get a cute, girlish diary with a lock. Where did she get it anyway?"

"A coffee exporting company gives them out every year." I laughed at the memory. "Mom forgot to buy me a diary in the city. At the last minute, she remembered putting *The Coffee Diary* away in a drawer. I was disappointed with it at first, but Dad came to her rescue, trying to justify the gift since it was filled with coffee information."

"That was the year he began teaching you about coffee production, wasn't it?"

I smiled in agreement. Lots happened that year. I didn't want to think about much of it just yet. I remembered Ana's party and my crush on her brother. He was the only boy in Moyuta I'd really been interested in. "Do you remember your birthday that year, Ana?"

"My thirteenth? We had a party here and you brought the ATV. Remember how you gave us all rides around the park?"

It was the first time Dad let me take one out alone. Ana's friends and relatives were there, and Santiago had come home for the weekend with some of his classmates.

"That's when Santiago first noticed you as more than just his little sister's best friend. When did you two become an item?"

"When he came home for mid-year break. I had a huge crush on him. Just after our first kiss, Mom and I left Guatemala for those months. I hardly saw him after that."

Though fourteen years had passed, the memory hadn't faded. After the party, Ana had told me that Santiago liked me and I told her my father wouldn't let me date until I was eighteen. She responded that hers wouldn't let her date until she married.

"So did your father ever let you go out with boys, or did you have to marry first?" I laughed.

"Once I left Moyuta for school in the city, he didn't have much choice. He was too far away to keep me reined in."

I couldn't imagine Ana being wild.

She got up and poured me another cup of coffee. "But I want to hear about you. What have you done since you've been gone?"

"Too much to tell you. I hate to say it, but I've hardly thought about home since I left. You know I couldn't wait to leave Guatemala after high school."

"I remember you came home from California resentful."

"That taste of freedom in San Diego." I shook my head. "It was the beginning of my rebellion toward Dad—well, maybe it started with Juan José. I left right after my eighteenth birthday."

"My parents told me you'd gone. It was as if the United States swallowed you up. You never came back, even to visit. You went to UCSD, didn't you? What did you study?"

"Languages."

"You had a good start with two. That must have made it easy to learn others. What did your parents think about your choice of majors?"

"Dad was thrilled. I couldn't do wrong in his eyes. He looked into Foreign Service and Diplomacy. He talked to his friends and contacts about jobs and careers. Every time he came up with an idea, I threw it out as a possibility. I didn't want him running my life."

The sweet smell of citrus blossoms wafted in, distracting me. I glanced outside at the tangerine tree in their courtyard.

Ana searched my face. "What happened? You and don Quique had been so close. I was always envious of your relationship with your father, since I rarely even talked to mine."

"I don't know. Why do any teenagers act the way they do?"

"How come you never came back to Guatemala?"

"Resentment, I guess. I was angry with my father for being so controlling. He wanted to know every move I made, every place I visited. He needed to know every boy I dated, asked questions about their families. I hated that."

"*Puchica*, Veronica. Aren't most fathers like that?"

"Maybe. But I never got over what he did to our family."

"You mean the affair?"

"Or affairs. The year Juan José came to live with us, when Mom and I left, I guess it changed my attitude toward Guatemala and how I felt about Dad." I stared pensively into my coffee mug.

A rooster crowed nearby. I turned toward the noise.

"My father has a new fighting cock," Ana said.

"He's still raising them?"

"Of course. He hasn't been to the fights since he's been ill, but he loves to handle the roosters. Would you like to see them?"

I smiled, thinking how scandalized my friends back in California would be to hear about don Guillermo's collection of fighters.

She led me to a storage shed where wooden cages lined one wall. "This is Felix." She pointed at a colorful cock with iridescent black and green neck feathers.

"He's beautiful."

"He's still young, but *Papi* has high hopes for him."

I examined the birds. There were eleven. A twelfth cage was empty.

"That was Tomás' cage," Ana said, when she saw me gazing at the empty box. "Don Tono took him last weekend and returned with just his carcass." Her expression was wistful. "I always liked that old rooster."

"Do you ever go to the fights, Ana?"

"Oh, no! I've been a few times, only briefly, looking for *Papi*, but it's not a place for women. The men all drink and place bets." She shook her head. "The thought of those poor birds injured and bloody—I just don't see the attraction."

We walked back to the kitchen. "Did you see your mother much after you left?" Ana asked.

"More often than I saw Dad. She visited my grandparents in San Diego at least twice a year. My father was never welcome there."

"What about Juan José? You're the only sister he has."

I shook my head, feeling guilty. "I didn't even make it to his wedding last year. I was speaking at a conference and couldn't get away. The first time I met Ita was when the two of them picked me up at the airport."

"I'm sure Juan-Jo forgives you."

"More than I forgive myself."

She refilled our coffee cups and sat down on the other side of the table. "Why didn't you keep in touch?" she asked. "I wrote you a few times."

"I should have. I just didn't want to know about home. I barely wrote my parents."

"You were so hard on everyone."

"I know." I looked absently at doña María as she poured *palanganas* of water over the plucked hen. "It's been hard coming back after all that. But I'm glad I'm here."

"I am, too. But I was hurt, Vero. I was your friend and you dropped me."

"It wasn't like that. I just didn't want to be the same person anymore. I wanted to reinvent myself."

"Still." She hesitated. "I thought you should know."

"Thanks. No one knows better than I how much I've screwed up my life. I never got to apologize to Dad. The next thing I knew, he was gone."

She changed the subject. "What about after you graduated? What did you do then?"

"I was offered a job by a computer company in Silicon Valley developing computer languages. I've been working there ever since. I didn't think about home. I put it out of my mind until that day your father called to tell me about Dad. My employer gave me a month's leave, but I was only gone two weeks. I couldn't stand to be here longer."

"Vero, I'm so sorry."

"I've been meaning to come back, but just haven't been up to it. My guilt dragged me down. I was angry with myself for waiting too long to make amends with Dad. When you're young, you expect your parents to be there forever."

A fleeting look of pain passed over Ana's face.

"When the lawyer read the will, I could hardly believe it. Dad always told me the farms would be mine, but somehow I thought Mom would keep them, or they'd be shared with Juan José. My first thought was to sell immediately, but I just couldn't bring myself to do it. Then when the mayor's offer came, I realized I wasn't so sure after all. It's been too long. I needed to come back."

"What about Juan José? Why didn't your father leave one of the farms to him?"

"His interests are in the city. Even though his mother's family is from Moyuta, he was never in touch with them. From the time he was young, Juan-Jo's ambition was to be a doctor. Dad knew that; he left him property in the capital. Dad wanted the farms to stay in the family, so I guess I was the best choice."

"What's Juan José doing now?"

"He's finishing a pediatrics internship at Centro Médico."

"What does he say about the farm?"

"I haven't talked much to him. I was only at his house briefly. But I don't think it ever occurred to him I would want to keep *Las Marías*. I haven't shown any interest in the farms since Dad died."

"You still feel that connection with the land, don't you?"

I nodded. "I keep thinking about Dad. I thought I'd put his murder behind me, but maybe I just haven't dealt with it yet."

Tears had welled up in my eyes and begun to run down my cheeks. Ana came over to my side of the table and hugged me.

"Vero, we love you. I know you went through difficult times. But you're home now. That's all that matters."

Just then, Santiago entered the room. He was even better looking than when I had known him as a teen, more mature and confident.

"Vero?" he said. "I can't believe it's you."

"*Hola*, Santiago." I wiped my eyes quickly and got up to greet him. He gave me a hug that lifted me off my feet.

"Hey! Put me down," I protested.

"It's about time you came home." He stepped back and grabbed my hands. "You look great."

His warm smile drew me to him once again. I kept hold of his hands. "How have you been, Santiago? It's been a long time."

"I've had my ups and downs." He didn't go into specifics, but I remembered what Ana had told me. "Let's see, I guess the last time I ran into you, I was a student at the Landivar University and you were getting ready to graduate from high school. Then you disappeared."

"Now resurfacing, at last." I looked up at him, but tried to avoid his eyes.

"I was gone four years as well."

"I heard we were practically neighbors in California. And I never knew."

"You didn't want to know anything about your past, Veronica."

I nodded. "True enough. I wasn't ready."

"Are you ready now?" He gazed down at our interlaced hands. He lifted them and examined my left hand as though looking for a wedding or engagement ring.

"I think so," I told him.

"And what have you been doing all this time? We thought we'd never see you again."

"Living in San Francisco and working in Silicon Valley."

"You were lucky not to be here for some of that time." I knew he was referring to my father's troubles. He dropped my hands and motioned for us to sit. "How long will you be here, and what are your plans for the farms?"

"I'm here for a month. At least that's what I'm thinking now." I hesitated. "Mayor Jaime called me several times while I was in California. He's determined to buy *Las Marías*. I met with him yesterday, and I'll speak with him again in a few days."

"What have you told him?"

"That I need time to decide. He said he'd give me two weeks. But he sent a message this morning with two of his goons that he needs to talk on Thursday."

Concern flickered across his face. "I wonder why he needs to see you again so soon."

"I have no idea."

"Be careful, Vero. The mayor is dangerous."

"So I hear."

"*Buenos días!*" A slender young man with sandy brown hair and wire-rimmed glasses walked into the kitchen.

"Oscar, I thought you'd never come," Ana said. "This is Veronica, the friend I was telling you about."

"*Hola, Oscar.*"

"*Mucho gusto.*" Oscar kissed my cheek. "Ana has told me so much about you. Does Moyuta seem any different?"

"Yes and no. Things were quieter ten years ago. Less dangerous. But the world isn't as safe anywhere as it used to be."

After chatting with the three of them for a half hour, I excused myself. "I need to get back. Tio Carlos will wonder where I am."

"Can't you stay for lunch? We're having your favorite, *caldo de gallina*."

"Perhaps I can make it another time." I hesitated and turned. "Really? You're having old hen soup? It's been forever since I've had that Moyuta treat."

Ana laughed. "It was *gallo en chicha* last week. But I couldn't eat poor old Tomás!" She made a face. "Vero, will you be here next weekend? Saturday's my mother's birthday and we're planning a party for her. Can you make it?"

"I'd love to."

"Let me give you my phone number." She looked through her purse for a pen. "Call me if you need a place to stay in the city. I want to keep in better touch." She wrote down a number on the back of a card and held it out to me.

"Thanks, Ana. I promise you'll be hearing from me." I put her card in my purse.

"Vero, I'll be back by noon on Thursday," Santiago said. "I'd like to get together with you. You will have met with Mayor Jaime by then. You can tell me about the meeting."

I suppressed a smile at the thought of spending time with Santiago again. "I'll see you then."

I gave them all hugs, said my goodbyes, and left.

When I got to my uncle's house, María Celia was setting the table. "Veronica, you're just in time."

Tio Carlos came in moments later. "How was your morning? How does *Ojo de Agua* look?"

"It needs some work, but still it felt great to be there."

"Rainy season will be here soon; time to start planting. I hope you're here for the blossoming. That's always such a treat."

"Two guys met me on the road as I was coming back. Chico Negro and Montaña Ocho. I didn't get good vibes from them."

My uncle shifted his weight nervously. "What did they want?"

"They gave me a message from the mayor. He wants to see me again on Thursday."

A strange expression passed over my uncle's face. I couldn't quite place it, but it seemed a mix of fear and satisfaction. Then he composed himself and sat down. "What else have you done?"

"I met with Ana and Santiago. I found *The Coffee Diary*, the journal I kept as a teen. It's bringing back memories, lots of things I'd forgotten."

"*Ojo de Agua* has such a history," Tio Carlos said wistfully. "It's the oldest coffee farm in the area. I've always loved that place. I remember going out there as a boy on horseback, taking food to my father as he worked planting and replanting, harvesting and pruning."

"I was remembering something similar this morning."

He shook his head as though shaking off the thought. "You're right to look to the past. History and family stories. They aren't that easy to give up."

At one time, I'd thought they were. I chose not to say that.

I gazed at Tio Carlos. He seemed so introspective that I wasn't convinced he was speaking to me. But he was right about one thing. Family roots, like those of the coffee trees, were deep.

## CHAPTER NINE

I SLEPT FITFULLY AND AWOKE TIRED. I PULLED THE COVERS OVER MY HEAD to keep the sunlight and morning noises from rousing me. Another day and still no decision. From the distance of my life in San Francisco, I thought everything would be clear when I arrived, but visiting Moyuta only seemed to have complicated things.

I decided to spend the day looking around *Las Marías*. Perhaps familiar sights would illuminate me. When I told my uncle, he suggested I do some target practice. He went to the back room to get extra bullets.

"It's been a while since the gun was used," he said as he handed me a small box of bullets. "Try it out and get accustomed to it."

"I haven't fired a gun in years."

"Quique always kept his guns ready, and was prepared to use them. What's the point of carrying one, if you aren't ready to use it?"

"Sure, Dad was always armed." A bitter taste rose to my mouth remembering how he died. "But maybe he shouldn't have been so prepared."

"It could have been worse, Veronica. He took two murderers with him. That's something."

I raised my eyebrows. Did it make a difference? Dead is dead.

"Go to *Las Marías* and stay as long as you want. Juan Bautista is working there this week so you won't be alone."

"You didn't need to set that up with Juan Bautista. I told you I'd take care of things when I got here."

"I know you did. I'm just hoping if it looks nice, you might stick around. Besides, it's safer if you aren't alone. You are the only thing that stands between Mayor Jaime and *Las Marías.*"

"If I'm dead, how would that help him?"

"Either Liz or Juan José would sell. No one else in your family is interested in Moyuta."

"I guess that's motive." My thoughts turned back to Juan Bautista. "If I give up the farm, you will have wasted your money fixing things up."

"Perhaps, but I will have given it my best shot."

I gave Tío Carlos a hug and started for the door. "I'm going to walk. The exercise will help clear my head."

A daypack hung from my shoulder with water, snacks and my diary in case I had a chance to read. The handgun and ammunition weighed it down.

I waved to people as I walked out of town. I passed the mechanic shop. "*Buenos dias, don Lee.*"

He raised his hand and smiled.

I waved a greeting to the woman behind the counter at the corner store. "*Mucho gusto, doña Meches.*"

"*Que Dios vaya con usted, Vero,*" she answered.

Slowly the names of neighbors and townsfolk were coming back.

*Las Marías* was one kilometer from town and there were no cars on the road this early. Walking was pleasant in the cool morning air.

Several peasant laborers passed me and called out the familiar *campesino* greeting.

"*Adios,*" I said back.

The men wore rubber boots and ragged but clean work clothes. They carried sheathed machetes and hand-woven brown and tan bags, *morrales,* which held their lunches.

*Las Marías* flanked the highway. I hadn't noticed the back side of the farm from my car. Grass was dry and sparse in the rocky soil, and reddish clay showed through. Farms in this area had such poor topsoil they could only support pine trees or coffee. Subsistence farmers in the region barely harvested enough corn and beans to survive.

I rounded the corner, arrived at the gate, and walked down the driveway toward the pump house. Assessing the farm, I was forced to agree with Mayor Jaime. This was an ideal place to create a housing project. The thirty acres of flat pastureland would be enough space for the proposed homes and there were sufficient trees to provide the necessary lumber.

Not much original forest remained in Moyuta, but this pine-covered hill had been special to my father. Each year in December, he and an armed helper had patrolled the area to warn off any would-be Christmas tree poachers.

I asked him once if he would really shoot someone for chopping down a tree.

"No, Vero. I wouldn't," he replied. "Not just for that." He winked and said in a lower voice, "Let that be our little secret."

During dry season, men dug ditches around the farm and cleared the perimeter to protect against fires on neighboring lands. Slash-and-burn management is common to prepare the ground for planting before rainy season. My father told me the Mayans farmed this way, working the land for a year or two before moving on. After two consecutive years of burning, the soil died, the nutrients gone up in smoke. Today, these descendants of the Mayans labor the same land year after year. Those who continue to slash and burn find it necessary to use expensive chemical fertilizers to enrich the earth.

That was never Dad's way. He composted coffee waste and animal manure. He and his workers dug holes for new coffee trees a year before planting and filled them with the nutrient-rich loam. He taught the value of soil conservation and terracing to his workers, neighbors, and anyone who would listen. He farmed using environmentally friendly methods. Some took the ideas home with them, and others didn't.

I lay back on a boulder under a prickly jocote tree. It was almost leafless and would bear fruit during rainy season after the last of its leaves had fallen.

I took the diary out of my bag. Santiago, I thought.

Flipping through the diary, I found the entry I wanted.

*June 14, 1991*
*Dear Diary,*
*I had the best day ever! I think I'm falling in love! I ran into Santiago on the way back from Ojo de Agua. He said his mother had some fruit for us, but I think it was just an excuse to ride home with me. When we got to the farm, butterflies were fluttering all over the fields. It was amazing!*

*He's so cute. He kissed me and said he'd call me! Ana was right,*
*he does like me!*

I closed my eyes and stretched out on the boulder, enjoying the sunshine and thinking about the day I fell in love.

After harvest, the busiest times at the farm were the first months of the rainy season: May, June and July. That's when planting took place, both of coffee and shade trees. I often took meals to my father and spent time with him while he worked.

That particular day, I was riding my horse back into town when I spotted Santiago at a *tienda*. I slowed to say hello.

"Hey, Vero. Where're you going?"

"On my way home from *Ojo de Agua*. And you? You're back from school?"

"It's our mid-year break. We were on the coast yesterday and brought back a sack of mangos for your family. Come with me to the house and I'll get them for you."

I dismounted and we walked together, leading Estrellita.

Suddenly, I was tongue-tied. "Is Ana around?" I asked, fumbling for something to say.

"She went to visit our grandparents in Jalpatagua. Do you want to come in for a minute?"

"No, I'll wait here."

He came out a few minutes later with a bag of Tommy mangos. "I'll ride with you and then walk home."

He swung himself into the saddle and pulled me up behind him. I put my arms around his waist and felt the warmth from his body. I could smell his boy scent. We took the back road, passing the cemetery to our right. I'd hoped the ride would last longer, but before I knew it we were there.

As we passed through the farm gate, heading toward the stable, we were greeted by a vibrant cloud of migrating butterflies. They flickered and flew in a kaleidoscope of color, alighting in the trees, on the bushes, fences, and grass, blanketing the lower meadow.

Santiago dismounted and helped me down. I took the horse to the stable and handed her over to Chepe, one of our workers.

"*Cuando vinieron las mariposas?*" I asked.

"They came a little while ago."

When I returned, Santiago was in the field, arms and legs spread, inviting butterflies to land on him. Several were already resting on his arms and shoulders.

"This is fabulous!" he said. "Try it."

I positioned myself where the butterflies were thickest. I felt the breeze from their wings as they brushed past me. They landed on my wide-spread arms like soft, fluttering kisses.

"I wish I had my camera," Santiago said.

"I'll go up to the house and get mine."

"Don't go. They might leave soon."

In the soft breeze of fluttering wings, I twirled around and around, scattering them in a medley of colors, until I fell down dizzy, laughing with delight. Santiago sat on the grass with me and held my hand as we watched the butterflies disperse.

"Veronica, that was so cool," Santiago said, pulling me to my feet. "I'll always remember this." He stood in front of me and took my hands. He noticed chill bumps on my arms as the late afternoon cooled. "Are you cold?"

He rubbed my arms, then held me close. He stepped back for a moment and looked at me. "Close your eyes."

I felt something like a butterfly on my lips. Then I tasted Santiago.

"I've got to go. I'll call you. I'd like to see you again before my break's over and I go back to school." He gave me a quick second kiss and left.

I watched him saunter to the road. He turned back and waved. I waited until he disappeared from sight.


Though it didn't seem like Santiago had changed much over the years, I was a different person from that fourteen-year-old in the diary. The youthful innocence was gone, but the strong attraction for Santiago remained.

I climbed down from the boulder with my heavy knapsack and spied Juan Bautista to my left repairing fences. He waved as I approached.

"*Cómo está, seño Vero?*" he said.

"I'm fine, and you? I'm going to do some target practice in the woods. Don't worry if you hear a gun going off."

He nodded and continued working. I hiked up into the forest to a relatively clear spot. How long since this gun was fired? Tio Carlos was not a man who packed a gun or was willing to shoot, but I wasn't surprised he owned one. There were more firearms in this country than adults.

I took aim.

*Bang!*

The gun's kick surprised me. Birds squawked and flew out of the trees. I was unaccustomed to firearms after so long. Dad had trained me to be a proficient marksman and we had practiced together. I was a crack shot back then.

I spent the afternoon firing the gun, loading, and reloading, until I felt comfortable with the weapon. When I was ready to put it back in my pack, I heard a shot. A bullet whizzed by me and buried itself in a nearby tree.

I jerked my head around. Did someone shoot at me? My knees nearly buckled from fright. I crouched down and tried to calculate where the bullet might have come from.

The neighbor's farm?

I panicked and took off in a pathless direction, going straight up the hill, stumbling and falling as I ran through the dense pines. What good would it do anyone if I were dead? Then I remembered what Tio Carlos had said. Perhaps the mayor would prefer to deal with Juan José or with Mom. But surely he wouldn't try to kill me before I said no. Who else?

An accident? A random bullet?

That didn't seem likely. *I'd better give the mayor what he wants and get out of Moyuta.*

When I reached the backside of *Las Marías,* I took a trail that led to a small settlement above the public school. My hair was a mess, my clothing torn and my arms scratched by branches. I hadn't noticed hurting myself, but my palms were scraped and bruised.

I hurried to Tio Carlos' house, my heart pounding with fright. In the kitchen, I spotted a bottle of rum on the shelf and helped myself to a hefty shot. My hands shook as I drained the glass. Immediate warmth spread through me.

María Celia stared when she saw me. "Vero, what on earth happened to you? Are you all right?"

"Yes…Well, no, not really. I was at *Las Marías* and a bullet whizzed past me, only inches away."

"What? Are you sure?"

"I wish I wasn't." I sat down, shaken, reliving the nightmare. "I've had a feeling that someone's been following me for the past few days. Now they've shot at me."

"Did you tell Carlos?" Her face showed concern. "This is serious."

"I haven't seen him."

I went to my room, composed myself, then squared my shoulders and picked up the phone. It was time to touch base with Mom again; I longed to hear her familiar voice.

She answered on the second ring. "Veronica, is that you? I've been worried sick about you. I tried to get you on your cell phone, but it didn't go through. Why did you wait so long to call?"

"Everything's fine, Mom," I lied. "It's only been a few days."

"What's going on, Veronica? You sound upset."

Mom knew me well. I couldn't fool her, so I relented. "I don't know what to do. I thought I might sell, but realize I don't want to. Now I'm frightened."

"Calm down. Why are you afraid?"

"I'm sorry, Mom. I shouldn't be telling you this. It'll just make you worry. I was at *Las Marías* today and a bullet went right by me. It was probably a random shot and I'm making too much of it."

"A what? A random shot? I doubt it was random, Vero. Leave town for a while. Go to the city. Visit your brother. Come back to California. Forget about the farm. It's not worth it. It sounds too dangerous there and I don't want you hurt."

I was sorry now that I'd told her. She sounded hysterical. "I'll try to stay out of harm's way. And I promise to call more often."

# CHAPTER TEN

I OPENED THE DIARY TO THE WEEKEND WE CLIMBED THE PACAYA VOLCANO. Dad had walked into the house and announced, "I'm ready to take a break." He was sweaty, his hair flattened where the cap had been, his pants and boots muddy.

"Done with the planting?" I said.

"And in need of a change. The weather should be clear the next couple of days. Let's spend the weekend in the city. Get some things together while I shower."

"You'd better take your boots off. Mom won't be happy if you track mud into the house."

"Where is she?" he said as he unlaced them.

"In her office, working on the computer."

He went back to talk to her. "Good idea, Quique," I heard her reply. "It's been so long, I'd almost forgotten we have an apartment in the city."

We left that afternoon. About halfway to the city we were flagged down. I was dozing in the backseat when Dad's cursing woke me. "*A la gran puta!*"

"What is it, Dad?"

"A roadblock. It's okay, Vero. Go back to sleep."

I looked out. Ten men from the Special Forces had set up a checkpoint, stopping all cars in both directions, examining identification and other documents.

Dad rolled down his window. "*Buenas tardes.*"

"License and registration."

He fumbled in the glove box and handed them over.

"Is this your vehicle?"

"Of course."

The officer stared at the *tarjeta de circulación*. "Why is it registered to Elizabeth Johnson?"

"My wife."

He peered into the car, first looking at my mother, then at me.

"Does she have identification?"

Mom immediately searched for her license and handed it to him.

Dad drummed his fingers on the steering wheel. "Can I go now?"

"You can leave when I tell you to." He glared at Dad. "Where you headed?"

"The capital, what does this have to do with anything?"

"Get out of the car, sir."

"What?"

"Out of the car!"

He pushed Dad up against the side, frisked him, and smirked when he found the gun. "I need to see papers for this."

"Of course."

"It's against the law to carry this weapon on the highway."

"What are you talking about? Of course it's not."

"Are you questioning my authority?" Expecting a confrontation, two men behind him started forward. "I'm going to have to take you in."

Dad hesitated, glancing over at Mom and me.

The officer sneered. "Unless you want to make it worth my while not to."

"I'm not giving you a bribe."

"Suit yourself." He steered Dad toward his supervisor, a stout, bespectacled man taking notes on a clipboard. Dad's face reddened in anger. He gestured with his arms, making an effort not to raise his voice. He presented his identification then pulled a card from his wallet. The supervisor studied the card, stepped back and left for a moment to talk to the first agent. He returned, handed my father the gun, and ushered him to the car. "*Que le vaya bien.*"

When we were on our way again, I asked, "What was that all about?"

"A shakedown. They want bribes. I wouldn't pay so they tried to scare me. When I pulled out the card of a good friend of mine, an active general in the military, he saw the name and backed down."

I was no longer sleepy and Dad still trembled with anger. "Never give them money, Vero. It only encourages their greed."

Mom patted his arm.

We arrived at the apartment without further incident. While Mom fixed dinner, Dad downed a Gallo beer then retired to the sofa, his feet propped on the coffee table, nodding off.

I walked to the window and called my mother over, pointing toward the Pacaya Volcano. In the evening darkness, red lava glowed as it oozed down the mountainside. During the day, steam blew out, creating a cloud which hovered over the crater.

"I've always wanted to climb that volcano," Mom said. "Quique told me he'd take me, but hasn't said when."

"I'd like to go, too." I glanced over at my father. He opened an eye. He had been listening.

At dinner, Dad said, "Remember a few months ago when we talked about climbing Pacaya, Liz?"

She nodded.

"Juan Bautista Salazar recently went up."

Mom glanced at him and raised her eyebrows, waiting for him to continue.

"You remember him? We went to high school together. Anyway, he said we should go soon. Pacaya's building up for a large eruption. It could change the shape of the volcano. Let's go tomorrow morning."

Mom and I greeted the plan with enthusiasm.

The alarm woke us early. We packed sandwiches, snacks, and bottles of water, then piled into the car and drove toward Lake Amatitlán, a half hour from the city. After passing through the lakeshore town, we turned toward San Vicente Pacaya, a village halfway up the mountain. Eight inches of fine silt covered the road, hiding the ruts and holes. Everything was the same dust color: the coffee bushes, the boulders, the houses, and even the people who peered out of their homes to see who was passing.

The road went through the small village and ended abruptly at the trailhead. Dad asked several people where he could leave his car.

"*No tenga pena*. Leave it on the road," they told him. "*Aquí no pasa nada*." They said he shouldn't worry; bad things don't happen here.

Dad had been up the volcano in his youth and told us the hike would take only a few hours. He led the way up a narrow trail that wound through brush and trees. We followed. The first part was steep and we stopped to rest several times. When we reached an overview with wooden benches, we sat down for a snack. My watch told me we had been hiking only forty minutes. I checked to make sure it hadn't stopped.

The view was spectacular. The volcanoes of Acatenango, Fuego, and Agua peeked through the clouds to the west. Guatemala City lay blanketed under a thin layer of smog, and Lake Amatitlán, where Guatemala City funneled most of its sewage, flaunted its polluted green color directly below us.

"How long until we get there?" I asked as we trudged along. Though it was cool on the mountain, the hike was strenuous and we began peeling off layers of clothing.

He assured me we'd be there soon.

"Quique," Mom said, "are you sure this is a short hike?"

"This is the easiest volcano to climb in Guatemala, and the most exciting. You'll be glad we did it when you see what it's like at the top."

A half hour later, the trail opened onto a clearing just below the cone. Picnic tables were scattered among low, gnarled trees, and a few lonely cows grazed on the sparse grass. We sat down and took out our sandwiches.

Billowing white clouds rolled in on the wind, bringing a chill and hiding the peak. Loud thunder-like rumbles came from deep inside the volcano.

"Are you sure it's safe to climb to the top?" Mom said.

"Don't worry, Liz. Lava doesn't flow over the sides during the day." He pointed to the south side of the cone. "See where the lava beds lie? The flow is generally on that side."

That word "generally" worried me, but Mom didn't say anything.

We left the meadow and started up the trail for the final ascent. The ground changed from hard-packed earth to loose volcanic gravel and became steeper. A group of five European tourists passed us on their way down.

We focused on the upward climb. With each step, we slid back. I looked down to make sure we were moving in the right direction. The picnic tables were barely visible and I was surprised we'd come so far. The wind picked up and we were glad for our jackets.

The booming got louder. With each explosion, my heart raced. Mom lagged behind. Dad stopped and decided to go back for her. "Stay here and wait for us, Vero. Don't go up any farther."

I watched as he slid down through the loose gravel. I couldn't hear with the wind whistling in my ears, but I saw Mom's mouth move. Dad grabbed her hand and pulled her along, determined to finish the ascent. I was twenty yards ahead leaning against a large boulder when a violent explosion shook the area. I was terrified when I heard rocks falling around me.

The volcano was erupting.

Dad yelled. I could barely hear him, but I knew what he was saying. We needed to get off the mountain.

I gathered my wits and quickly stepped onto the trail. My feet sank in the loose, gravelly pebbles; I slipped and slid down a lot faster than I had climbed up.

When we reached the picnic area we felt safe, even though volcanic rocks were landing only a few hundred yards away. We sat at a table and emptied the sand and gravel from our shoes.

"Let's go home, Quique," Mom said. "This is enough excitement for one day."

We started back across a narrow ridge, Dad in front and me in the middle. Suddenly, a man stepped out from behind a boulder, his face covered with a blue bandana, hair invisible under a black ski cap. He waved a revolver and said, "If you have weapons, throw them down, or you'll all die."

In a split second, Dad had his gun out and was shooting.

"Get down, get down!" Mom shouted, pulling me to the ground. When I no longer heard shots, I looked up to see what had happened. Dad was standing, legs apart, gun in hand. I peered over the edge and saw the assailant rolling down the gravel embankment about thirty feet below us.

"Come on!" Dad ordered. Minutes earlier we had been exhausted; now adrenaline kicked in and we ran the rest of the way, silent and shaken. When we reached the base of the trail and saw the car, we realized our quick descent had surprised someone. The doors had been forced, the car ransacked, and the radio hung by one screw. We looked around for the culprit, but the streets were empty and the village silent.

We jumped in and breathed a sigh of relief when the engine started. We left in a hurry, the car jolting and bumping down the dusty road. We were quiet on the way home. The image of my father shooting at the bandit kept flashing through my mind.

After dinner, I couldn't hold my question any longer. "Dad, I know you carry a gun to protect us, but you were so fast. He didn't even get a chance to fire back."

Dad hesitated, carefully formulating his next words. "I had to make sure he wouldn't fire back. You could have been hurt. He might have been bluffing, but I couldn't risk it. Many years ago when I decided to carry a firearm, I promised myself I would be ready to use it if necessary. I envision scenarios, practice making decisions so if the time comes, I can react instinctively."

"What if there had been three or four attackers instead of one? Would you have tried to fight them all?"

"I would have reacted the same way. How could I throw down my gun and allow us to be robbed, perhaps killed? Criminals are encouraged when people don't fight back."

A few weeks later, bandits attacked a group of tourists on the mountain, beating and robbing them, raping the women at gunpoint. No one put up any resistance.

That's when Dad decided I should learn to use a gun.

# CHAPTER ELEVEN

I AWOKE TO THE MUFFLED SOUNDS OF TIO CARLOS ON THE PHONE.

"That wasn't part of our deal…Of course I understand, and yes I still want it…No, I didn't expect it to be so difficult…I don't want her harmed…"

What kind of a deal had my uncle made?

He sounded nervous. I went to the door to listen.

"I want out now…No, no, I didn't mean that…" The conversation abruptly ended. I walked into the kitchen. When he saw me, he started. "Oh Vero, it's you."

"Are you okay, Tio? You're pale."

"I'm fine. Maybe I'm coming down with a cold. It's the change of weather."

I drew in my lips, knowing he wasn't being truthful. "Mmm. I hope you feel better."

I wondered about what I had heard and it bothered me, but I could hardly bring myself to suspect Tio Carlos of duplicity.

The scheduled meeting with Mayor Jaime was fast approaching. I ate breakfast and like any woman, wondered what to wear. I didn't want to wear something that might look enticing. You never knew about men, especially about the ones from around here. I finally decided on something neutral: gray slacks and a light sweater.

I started getting ready at nine. By nine thirty I was pacing the floor. Why had they told me to go alone?

"Veronica, would you like some coffee?" María Celia asked.

"No, thank you. A tranquilizer would be more like it."

She laughed. "I'm sure Carlos would be happy to oblige. Don't worry. Your meeting is in city hall. He can't do anything to you there."

Though she meant to be reassuring, her comment only made me more nervous. "By the way," I said. "Santiago Godoy is coming over after my meeting. Have him wait for me if I'm not back yet."

"Santiago. Is he a friend of yours? His mother, Alba, and I go way back." She thought for a moment. "That's right. Your families were close when you were young."

"Ana was my best friend." I looked at my watch. "I'd better be going."

"Aren't you leaving a little early? It's only two blocks away."

"I'd rather get there early. I'm ready now and I'll only get more nervous waiting around here."

I left the house, strolled down the street to the park, and sat down on a cement bench. The morning air was fresh and the day clear, but I was anxious, eager to get the meeting over with. Though it wasn't time yet, I got up and entered the *municipalidad*. My footsteps echoed on the cement floor as I approached the receptionist.

"I'm here to see Mayor Jaime."

She looked at her appointment book. "You must be Veronica. You're early. Wait here a moment." A sign over the door behind her desk read *Alcalde*. She tapped on the door and went in. A few minutes later she returned and told me to take a seat. She said the mayor would be with me shortly.

I looked around. Toward the front, petty officials shuffled papers at cheap metal desks. Several people sat in chairs near the door. A small indigenous-looking woman suckled a baby at her dusky breast. I imagined they waited for help with official paperwork: taxes, identification papers, birth records, death certificates. I checked my watch; twenty minutes had passed. I asked the secretary again if the mayor knew I was here.

"I told him," she snapped. "You saw me go in. You're not so special that you can't wait like everyone else."

I sat down. My foot tapped on the cement floor.

The receptionist glared at me for a moment, then stepped into the office again, said something, and returned. She looked at me impassively. "*Pase adelante.* The mayor will see you now."

Mayor Jaime swung about in his chair to face me. "Señorita Villagrán. Thank you for coming. Please have a seat. I presume my messengers relayed my request."

"I got your message."

He laughed at some unshared joke. "I'm not the subtle type."

"I noticed. Why did you need to see me again so soon, Mayor Jaime? I thought we agreed on meeting after a week."

"Something came up."

To avoid his blatant stare, I focused my eyes on the diplomas and certificates that covered half the wall behind him. Among them was a framed photograph of the president of Guatemala embracing a smiling Jaime Ramírez. He turned toward my gaze. "It was a memorable moment. President Porta is like a brother."

I swallowed hard. Mayor Jaime had strong political connections.

"I'll be direct with you," he continued. "I need *Ojo de Agua*."

"You...what? I thought this was only about *Las Marías*." I tried to keep the panic out of my voice. "I would never sell *Ojo de Agua*. The farm has been in my family forever."

"I'm aware of its history, but I must have both farms."

"Why? Surely you aren't planning on subdividing that as well."

His lips curved down as though considering what to answer. "Personal reasons. I can't go into it."

"The answer will be no, then."

"You have time to think about it."

I shook my head. "I'm sorry, Mayor Jaime. This is unexpected."

"I went ahead and had my lawyer draw up the additional papers for *Ojo de Agua*. Would you like to see them?"

I got up abruptly, then decided I should let him think there might still be a chance I'd sell. "No, thanks. But I will consider it." He offered me his hand and I pretended not to notice. "Now, please excuse me," I said.

"Temper, temper." He had an amused look in his eye. "Beware, Veronica. Unexpected things can happen in Moyuta. Be sure you're here again next Thursday, ten o'clock sharp. Time is running out."

I was even angrier than after our first meeting. I knew he was toying with me and that he enjoyed upsetting me. I reminded myself not to fall into his trap. Playing the vulnerable woman could only hurt my prospects; besides, it was completely out of character.

I went straight back to Tio Carlos' house, walked in unseeing, and almost tripped over Santiago, who sat on a wooden bench in the hallway.

"Veronica!" He reached out for me and I fell into his embrace, my anger melting into tears. "Are you okay?"

"No, I'm not. I don't know if I'm strong enough for this."

"Sit down." He made room for me next to him on the bench and put his arm around me protectively. "Tell me what happened."

"Do you know the mayor?" I asked.

His mouth grew tight. "I've had few dealings with him. And the fewer, the better. He's a bad man."

"I was on the brink of giving in. But now he wants *Ojo de Agua* as well. What am I going to do?"

"What did you tell him?"

"I said no. He didn't accept it. He tried to intimidate me by saying that unexpected things can happen in Moyuta. Do you think I should give up?"

"It doesn't matter what I think. Knowing you, I seriously doubt you will."

I stared into the garden. "I've been followed and threatened. Two men approached me on my way back from *Ojo de Agua* yesterday. The mayor's men—Chico Negro and Montaña Ocho."

His eyes narrowed. "That sounds dangerous. Let me help you. You can't fight this alone."

"Are you certain you want to get involved?"

He ignored my question. "When is the deadline for your decision?"

"I have ten days."

"Okay. We have to come up with a plan. Who have you told about your comings and goings?"

"Only Tio Carlos and María Celia. But they're family."

Santiago bit his lip and thought for a moment. "Anybody could be on the mayor's payroll. From now on, don't trust anyone."

"What about you?"

"Be suspicious of everyone, even me." I tried to absorb this new information. "Remember, anyone can be bought. Everyone has a price."

"Ahem." We both looked up. Tio Carlos had appeared in the doorway. "Santiago, how good to see you! How are your parents?"

"Nice to see you, doctor. Everyone is fine, thank you."

"Don Guillermo?"

"Still hanging in there. He has good days and bad days."

"How did your meeting go, Vero?"

I shrugged. "Not well. The mayor wants *Ojo de Agua*, too."

A glimmer of satisfaction flashed across his face before he could control it. "That's too bad."

I remembered what Mom had said about Tio Carlos losing his inheritance. Was that what this was about?

Tio Carlos lingered. "María Celia told me you were shot at yesterday."

Santiago turned quickly, "Is that true, Veronica?"

"While I was doing target practice."

"I'd rather have a live niece than a dead one." I studied his impassive face. "Maybe you should sign those papers. I know I said I'd love to have you near, but I don't want you in danger."

"I'm thinking about it," I said noncommittally.

He stayed for a moment. We sized each other up, wordlessly. "Excuse me. I need to get back to my patients." The door closed behind him.

Santiago got to his feet. "I have to go, too, Vero. I'm meeting someone at the farm shortly. I'm free tomorrow. I'll pick you up after breakfast, around eight. You need to get away from here, some place where no one can follow you."

"That's a welcome idea. What are you planning?"

"It's better you don't know. Then you can't give us away." He smiled at his attempt at humor. "I'll see you tomorrow. Stay low today and don't go out."

We turned at the sound of the clinic door closing again. Had Tio Carlos opened it to listen to our conversation?

Was Santiago right? Should I not trust anyone?

In the kitchen, María Celia was fixing lunch. "How did it go?" she asked when I walked in.

"Okay," I said guardedly, afraid to give anything away.

"I told you it would be fine." She handed me a plate of steaming tortillas filled with melting fresh cheese. They looked delicious. "You forgot to have breakfast. This is just a snack to get you through the rest of the morning until lunch."

When I finished, I went out to the garden. A black witch moth with a wingspan of nearly seven inches landed near me on a post.

Was it an omen? I wasn't superstitious, but I remembered the last time I'd seen one. It was fourteen years ago, around the time I was falling for

Santiago. Out of curiosity, I went back to my room and skimmed through my diary to look for the entry.

> *June 18, 1991*
> *Dear Diary,*
> *I've been daydreaming a lot and Mom keeps asking me if I'm okay. I don't want my parents to know about Santiago. Dad would be so mad!*
> *I helped Mom in the garden today. We saw a papalota on the screen door. Juanita was terrified. I thought it was pretty funny. People believe anything.*

We were coming in from the garden when I spotted it. "Look, Mom."

A large black witch moth had attached itself to the screen door on the inside. We opened the door carefully so as not to disturb it and slipped in. Juanita, the young girl who helped with cleaning, had backed into the corner by the refrigerator, her eyes wide with fright.

"*Señora Liz*," she began, "*hay una papalota.*"

According to local superstition, these majestic moths were omens of death. I went back to inspect it more closely. At a glance, it looked black, but up close it was a dark brownish-gray with intricate black patterns.

"Mom, this is like a beautiful butterfly." As I spoke, the moth detached from the screen door and flapped through the house like a bat, searching for an exit.

Juanita screamed and backed farther into the corner, trying to hide behind the refrigerator. We opened all the doors and windows; I followed it with a broom, and chased it out of the house.

"*Juanita, mejor váyase a su casa.*" Mom sent Juanita home as she was too shaken to continue working.

The next evening, I didn't think the episode with the witch moth was so funny. The phone rang around seven. I was in the living room reading when Dad answered it.

"Hello?...*Dónde fue?*" Dad's comments were terse, his tone grim; his eyes examined the ceiling as the caller explained. "*A la gran puta, que desgraciados,*" he cursed. "Where is he? . . .Don't worry. We'll be there as soon as we can."

He hung up, pensive for a moment.

Mom came in from the kitchen, wiping her hands on a dishtowel. "Who called?"

"It was Antonia. She said May's brother, Sergio Conde, was murdered late this afternoon in his clinic. We have to get over there to represent our side of the family. Mario and May are making arrangements to come tomorrow morning from Chicago for the funeral."

Dr. Conde was Dad's *cuncuño*, his brother Mario's brother-in-law, a prominent doctor. He was building a new hospital in Jutiapa, a bustling commercial town of about twenty thousand people. My father knew him and my mother had met him several times. Apparently I had, too, although I didn't recall. Families extend so far and wide in this country it's impossible to remember everyone.

We put on our black mourning clothes, left our mountain town, and descended five thousand feet into a flat, dry region where long-horned cattle ranged in dusty pastures.

When Dad dropped us off at the *Pollo Campero* in the center of town, it was already nine in the evening. "Go ahead and get a bite to eat," he said. "I'm going to see if I can help with getting the body back from the morgue."

The police had marked out the area for investigation and ordered an autopsy. Why the autopsy, no one knew. It was obvious he'd been shot.

"I think the coroner just wanted the practice," Dad grumbled.

We waited, drank coffee in the restaurant and watched people stroll past. After an hour, my father joined us. "I hope you girls are ready for a long night. We can't leave until either Antonia or Herman get here from Guatemala City."

"Where is the wake going to be held?" Mom asked.

"At the Rotary Club. Sergio was on the board of directors."

We stayed a while longer, got our check, and left.

We parked in front of the Rotary Club's long, white building. Few cars had arrived. Inside, several men were setting up chairs and two ladies arranged *coronas*, large flower wreaths, in the front where the casket would be displayed. Hundreds of people would come and go all night until after the funeral service and burial the next day.

"Did you find out what happened?" I asked.

Dad glanced at my mother. I saw something pass between them, then Mom nodded. "Sergio was in his clinic at about four o'clock this afternoon. There were maybe twenty people waiting to see him. Two unknown men stepped into the waiting room. One of them wanted to see the doctor immediately and convinced an older woman to let him in ahead of her. The other man stayed near the door. Both were armed, but this is Jutiapa and most men are." He unconsciously felt for the weapon at his waist.

Dad continued, "He went in, shot Sergio three times, then turned and calmly walked back into the waiting room. 'Stay where you are for five more minutes,' he told everyone. 'Don't do anything stupid. We'll be watching.' Then they left."

"Quique, that sounds like hired assassins. Nothing was stolen?" Mom asked.

Dad shook his head.

We sat in the second row, not far from the coffin. Many came to pay their respects to the family. People around us discussed the murder in whispers.

"Does anyone know who could have done it?"

"No one recognized the men. They didn't even wear masks."

"They couldn't be from around here."

In a country where murder is commonplace, people sense death's nearness most closely at a funeral. "It could have been me or you," they think. "Who will be next?" They huddle together whispering, trying to make sense of a murder, trying to believe they won't fall victim to a similar fate.

Sergio had no known enemies. He was a respected community leader. One of Sergio's sisters sat next to Mom. "Who do you think could have done such a terrible thing?" Mom whispered.

"Sergio was a great man and a fine brother," the sister replied. "But his love life was chaotic—fourteen children by eight women. Who knows how many were wives, or girlfriends, or just casual one-night stands? I gave up keeping track long ago."

"Oh, dear," Mom said. "It could have been any of them."

"Or a father, brother, boyfriend of one of them, or someone else that we don't know about."

"Who stood to gain in his will?"

"He didn't have one," she told Mom. "It's a tragedy for all of those involved. He actively supported all eight families."

It was likely Sergio's disorderly love life that had done him in.

I closed the diary, once again reminded how Dad's adulterous behavior had changed my life. Adultery is overlooked in Guatemalan society. Women become embittered, but they are defenseless, with no option but to accept it. Infidelity is as common as drunks sprawled on the sidewalk on a Sunday afternoon, but it is also as dangerous as a rabid dog. It can bite back.

# CHAPTER TWELVE

I walked down the hallway of my childhood home on the coffee farm. The floorboards creaked under my bare feet and anticipation crept over me. Everything was just as it had been when we all lived at the farm. All of us, that is, except Juan José who hadn't yet arrived. Family photos hung on the cream-colored walls. Happy faces looked out from family moments: me as a baby, my christening, first communion, a grammar school graduation, a family portrait at Christmas. Suddenly, Dad appeared in front of me, in the way people often do in nocturnal wanderings.

"Dad? What are you doing here?"

My heart wrenched as I saw the bruises on his neck and wrists. Blood soaked his shirt front. A bullet hole gaped in his temple.

"I've been waiting for you to come home, Vero. It's been too long."

"Dad, I'm so sorry I never came back. I meant to, but it was just too difficult."

I stared at him, trying to fathom such brutality. He gazed back at me and said, "Don't feel bad for me, Vero. It was my choice."

"Why did you let it happen?" I asked. "Wasn't there some other way?"

"It was the right decision," he said. "I couldn't involve more people and risk their lives. I thought about it long and hard. I never meant to hurt any of you. I gave them a good fight, Veronica, but they were just too many."

"Dad, I want you to know I'm sorry for leaving like I did. I'm sorry for everything and I wish I'd had the chance to tell you."

"You have nothing to be sorry for," he said. "I love you very much, Vero, and I regret not being here for you. Especially now when you need me."

"Dad, what should I do?"

"That's your decision. Just remember, things are not always as they seem."

He opened his arms and embraced me. I laid my head on his shoulder, tears streaming down my face as he held me tight.

I awoke with a wet pillow and a heavy heart. Could I stand up to Mayor Jaime like Dad stood up to the extortionists? I doubted my strength, and I sure wasn't ready for the family mausoleum.

I ate a hurried breakfast and went to the store to buy a few food items for my trip. When I returned, Tio Carlos was waiting for me.

"Where are you going today, Vero?"

"Santiago didn't say. It's a surprise."

"Hmm. Under the circumstances, I don't think that's a good idea. I like to know where you are, in case something happens."

I shrugged, relieved that Santiago hadn't told me.

"When he comes, I'll talk to him."

I was waiting by the door when Santiago drove up. "My uncle wants to know where we're going."

"I bet he does." His voice dripped with sarcasm. "Get in quickly. I need to shake a car that's been tailing me."

"Why would someone be following you?"

"Perhaps because they know we're going out together today."

I remembered the noise from the clinic door when Santiago got up to leave. It was the only explanation. Tio Carlos.

I got in and sat quietly. I hadn't considered that anyone else would be endangered and was filled with remorse. It was bad enough that I was putting myself in a risky situation.

Santiago tossed my things in the trunk, then jumped into the driver's seat. We left Moyuta and headed toward the neighboring town of Conguaco.

"Where are you taking me?"

"Nowhere yet. I'm trying to get rid of the tail." A black Land Rover was some distance behind. He pulled out his cell phone and punched in some numbers. "Selvin? Hey, buddy. This is Santiago...Doin' good, doin' good.

Listen, I need a favor. I'm playing a prank on someone who's following me…Can we switch cars for the day? I'll be in front of your parents' business in five…Great. Veronica and I will get down in the back seat while you drive out…"

He didn't explain anything and I didn't ask. I trusted him. I turned around and glared at the car following us, but the windows were tinted and I couldn't tell who was driving.

"Don't be so obvious, Vero."

When we reached Conguaco, we had to slow down as people walked in the middle of the street, unaccustomed to traffic.

We parked in front of an electrical appliance store. Toasters and blenders with large green and yellow price tags brightened the front window.

"Just follow my lead," Santiago said as we got out of the car. "Act natural, like we're planning on buying a toaster or something."

We locked the car and I glanced back, trying not to be obvious. The dark car parked a half block away; no one had gotten out. We window-shopped on the sidewalk to make sure they saw us, then went in.

"Santiago, over here!" A short, husky man in his early thirties came into the showroom from the back.

The men embraced quickly before turning to me. "Selvin, I want you to meet a very special lady. This is Veronica."

"You've been holding out on me."

"I found her first!" Santiago winked at me.

Selvin rubbed his hands together. "I love intrigue." He led us through a back door to a small garden area and into a garage on the other side. "Don't tell me the details. It's better I leave them to my imagination."

A bright red, double-cab, four-wheel-drive pickup sat in the enclosure. The garage door emptied onto a side street. "Isn't she gorgeous? I just bought her."

"*Puta*, Selvin. You couldn't have picked a louder, more visible car, could you?" Santiago said as we got into the pickup.

"You two stay down just in case. The guys who are following can't see you anyway through the darkened windows. They only have one vehicle, right?"

Santiago nodded.

"They won't expect you to come out on this street in a different car. Especially not in a hot rod like this."

We squeezed in and Selvin started the engine. "It's not loud. Unless I rev it! Listen to this—I love the way the motor sounds. Purrs like a cat!"

"More like a lion," Santiago muttered.

"Here we go!" The garage door opened automatically, and with a jerk the pickup pulled out onto the street.

I glanced back, but didn't see the Land Rover. "You don't think they'll follow us?"

Selvin grinned. "I'd like to see them try."

"They probably think we're still inside buying a toaster," Santiago said. "By the time they go in to look for us, we'll be long gone."

"I can't wait to see their faces." A slow smile spread across Selvin's face. "Did you see who they were?"

I remembered the mayor's messengers. "No, but I have a pretty good idea."

"Don't worry. Whoever was driving would never connect me with your disappearance."

Santiago and I hunched down in the backseat. As we left town, he picked up speed, then abruptly slowed to a stop. "The coast is clear! You drive now, Santiago. I'll walk back."

"Are you sure, Selvin?"

"The walk will do me good." He patted his slight paunch. "I don't get enough exercise anyway."

"Thanks, Selvin. You're the best."

"You bet."

We climbed into the front seats and headed back. As we approached Moyuta, we turned onto a side street and drove toward the volcano.

About five minutes outside of town, Santiago stopped near a small wood-framed house. He honked twice and a boy about twelve came out, the same boy I'd seen playing ball on the street a few days earlier. He opened the gate and we parked the truck under a palm-thatched carport. Two horses were tied nearby.

"Thanks, Chepito."

"*Si, señor Santiago.*"

The boy looked at me curiously. "*Hola, Chepito*," I said. "*Yo soy Veronica.*"

"*Mucho gusto.*"

Chepito brought out saddles for the horses. "This is where we change transportation again." Santiago glanced at me as he saddled the mare. "You do remember how to ride?"

I nodded and admired the mare. She was a roan, well filled out, a cut above average for the town. "Nice horse."

"I bought her the other day. Did I tell you to pack a swimsuit?"

"You left that part out."

"We'll improvise."

"Now I'm really intrigued."

The boy went back into the house and returned carrying a bag, which he attached to the back of Santiago's saddle. Our lunch, I hoped. We hadn't given a second thought to the food I'd brought; it was still in the trunk of Santiago's car in Conguaco.

Santiago took off his shoes, put on cowboy boots and a hat Chepito offered him. Then he slipped a semiautomatic pistol into the holster at his waist. He saw me watching him. "Hey, I need to look the part! I've got a girl to impress."

"You orchestrated this well."

"What do you think I was doing all yesterday afternoon?"

I laughed. "Santiago, you look like a character out of a John Wayne film."

"And you must be the lovely heroine," he returned, then got up on his horse. He pressed his spurs into the stallion's flanks and the horse reared and whinnied in protest.

"Are you ready?"

"As ever."

I mounted the mare and waved goodbye to Chepito. He shut the barbed-wire gate.

Villagers called out greetings as we passed. Santiago stopped several times to chat.

"You're a pretty popular guy around here, aren't you?"

"Our farm is close by. We know everyone in the area."

I must have looked concerned, because he continued, "Don't worry. These villagers aren't on the mayor's payroll. He made a lot of enemies around here. The people from this *aldea* decided not to vote for him, despite the threats. He and his henchmen are not welcome."

Houses along the dirt road we traveled were small and poor, some sided with plywood, others with metal sheeting or plastic tarps. A few had outhouses in back, draped in tattered plastic or old sheets for privacy. Family wash hung on wire fences, drying along the roadside. A few children peeked out from doorways. The road narrowed into a trail. The last few homes were one-room shacks with dirt floors.

It had rained during the night, the first rain of the season, and the steamy smell of plants and shrubs filled the air. The ground absorbed the moisture and seemed spongier, less hard and dry than when I'd gone to *Ojo de Agua* a few days earlier. I knew it wouldn't be long before grasses and weeds sprouted, and then everything would be green.

"What a gorgeous day it is," I said. "Thank you for bringing me out here."

We arrived at a gate set in the middle of the trail. Santiago dismounted and opened it. Most trails and many roadways in the countryside ran through private property; wood and wire gates marked property boundaries and were designed to keep animals from going in or out.

A few minutes later, we came to a middle-aged man cutting brush with a machete. He looked up. "*Don Santiago, buenos dias! Que bueno verlo!*"

"*Buenos dias, don Jorge.* What have you been up to?"

"I work here now. This is my home," he replied, and gestured to the property we were on. A humble house was partially hidden behind the banana trees. "I keep beehives and harvest the honey."

"Who is he, Santiago?"

"He worked for my father for several years as foreman."

We got off our horses and he helped us tie them to a nearby tree.

"*Pasen adelante.*" He invited us to approach his home. "*Bienvenidos a mi casa.*"

"Please sit here," he said, indicating a homemade wooden bench on his porch. "My daughters are making banana bread now to sell in town." His wife approached quietly and handed us each a glass of warm lemonade followed by a piece of banana bread.

His house was made of three-inch-diameter sticks tied together with thin rope and topped with a thatched roof. Through an open door I saw a young girl sweeping the hard-packed dirt floor in a bedroom area. In a separate outdoor kitchen, two older daughters tended an igloo-shaped adobe oven. The kitchen area had no walls; bamboo poles supported the tin roof. The homemade oven sat on a wooden platform at waist level.

After we finished our snack, we followed don Jorge as he showed us his beehives and proudly explained that on his two acres of land he grew his own bananas for the bread.

We returned to the house, and after some conversation about the approaching rainy season, we got up to leave.

"*Muchas gracias don Jorge y señora, ustedes son muy amables.*"

"It is a great honor for me to have don Santiago at my humble home. Any friend of yours is a friend of ours," he said, looking at me.

We thanked him again and continued on our way, armed with two loaves of banana bread.

The smell of sulfur reached us. "You're taking me to the *ausoles!*" I exclaimed. "I haven't been here since I was a child."

The area surrounding the hot springs was overgrown with weeds. It held little appeal to locals, who were more interested in fresh, cool water. Hot water bubbled out around haphazardly strewn rocks, forming a series of small ponds of varying temperatures. A small cement pool had been built for medicinal bathing, the sides slick with yellow and orange algae.

"I'm not going skinny-dipping with you, Santiago Godoy. I hope it isn't part of your plan to seduce me."

"Don't worry," he said. "If you prefer, bra and underwear are acceptable. But it's not like I haven't seen it all before."

"Maybe you've seen others, but you haven't seen me."

"Yet."

I glared at him in a teasing way, then stripped down to my underclothing. "Don't push your luck."

He whistled in admiration.

"Thanks, I guess," I said with a wry face.

Santiago undressed to his boxer shorts and we slipped into the hot water.

"My mother likes to come here. At least, she used to like to come. It's great for aches and pains, but the horseback ride is too much for her now. She has arthritis. I'm afraid I'll have to buy her a Jacuzzi instead." He made a distressed face.

"Cheapskate!" I laughed and splashed water at him.

"My father had a friend who drank the water," I offered after a moment. "He said it helped keep him stable. I think he was manic-depressive. The same lithium used to treat mental disorders is abundant in hot springs."

"I'm afraid if I drank it, I would be anything *but* stable," Santiago said. "And I would worry about your sanity if you did!"

"I don't feel stable, at least around you. Pass me a glass, please. I need some hot water to cool my thoughts."

"I like a girl who thinks hot things."

The pool was small and we kept touching each other under water. Santiago grabbed my foot and began to massage it.

"While you're at it, how are you with backs?" I said.

"I'm a regular masseuse." He moved behind me and began to knead my back. "It'll work better if I unhook your bra." I started to object, but his comforting hands quieted my protests.

After a few minutes, I scooted back slightly and felt his erection. Startled, I jumped up, my arms covering my chest. I wasn't sure how to react. "Let's get out, Santiago. I've had enough for now." I turned, fastened my bra, and pulled myself out. I sat on a rock and hugged my knees, waiting for my underclothes to dry.

"Wait a sec, Vero. I didn't mean to give you the wrong impression. It's not like it's something I can control."

He got out a moment later.

I waved it away. "Don't worry. It's just that I'm not sure I can deal with that right now."

After an awkward few minutes, Santiago got our food out. We sat in a shady spot in our wet underclothing to eat lunch. The breeze felt deliciously cool.

When our underclothes were somewhat dry, we dressed, mounted our horses, and rode back to where we parked the truck, avoiding cattle and chickens that strayed near the path.

We left the horses with Chepito and got into Selvin's pickup. "You don't have to come with me to Conguaco. Would you like me to leave you at Dr. Carlos' house?"

"I don't have anything to do there. I'd rather go with you."

"It's been great spending the day with you, Veronica. I've wanted to go to the hot springs with you since we were teens, but never had the opportunity."

I smiled pensively. "If Juan José hadn't shown up that day, things might have been very different."

When we got to Conguaco, the black car was no longer on the street and I saw Santiago's car still parked in front. A quick honk of the horn and the gate opened.

Selvin greeted us. "Santiago, my friend, how was your day? The two guys tailing you were pretty unhappy not to find you in the store."

"Did they say anything?"

"No. They just looked around and left."

"Thanks, Selvin. I owe you."

"Listen, I have bad news. Arturo Buencamino was kidnapped this morning, a few hours after you left here. A villager found his mutilated body tossed on the road near the cemetery."

"What? Don Arturo from the ice factory?"

"The same."

"Who had it in for him?"

"Rumor has it Mayor Jaime was behind it. He wanted the parcel of land where they draw spring water. Of course don Arturo wouldn't sell. It was his livelihood. One of the mayor's men was spotted in the area where the body was dumped."

My legs went limp and I felt dizzy. Don Arturo's situation sounded a lot like my own. "Can I sit down for a moment?"

"Veronica, I've got to get you out of here," Santiago said.

"Why? Is she in danger?" Selvin asked.

"The mayor is after her to sell her properties."

"Go into hiding, girl."

# CHAPTER THIRTEEN

"I think we're making way too much of this," I argued on the way back. "Mayor Jaime won't do anything to me until the time to decide has passed and I've refused to sell."

"But he can threaten," Santiago said, turning to me. "You've seen for yourself how persuasive he can be. What about the people following you? What about the 'stray' bullet? He could have you kidnapped, beat up, who knows what."

"No, Santiago. I'm not going into hiding. At least not yet."

"Veronica, this is serious. Aren't you afraid?"

"Of course I am. But I refuse to let fear rule my life." I crossed my arms defiantly. "I just have to push it out of my mind. I won't give in to this." I wasn't planning to back down, not unless it was absolutely necessary. I was my father's daughter.

"Okay." He put his hand on my arm. "At least promise me you won't wander down deserted roads alone."

"I promise. Anyway, that'd be pretty foolish after all that's happened."

He stopped the car in front of Tio Carlos' house. "I guess this is where we say goodbye." He put his arm around me and pulled me closer.

Children leaned against the vehicle and peered in, an old woman stared at us, and some young boys quit their ball game to watch us. A small town afforded little privacy.

"Come in for a minute. Don't say goodbye here, everyone's a spy."

We laughed, then Santiago turned serious. "Before we go in, I want you to know I don't trust Dr. Carlos."

I sighed. "If you told me that a week ago, I'd have been furious. You know he's been good to me since Dad died. He's given me advice, helped me with the farms, and hasn't charged anything. But I'm beginning to have doubts myself."

"Vero, be honest. Have you noticed anything suspicious?"

I told him about the phone call I overheard that morning.

"He's in cahoots with Mayor Jaime, I'm sure of it. I just wonder why. Have you noticed anything different about him?"

"I don't know. He seems to have more money. He said the clinic is doing well."

"And you believed him? Come on, Veronica. People around here can't afford to pay doctors. You should know that. They pay with hens, mangos, and eggs."

"I guess you're right about most of the people. But there is more wealth around here than there used to be."

"Narco wealth. But they don't spread it around. It leaves the country or gets invested right away, usually in property."

My heart sank as the truth filtered in. He was right. "I feel really naïve. Now what?"

"Be careful what you say. He's been tipping someone off about where you're going and what you're doing. That's the only thing that makes sense."

"What would he stand to gain?"

"I don't know." His eyebrows drew together in thought. "How have the harvests been?"

"Not great. But I figured it's because no one has been managing the farms. I never expected to make much money from them."

"Just so you know, these have been excellent crop years and the price of coffee has been on the rise. All the coffee farms show strong profits. People who have never before grown coffee are considering planting."

"Hmmm. He offered to show me the books."

"Take a look at them. Then tell me what you think."

We got out of the car and went into the house. It was quiet except for sounds from the kitchen.

"Vero, I want you to be safe." He tilted my chin up so he could look into my eyes. "Don't do anything risky." Then he kissed me lightly on the lips.

"Thanks for a wonderful day, Santiago."

"I'll see you tomorrow morning. Around eleven."

I looked at him, questioning.

"My mother's birthday. Ana invited you. If she hadn't beaten me to it, I'd be asking you myself."

I went out to the patio to sit down for a few minutes. Tio Carlos was at a table with the newspaper spread out in front of him, reading glasses perched crookedly on his nose. He turned to me as I approached. "Vero, how was your day? Where did you end up going?"

María Celia came out of the kitchen with her hair tied back in a scarf, a potato peeler in her hand, also waiting to hear my answer.

I hesitated a moment, wondering if I should reveal where we went. Then I figured it didn't matter anymore. "We rode horseback out to *los ausoles.*"

"That sounds wonderful, and very romantic," María Celia said. "I haven't been out there for years."

"It only took an hour and a half to get there on horseback. And it was such a pretty day."

"Did you hear about don Arturo?" Tio Carlos was visibly upset.

"I heard."

"He was a friend of mine, and of your father, as well."

"I'm really sorry. What happened?"

He looked out toward the garden. "Don Arturo refused to sell to the mayor. Damn it, I can't believe people resort to violence instead of talking things out." My uncle's eyes showed fear. "This is more reason for you to sign over your properties. Go back to your life in California. I'm afraid for you. I wish I could protect you, but I can't."

"I told you, I still haven't decided."

"Veronica, don't you understand? Mayor Jaime doesn't play around when he wants something. Don Arturo's murder proves that."

"Are you sure he's behind don Arturo's death?"

"Chico Negro was the last person seen with Arturo. Doña Violeta saw him force Arturo into his car."

Chico's face flashed in my mind. I remembered him only too well. He and the other creep had been waiting for me on the road from *Ojo de Agua.*

"He's Mayor Jaime's right-hand man. He takes care of all the dirty work." I felt my stomach sour at the turn of events.

"The wake is tonight at don Arturo's house. We're leaving shortly. Would you like to come with us?"

"I'm tired. I think I'll pass."

"The funeral service is at eight tomorrow morning, followed by the burial. You should consider showing up for one of them, since don Arturo was your father's friend."

"Maybe tomorrow." Remembering my conversation with Santiago, I asked, "Tio, can you show me the farm's account books you mentioned earlier?"

I thought he sounded nervous when he replied. "Of course. Any particular reason you want to see them now? I didn't think you were interested."

"Just curious."

As he went to get them, my cell phone rang. It was Mom. "Veronica. I'm so glad I was able to get through. How is everything?"

I walked to my room and shut the door. "Well, the early part of the day was delightful. Santiago and I went to the hot springs on horseback."

"Ana's brother?"

"Mmm. But when we got back we learned that don Arturo, the man from the ice factory, had been murdered."

"Arturo Buencamino?"

"Yes. It was a property dispute."

"A property dispute? With who?"

"The mayor."

"Veronica, I'm afraid you've bit off more than you can chew. Have you made your decision?" she asked.

"Mayor Jaime wants *Ojo de Agua* as well. How can I give it all up?"

"Your life is more important than a piece of property. Your father was murdered because of his principles. I don't want the same thing to happen to you. You're so much like Quique. If you don't plan to sell, leave town. Go where Mayor Jaime can't reach you."

"You're right. I'll leave for a few days."

"Take care of yourself, Vero."

"Bye, Mom. Thanks for calling."

It suddenly dawned on me that I wouldn't be able to go to the funeral tomorrow because of doña Alba's party.

I hurried out of my room.

Tio Carlos was taking his keys from the hook. He and María Celia were on their way out. "The books are right here on the table." He motioned towards some notebooks that sat in a jumble, loose papers stuck in folders. The whole mess looked very haphazard.

"Thanks. I think I'll go to the wake with you after all," I said. "Can you wait a sec while I change?"

Five minutes later, we were walking down the street toward the park. Several other people, also dressed for mourning, headed in the same direction.

We reached a modest cement-block home and walked in. Grim-faced people looked up, barely managing to greet us. I found an empty chair and sat down next to an older woman, her hair covered by a black scarf.

She turned to me, her eyes swollen from tears. "He was my youngest son. He was almost forty, with a wife and children of his own, but he was my baby," she said. "Children shouldn't die before their parents. He was in his prime."

"I'm very sorry for your loss."

"The culprits will burn in hell." The tone of her voice was bitter. "I'll make sure of it."

I listened to fragments of conversations around me.

"His body was thrown out of Chico Negro's car..."

"...the audacity of not even disguising himself."

"It's blatant lawlessness."

Flowers and floral wreaths filled the room and surrounded the coffin. People sat in plastic chairs against the walls. Others mingled and whispered outside. Smells of fresh and wilted flowers filled the air and smoke from burning candles stung my eyes.

The scene brought back memories of my father's funeral. A sorrowful glance, a sympathetic smile, the feeling of helplessness I struggled to put aside. I remembered the horror of it. I panicked and jumped from my chair, almost knocking it over.

"Excuse me, I'm not feeling well." I fled into the night to escape the overwhelming memories.

Once outside, I breathed easier. The street was well lit, but empty. A block later, I heard someone calling me. "Veronica, Veronica."

I looked up and saw Santiago running toward me. "What are you thinking, walking around alone?"

"I'm on my way home."

"Do you have a death wish or what? Let me walk you back."

"I wasn't thinking clearly. I got claustrophobic."

When we reached the house, I turned to him. "Please come in for a moment."

He put his arms around me. "You've had a tough week, Veronica. Why don't you just get some rest?"

"Wait, Santiago. Tio Carlos got the farm books out. Look at them with me."

I unlocked the door, turned the lights on, and then spread the books out on the table. It was apparent at a glance that they were fudged. Some entries were erased, others written over, and entire pages were missing.

Santiago raised his eyebrows.

"Well," I said defensively, "Dad's books were always a mess, too. It's hard to keep them clean when you're working."

"Vero, your uncle didn't do any farm work. He just wrote down what the farm boss told him."

"Maybe *el caporal* wasn't clear about the data."

He moved his head slightly back and forth. As we looked through the pile of papers, the figures were so muddled we couldn't make any sense of them. Some pages were clean and neat, others a mess.

"Why are you still defending him?"

I shrugged. "Habit, I guess. He's family."

"Vero, the bottom line is the money intake. Your farms produce a lot of coffee. How much money did he send you?"

"Something like twenty thousand dollars this last year, between the two farms."

"I've been thinking about your farms and how much they should produce. It should have been three times that after expenses, even though they're semi-abandoned."

"You randomly calculate farm productions, Santiago? Why do you have mine so fresh on your mind?"

"Because I'm trying to help." He looked hurt.

I suddenly felt very tired. "You should go."

He leaned down to kiss me. The warmth from his kiss was reassuring, but not enough to dissuade my doubt.

"I need to spend some time at the wake, anyway," he said. "I'll come by for you tomorrow around twelve-thirty, a little later than we'd planned.

We're only doing a simple lunch because of the burial in the morning."

I nodded, wordless. There was just too much to think about.

"Take care of yourself. We'll get through this."

I closed the door and leaned against it, then returned to my room. I was shocked to think that Tio Carlos might be stealing. And Santiago— why was he calculating my farm's income? Was it really to help me, or did he have some other motive?

Sleep was impossible, so I picked up The Coffee Diary. I hadn't had much time for reminiscing in the past few days. I flipped through and went back to a passage I skipped over earlier.

> *March 24, 1991*
> *Dear Diary,*
> *We went to Palm Sunday service today. The church smelled like our forest. The floor was covered with pine needles.*
> *I saw that man again. He glared at me while I was standing in line for communion. No one else noticed. I asked Dad who he was. Apparently, he is the son of a former employee.*
> *Tomorrow we go to the beach house. I'm so excited. All my cousins will be there.*

I was now beginning to think that young man had been Jaime Ramírez, Moyuta's mayor. What I didn't know was why he had resented us so much.

Though we arrived early for Mass that Palm Sunday, the church was already half full. We found seats toward the back. Mom scooted in first, then me, with Tio Carlos and Dad filling up the narrow bench. A few minutes later all the pews were taken. People jammed together in the entrance and lined up along the inside walls. Heat from the crowd pressed in on us.

Though far from the front, we had no trouble seeing. Most of the people were from impoverished *aldeas*, outlying villages, and were only four and a half to five feet tall. The townsfolk interspersed in the congregation were somewhat larger. On our bench, only Tio Carlos blended in.

Father Octaviano spoke with an Italian accent. "*El poder de Cristo, este con vosotros.*"

"*Y con su espíritu,*" answered the congregation.

During the service we stood, sat, knelt, sang, and chanted. We gave our neighbors the brotherly greeting then lined up to receive communion wafers. While waiting, I felt someone staring at me. I glanced around and recognized the hostile young man from the market and later from the procession. His father sat next to him. Dad nodded to the older *campesino*.

"Who is that?" I asked.

"He used to work for us."

With the last "Amen" said, we stepped outside the church and paused, drinking in the fresh air.

# CHAPTER FOURTEEN

"So, how is your mother?" doña Alba asked when I arrived for her birthday luncheon. "I haven't heard from her for a while."

"Doing well," I said.

"Does she go out? Any gentleman callers?"

I shook my head. "She says she isn't interested in having another relationship. Dad was the love of her life."

"Not enough time has passed. She'll change her mind if someone else comes along. It's always like that."

"She goes out occasionally with another teacher from work. She swears they're just friends, but you never know."

"Excuse us, Mama," Ana said. She grabbed my arm and steered me to a pair of isolated chairs. "I heard something is going on between you and Santiago. Tell me all about it."

"Don't you think I'd share with you if there was? There's really nothing to tell."

Ana looked doubtful. "That's not what I heard. And no, I don't think you'd share the information with me. We haven't shared much of anything for fourteen years. Haven't you two been going out?"

"He took me to *los ausoles* on horseback yesterday. That's all."

"He didn't kiss you?"

"Like a brother."

"I bet he doesn't kiss *me* that way." she said. "I know my brother, and I think he likes you...again. You two always had chemistry. There's more to this than you're telling me." She narrowed her eyes and tilted her head slightly, still searching my face.

"Think what you want, Ana. I'm not hiding anything."

"No? Then why are you blushing?"

My hands instinctively went to my warm cheeks. "I'm sunburned from our ride yesterday."

"Fine. I'm not getting anything from you, so come on. Let's get good seats before they're all taken. Lunch will be served soon."

White linen stretched over a table under the guava tree in the courtyard. Ana and I sat across from each other; I put my purse on the empty chair next to me, saving it for Santiago. Only aunts, uncles, cousins, and close friends were invited. "We'd hoped to have a bigger celebration," Ana explained. "But don Arturo's murder put a damper on our plans. It wouldn't be right to have a big *fiesta* with neighbors in mourning."

People spoke in low voices about the murder. "Why did they have to kill him?" an aunt asked.

"Because now the family has to sell," don Guillermo explained. "They'll be afraid not to, even if they don't need the money."

"It's terrible the way the mayor takes whatever he wants," another guest said.

"It's not just him." Don Guillermo looked out over the faces at the table. "Chico Negro has gotten greedy. He's the most ruthless of the three. I wonder if he doesn't do a lot on his own." He paused and coughed into a napkin. "Jaime splits his earnings with those other two. He gives them half to share—just enough to keep them satisfied. At least, that's what I hear."

Doña Conchita, from the store, turned to Guillermo. "Are you defending the mayor?"

"I'm not defending anyone," he continued. "I've just noticed that Chico's out of control."

"Look where they came from." Doña Conchita's mouth drew down in disapproval. "Chico's father was a drunk and a two-bit criminal. Mickey Montaña's family was no better. Jaime's mother used to do our laundry, and his father was killed by vigilantes. Who do these scumbags think they are? And to be running our town at that."

Santiago arrived and took the chair next to mine. "Thanks for saving me a place."

Plates with avocado halves, bowls of rice, and various types of chili were scattered on the table. Then baskets of hot tortillas were set out. Finally, doña María served the main dish: *kakík*—stewed turkey in a complex sauce of spices, ground nuts, and seeds. Conversation ceased as people began to eat.

After the guests had their fill and coffee was served, Santiago stood up and tapped his glass with a fork. "I'd like to make a toast. Today is my mother's birthday and we're here to celebrate with her. I honor her as a wonderful mother, a good friend, and a loyal wife."

He acknowledged his father who sat at the end of the table, then walked over to doña Alba and put his hands on her shoulders. She looked up at him affectionately. "We took up a collection and got you something special, Mom." He signaled two younger boys and they pulled a tarp off a large object in the yard, exposing an empty Jacuzzi. White insides gleamed in the sun. Cedar slats decorated the outside.

"Oh, Santiago, it's beautiful," Alba cried. "I had no idea. I'll be the envy of everyone in town."

"Remember, Mom, this is not for household water storage," he joked.

He looked over at me and winked. He might just as well have said, "So much for being a cheapskate."

As the guests began to leave, I wished Alba a *feliz cumpleaños*, and told her how good it was to see her again.

"Thank you, Vero," she replied. "You're always welcome here. Consider this your home. And say hello to your mother for me, when you talk to her."

I gave her a hug and got ready to go.

"Vero, don't leave just yet," Ana called. "If you're free for the rest of the day, why don't you and Santiago come to the beach with us to watch the sunset? We'll return tomorrow. You're welcome to stay with us overnight."

"That sounds fun. I'll get some things together. Thanks for the invite, but I'd rather stay at our beach house. As long as I'm down there, I need to see what kind of shape it's in. I haven't been there since I was a teenager, and I guess it's mine now."

As I started for the door Santiago came over. "Leaving so soon?"

"I'm going to pack a few things. Ana and Oscar invited me to join them at the beach. Would you like to come?"

"I'd love to. You know what they say…three's a crowd, four's a double date."

"Is that how the saying goes?"

"Drive with me. I don't have to be back to work until Tuesday. I'll go directly to the city from the beach. That way we can spend more time there. Don't you have family you can visit in the city?"

"Yes, when Juan José and Ita met me at the airport, I promised I'd spend a few days with them. This would be a perfect time."

"It's probably wise to stay out of Moyuta for a while. When do you have to be back?"

"I meet with the mayor Thursday morning."

"I'm coming back early on Thursday. By then, maybe you'll have made a decision."

At Tio Carlos' house, I packed a few items of clothing. As I looked around to make sure I wasn't forgetting something, María Celia appeared at the door.

"Are you going somewhere?"

"Down to the beach house for a few days. Sunshine, sand, and warm water will be a welcome break."

"Did you tell Carlos?"

"I just decided."

"I'll let Julián know so he can get the house ready." She disappeared, and a few minutes later Tio Carlos poked his head into the room.

"Vero, you'll need sheets and towels." He handed me a bag María Celia had prepared. "Also, here's some coffee, and take our ice chest for your cold drinks."

"Thanks. I'm going with Santiago, Ana, and Oscar. I'm leaving my car here for a few days."

"Be careful," he said. "Carry your gun, even on the beach. I don't trust the mayor or his men. They might try to follow you."

I searched his face. He appeared earnest and concerned, but the thought that he'd been betraying me rankled. "Please don't tell him where I've gone."

Surprise and uncertainty flashed across his face. He didn't say anything.

"Or anyone else, for that matter."

His mouth slacked open. "How can you say that, even think that, Vero?"

Anger coursed through my veins at the thought of my uncle's deception and my voice hardened. I hated that he was playing innocent with me. "Obviously someone's been tipping him off."

He looked at the ground, crestfallen. "I never thought I would be suspect." "Neither did I."

He didn't say anything but his face was ashen.

"I'll be back in a few days to collect my stuff," I said curtly, and left my room.

María Celia hadn't heard our conversation. She was waiting for me in the hallway. "Good luck and enjoy yourself, Vero. Call us if your plans change," she said. When she hugged me, I stiffened, not knowing how much she knew about my uncle's involvement. "Are you okay?"

I nodded, not trusting myself to speak. She followed me out, carrying one of my bags.

Santiago pulled up in his blue sedan, got out and opened the trunk. When he closed the lid, it rang of finality.

"May God be with you," María Celia said, making a sign of the cross in the air.

We drove out of town and down the mountain toward the coast. Following the first rain, the brown hues were already fading; new grasses and weeds sprouted bravely near the edges of the road. There were more turn-offs than I recalled, but it was many years since I'd traveled this way. A silver Porsche Cayenne sped by, followed by a deep blue Lincoln sports utility vehicle. A large Toyota SUV was parked at *la vuelta de la u,* or the hairpin turn. Several men stood at the edge of the cliff, pointing something out in the distance.

"Isn't this highway just used by locals? What's with all these expensive vehicles?"

His face grew serious. "Most of these cars are owned by young men who grew up in nearby villages and got involved in the drug trade."

"It's that common?"

"Coffee is no longer Moyuta's main source of income."

New houses and businesses disguised the old landmarks I remembered, fancy homes incongruous in small villages where years earlier only modest farmhouses dotted the landscape.

I thought back fourteen years to the last time our whole family had gathered at the beach for a vacation of sun and fun.

—

*Semana Santa:* the week when the towns and cities empty out and a mass exodus of people head for the seashore. We grabbed our beach towels, put on sunscreen, and prepared to soak up some sun. The whole family would be staying at the beach house—aunts, uncle, and cousins from the city. I had especially been looking forward to it. We didn't get together very often.

We took the double-cab pickup, loaded down with supplies and pulling a small trailer with our two new ATVs. The highway from Moyuta was fast, and we traveled from mountain temperate to coastal hot and humid in about twenty minutes. But when we reached the junction with the coastal highway and turned onto a dirt road, we slowed to a crawl as the next fifteen kilometers of road was riddled with ruts and holes.

The beach house was simple, with no air conditioning and few modern conveniences. At night the mosquitoes swarmed out of their daytime hiding places looking for warm bodies. If there was a breeze, it was bearable. If not, we all suffered the whiny buzzing around our ears, since it was too hot to hide under the covers.

Julián, the caretaker, had opened up the house to air it out, prepared the pool, plugged in the refrigerator, and was waiting for us at the gate when we pulled up. He was about thirty-five, dark-skinned and thin in a wiry sort of way. He wore shorts and a ripped T-shirt. His family had worked for my father's family for generations.

When Julián married, Dad gave him and his wife a job on our beach property as caretakers. We paid them a modest salary and provided them a place to live next to our house. María Santos did some cleanup when the beach house was occupied and made tortillas for the family. Julián took care of maintenance, worked odd jobs, and did some fishing on the side. Now, they had five children ranging in age from a toddler to an eleven-year-old. Whenever my family came, we always brought clothes and treats for the children.

My father parked the pickup in the driveway. As I got out, I saw a flash of movement from inside Julián's house. A face peeked out and the couple's oldest son, Junior, ventured out and approached me hesitantly.

"*Buenos días,*" he said shyly, looking down at his dirty bare feet, his toes fidgeting nervously in the dirt.

"*Buenos días, Junior,*" I returned.

His siblings were hiding in the shadows of their small home. He glanced back at them then looked up at me expectantly. Little brown faces began to appear in the doorway.

"*Hola, niños,*" I called to them. I heard giggles from inside the house. I handed Junior a bag containing sweets and toys that we had brought for the kids. He snatched it out of my hands and raced back to his house to share the prize with the others.

"*Niños…*" Julián demanded. "*Qué dicen?*"

"*Muchas gracias,*" answered a chorus of little voices.

I took my things into the small room I would be sharing with my girl cousins. The air was hot and heavy. When I went outside, I saw that the swimming pool was already halfway filled. I climbed down the stairs at the side of the pool and into the cool water. I liked to go in when it was filling; it never stayed cool for long.

"Vero! Vero!" I heard my mother call. A car bounced into the driveway. My aunt had arrived with her two sons. Since my *abuelita* died, Aunt Antonia, the eldest daughter, had taken over as the matriarchal figure of Dad's extended family. She was dignified and fairly tall for a Guatemalan woman, about five foot four. Her hair was often brown, occasionally red, once maroon-colored, but never grey. Everyone had long forgotten what her natural hair color was. Her husband had been murdered in a carjacking several years earlier, yet somehow she managed to be a tower of strength for her family through all of it.

Her eldest son, Antonio, was a handsome young man with a boyish smile. His father's death had affected him deeply and his eyes still carried sadness. His girlfriend, Sara, was with him on this trip. They were inseparable.

His younger brother, Mario, was heavyset, good-natured, and playful. He was one grade ahead of me in school. His greatest defense against life's challenges and tragedies was his innate good humor.

About an hour later, Aunt Marielos and Uncle Herman arrived with my two other cousins. Melinda was a good-natured chubby girl. Her sister, Karla, was pretty, but vain and self-centered.

"Mom, I don't know why I couldn't have gone to Chula Mar," Karla whined as she got out of the car, ignoring us. "I won't be able to go to any of the good beach parties from here."

She shook her hair off her face in that annoying way that teenage girls have. "Oh," she said, when she noticed me. "*Qué tal*, Vero? How are you?"

She put her cheek out so I could give her a peck.

"Vero, it's so good to see you," her sister Melinda said and gave me a big hug. "Don't pay any attention to her." She glanced at her sister, whose back was turned, and stuck out her tongue. "You know how she is."

While three of us hung out in the pool chatting, Karla sat to the side in a chair under an umbrella, wearing a hat, sunscreen, and sunglasses.

"She's worried about premature aging," Mario said in a low voice. Melinda and I giggled. Karla glanced at us sullenly.

After a few days of hot sun, shrimp cocktails, ceviches in the afternoon, and jokes in the evening, even Karla had begun to warm up. But it all came to an end quickly when we got a phone call on Saturday. The house on the farm had been broken into.

My mind came back to the present. I hadn't thought of the break-in for years, and decided to look up that entry in the diary sometime in the next few days while I was at the beach. I also made a mental note to call Aunt Antonia.

When we reached the turnoff, I was astonished to see the road paved. Noticing my surprise, Santiago said, "Things have really changed here, haven't they, Vero?"

"I'll say. I never thought this little access road would be improved."

"Shall I take you to our house or drop you off at yours?"

"At mine, please. I'll walk up to your house in a little while. I need to say hello to Julián and María Santos."

When we arrived at the gate in front of my beach house, Santiago honked the horn and got out of the car to help me with my things. María Santos peeked out the door of the guard's cottage.

"*Buenas tardes, María Santos,*" I called.

"Veronica Villagrán?" she asked, as she walked towards the locked gate.

"*Sí, soy yo.* I'm back visiting from the States."

If I hadn't known it was María Santos, I wouldn't have recognized her. She had grayed and thickened in the way many Guatemalans do when they hit middle age. The heat and sun had lined her face and given her patches of dark spotting.

I asked her how she'd been and how her family was getting along.

"*Bien,* Vero. It's a miracle you've come."

She opened the gate for me. I waved to Santiago as he started the car and continued down the road to his family's beach house.

We embraced. María Santos had the combined scent of ocean salt and perspiration on her skin.

I took my things into the house and looked around. The house was clean, but the interior furnishings were shabby. Furniture needed replacing, the curtains were in tatters, and it smelled damp and musty.

Putting my duffle in the master bedroom, I quickly changed into my swimsuit and went outside. The small pool in front was empty and in disrepair, the bottom cracked so it no longer held water. I walked out past the pool toward the ocean.

When I went to the seashore in San Francisco for the first time, I marveled that it was the same Pacific Ocean. The sea smells were so unlike the beaches of my childhood. There was no warmth to either the water or the air, only a crisp ocean wind that stung my cheeks with its salty coldness.

Here both the water and the air were warm. A prevailing breeze cut through the heavy humidity and brought with it the odors of damp nets and the day's catch. Several small wooden boats with motors, manned by local fishermen, bobbed up and down just beyond the surf. There were three speed boats as well, looking incongruous among the local craft.

Upon reaching the water's edge, I stopped, let my towel and beach bag drop, slipped off my sandals, and let the water lap at my feet. An inch-long sand crab scurried past, looking for refuge in one of the small holes made in the damp, black volcanic sand.

Thinking to savor some time alone before going over to visit my friends, I spread out my towel and sat down. I hugged my knees to my chest, took a deep breath of the ocean air, and watched as a flock of pelicans skimmed close to the breaking waves, looking for fish near the surface.

It was late afternoon, but the rays were still strong. I applied sunscreen, stretched out, shut my eyes, and listened to the swooshing of the waves.

I must have dozed off, because when I opened my eyes, Julián was looking down at me with a coconut in his hand. It was cut across the top, with a straw sticking out. "*Vero, buenas tardes.* My wife told me you'd come. *Tenga.*" He offered me the coconut.

Unlike his wife, Julián looked much the same as he had ten years earlier, lean and sinewy. He even wore what looked like the same ragged shorts and ripped T-shirt. He was a little grayer, but I would have recognized him anywhere.

"*Muchas gracias.*" I took it, and sipped the coco water through the straw.

He squatted down next to me.

"How are your children?" I asked.

"Junior is married and lives in the capital. Only the youngest is still at home. The rest have all left."

"Are you still fishing part-time?"

"Few are fishing anymore, Vero. Times have changed. I pick up odd jobs on boats when I can, do some gardening for those who can afford it, and other things."

"What about these cigarette boats?" I asked, pointing at the long fancy boats not far away.

He made no comment.

When I finished sipping the coco water, he pulled his machete out of its sheath and cut the coconut in half. Then he fashioned a scoop from the outer part of the husk to take the meat out.

"*Gracias,*" I told him.

"*Estoy para servirle.*" He sauntered back toward the house, his splayed bare feet so callused that the hot sand didn't bother him.

The beach was fairly deserted. Only locals were out. Youngsters fished in the surf and others combed the beach for small crabs.

I took my cell phone from the beach bag, looked up the number, and called my aunt. Her familiar voice answered.

"Aunt Antonia? This is Veronica."

"Vero, I heard you were in the country. I've been wondering if you would call."

"I came right out to Moyuta, but I'm coming into the city on Tuesday. I'd love to see all of you. It's been so long."

"That's *your* doing, dear," she said, a note of resentment in her voice.

"I've been planning to phone you, but I've been so busy. The mayor of Moyuta wants to buy the coffee farms."

"Really?" Aunt Antonia sounded genuinely surprised. "Are you going to sell?"

"I don't want to, but he's been pressuring me."

"What do you mean?"

"Oh, I'll tell you about it when I'm in the city."

"How long will you be here? Everyone's looking forward to seeing you. I certainly hope you won't leave without saying goodbye this time."

"I'll be in Guatemala City until Thursday morning, then I'm going back to Moyuta."

"Where are you staying?"

"With Juan-Jo and Ita in Zone 14."

An awkward silence followed. "Well, I guess I'll have to invite them as well." She paused. "Wednesday night it is, then. I'll have a dinner in your honor and see you at seven at my house."

Her invitation sounded like an order and I was a little taken aback. "Okay. That sounds wonderful. I'll be there." The same old thing. She didn't accept Juan José, and had never welcomed him into the family. He was my father's son, wasn't he?

# CHAPTER FIFTEEN

"Vero! Wake up. We've been waiting for you." I opened my eyes. Santiago stood over me wearing wildly colorful shorts.

"Sorry. I must have dozed off." I shaded my face with my hand and sat up. "The sun feels so good. It's been a long time since I've been able to relax on a beach, at least on a warm one." I scooted to one side of the towel. "Have a seat."

"It's a beautiful afternoon." Santiago reached down and pulled me to my feet. "Come on, let's get wet!"

I waded out, turned my back to brace myself against the waves. The ocean was warm as a bath. Santiago ran in and dove under a breaking wave. I watched as his lean, tan body disappeared in the foaming water.

A big wave came toward me and the force of it stung my skin with sand and salt. Santiago swam in front of a swell; it lifted him up and carried him to the beach. I followed his lead. Several waves later, we dragged ourselves onto the sand.

"Nice bodysurfing, eh?"

"Very nice," I replied. "Tires me out, though."

"Come back to our house with me. We've got cold beers."

"I can't wait to have a Gallo."

I followed him down the beach, thinking about how crazy my life had become in one week. I glanced quickly at the date on my cell phone. I could hardly believe it was only seven days since I arrived.

A thatched roof topped their whitewashed, clapboard beach house, and a wooden porch encircled it. Ana and Oscar bustled around the barbecue.

"We thought you'd gotten lost," Ana said as I approached. "I sent Santiago to look for you."

"I fell asleep on the beach. I meant to come sooner."

"Take a seat. Have a beer." Oscar handed me a sweating bottle. "I was just about to start the grill."

"Let's relax, Vero, and leave the barbecuing to the men." Ana plopped down on the lounge chair next to mine.

I slipped on my sunglasses and gazed out at the ocean. "If I lived in Moyuta, I'd spend a lot of time here."

"No one from your family uses your beach house anymore. I can't remember the last time I saw someone there."

"It's clean, but it's falling apart from disuse. My relatives in the city have vacation houses closer to Puerto San José. Tío Carlos was never interested in the ocean."

Santiago, in a bib apron and brandishing a spatula, announced, "I'm taking orders. Hot dogs or hamburgers?"

"Hot dog, please," I said, then turned back to Ana. "Sun, sand, cold beers, and men doing the cooking. This is the life."

The sky filled with color. The clouds, no longer white on blue, glowed silver against the rosy-hued sky. The ceaseless churn of the waves lulled me and in my relaxed state my eyelids grew heavy. Good friends, good beer, good food. I felt like troubles might easily be forgotten in such a place. But my happiness was tinged with worry when I remembered the past week's concerns.

After eating, we sat in the lounge chairs and gazed toward the water. "What's next?" Ana asked.

"More beers, of course," answered Santiago, and sat down on the end of my lounge chair. "I think it'd be great fun to get Vero drunk."

I threw my rolled-up towel at him. "You get off! You're going to tip my chair over."

"Any other ideas, besides more beers?" Ana held up her soda can and patted her growing midsection. "I'm left out."

"Let's watch the *arribada*," Oscar suggested. "There will be a high tide tonight and likely plenty of activity on the beach. We shouldn't miss it."

"What kind of activity?" I asked. "What's an *arribada*?"

"The sea turtles are nesting. During high tide they come ashore at night by the dozens along this strip of the Pacific. They dig nests and lay their eggs."

"I'd love to see that."

"They don't arrive until very late. We'll have to hide in the sand dunes," Santiago said. "If they sense humans or other predators on the beach, they return to the water and wait for a better time."

"I have friends who go to Monterrico and La Candelaria beaches every year and volunteer to guard the nests at night," Ana said. "Poaching is such a problem that sea turtles are now on the endangered species list."

"Surely not for their meat?" I questioned.

"People do eat them, but it's mostly for the eggs," Santiago replied. "They're sold by the dozen. They run about a hundred quetzals for a dozen eggs, or about fifteen dollars."

"That's a windfall for a poor family," I said.

"You'd better believe it. Each nest contains up to twelve dozen eggs. That's more than a month's wages for a villager, and in one night, from only one nest."

"Are they any good?" I asked, wondering why anyone would want to eat turtle eggs.

"You don't really taste them. People eat them raw. Swallow them whole. The covering is kind of tough, but pliable. I tried one once on a dare."

"Why would anyone eat them?"

"People believe they're good for hangovers. They're aphrodisiacs as well, or so they say."

"Do you think there'll be poachers tonight?" I asked.

"I doubt it," Oscar said. "This is a pretty quiet section of beach. Few people live around here."

As the evening wore on, I began to feel sleepy and tipsy. "What time is it?"

"Eleven thirty," Oscar replied. "Let's grab some towels and find a place in the sand."

Santiago went into the house and came out a minute later. "*Lástima*, I only found one towel. I guess that means we have to double up. You take this one Ana, Vero and I will share hers."

We walked out to the dune area, far enough from the beach not to frighten any turtles. A few tough plants grew in the sand above the high tide water line. The full moon spilled a silver light over the ocean. Each crashing wave sparkled with phosphorescence, as though touched by a fairy's wand, lending a magical quality to the night.

We spread our towel a short distance from Ana and Oscar. Santiago stretched out on his half. "I know it's tight," he said when I hesitated. "But you don't mind, do you?"

I lay down beside him. Our bodies touched; his bare foot found mine and covered it. I was acutely aware of his earthy pine-forest scent.

"The sand is chilly," I commented.

"Are you cold?"

I shivered my answer. He wrapped his arms around me, and I felt the heat of his body seep through his sweatshirt. I buried my face in his chest.

"Hey, you." I looked up and he kissed me. His tongue explored my mouth and I felt my body drifting off, warmed and tingling at the same time.

"I've wanted to do this for longer than you can imagine," he said hoarsely. Our bodies intertwined.

"Santiago." His name was all I could manage to say. His hands roamed, touching and stroking me. I was aroused, my chill forgotten.

A pebble landed nearby, kicking up sand, followed by a barrage of small rocks, breaking the spell. It was Oscar signaling towards the beach.

Huge female turtles, weighing up to eighty pounds, awkwardly propelled themselves over the sand in our direction. Their dark olive shells glowed wet in the moonlight. Santiago kept his arm around me as we quietly watched.

Finally, satisfied with the location, the massive female nearest us stopped and began digging, using her front flippers as shovels. After about fifteen minutes, she nestled into the hole and began excavating with her back flippers.

"What's she doing?" I whispered.

"She's digging a cavity where she'll deposit the eggs."

A half hour passed before the turtle climbed out of the hole and covered her eggs with sand. When they were successfully disguised, she began the arduous trip back into the ocean.

"Can we open the nest and look at the eggs?" I asked.

"We probably shouldn't." Santiago thought for a moment. "Well, what the heck…we'll look then leave them as they were."

With our hands, we dug into the spot where the female had left her clutch. I felt something slimy in the sand. "I think I found them!" I whispered, trying not to disturb other nesting females in the vicinity.

The eggs, enclosed in a soft mucous film, looked like ping-pong balls. They were soft and spongy to the touch, their shells like paper-thin leather.

"How long does it take for them to hatch?" I asked.

"It depends on the temperature, but I think between forty-five and sixty days."

"Let's cover them well, so no one steals them."

"Shall we take a few and try them?"

"No!" I whispered, aghast. "What a horrible thought."

Santiago smiled. "I don't need turtle eggs for an aphrodisiac when you're around, Vero."

"We should get back, Santiago. I'm pretty sleepy."

"I can't say that sleep is what's on my mind right now."

I ached for him, but was fearful at the same time. Was I ready for this? Or would it just complicate my life even more? I knew sex could make or break a relationship.

Just as we started to get up, the buzz of a small airplane shattered the quiet.

Santiago pulled me back down. "We can't let them see us."

A strong beam of light shone into the water from one of two black Land Rovers parked several hundred yards down the beach. With the excitement of the sea turtles, we hadn't noticed them.

"What's going on?" I whispered.

He put his index finger over his mouth. "Shhh. It's a drug drop."

The aircraft circled low.

The three speed boats I'd seen earlier roared over the surf towards the lit area.

The plane made several circular passes as we watched. White packages dropped into the sea. A driver, two heavily armed guards, and another man stood in each boat. As the packages fell into the water, the boats raced to retrieve them. The airplane continued flying low, dropping more packages. After five passes, it left. When the packets were all picked up, the boats turned and headed toward shore. They sped over the breaking waves and slid up onto the sand.

Men jumped out, unloaded the packages, and pushed the boats back into the water. The drivers started up the engines, and the boats quickly disappeared into the night.

A large man got out of one of the cars and counted the packages several times. Apparently satisfied, he gestured, and they were loaded into the vehicles.

When the Land Rovers left, the other men took off down the beach. A few minutes later the beach was silent and empty.

We waited until we were sure everyone was gone, then the four of us went quickly back to the house.

"Does that happen often?" I asked.

"This is the first time I've seen it, but I've heard it happens regularly," Ana said. "Drug runners choose different beaches and different times to make it difficult for anyone to intercept them." She studied my face. My eyes must have revealed my shock over what we'd just seen. "Why don't you stay with us?"

"Thanks, Ana, but I'd rather go to my house. Can you walk me back, Santiago?"

"Of course."

As we started off, Santiago took my hand. The black sand was damp and sticky under our feet.

I turned to him. "Those black Land Rovers look like the car that tailed us the other day."

"There are quite a few around," he said. "They're popular with the narcos."

When we reached the house, we washed the sand from our feet at an outdoor faucet and climbed the stairs to the porch. My hands shook as the key went into the lock. I opened the door, took a deep breath, and said, "Come on in."

We passed through the living room and kitchen areas to the bedroom. The door was ajar. María Santos had made the bed and put away the things I had haphazardly strewn around when I changed clothes.

"Vero." Santiago pulled me toward him. His kisses were soft but demanding. This time I didn't hesitate. We stripped our clothes off, discarding them thoughtlessly on the floor. My body tingled at the touch of his warm skin. He lifted me up and we fell onto the bed together.

I was ready for him when he entered me. Afterward, as we lay locked together in each other's arms, I laughed.

"What's so funny?"

"I'm just happy," I said. "What a day."

"It's two thirty in the morning, Vero. The day is just beginning."

# CHAPTER SIXTEEN

*KNOCK, KNOCK, KNOCK...* THE NOISE FILTERED IN THROUGH THE HAZE OF MY SLEEP.
"Who is it?" Santiago called, pulling on his pants and heading for the door.

"Sorry to wake you lovebirds," Ana called through the door. "But we're leaving. Just wanted to say goodbye and make sure you have the key to the house, Santiago. You don't need to open up."

He reached down and felt the front pockets of his pants. "Got it. Thanks, sis."

"Love you guys. Have fun! See you later."

"Bye, Ana," I said, groggily.

"Good morning, Sunshine," Santiago said as I opened an eye. "I'm glad you're still alive."

I laughed. "You mean after our romp last night? Ha! I've had better." I threw the pillow at him.

"You ain't seen nothin' yet." He grabbed me and we wrestled on the bed. I let him pin me down. "Anyway, I was referring to your hectic week."

"Hey, now that Ana's gone, there's no one to disturb us."

"I'd like to disturb you."

"Disturb away," I said.

At eleven o'clock, I got up, showered, and got the coffee going. It was quite a while before Santiago came into the kitchen; he'd just showered and wore a towel around his waist.

"Did you fall asleep again?" I asked.

"Just sidetracked. I'm getting hungry, Vero. How about you?"

"Famished."

"I'll go out and look for some fresh catch. Maybe we can talk María Santos into preparing us a meal."

While I waited for him to return, I hung two hammocks on the corridor hooks. I went into the bedroom and picked up *The Coffee Diary* from the nightstand. I hadn't remembered getting it out of my bag. I settled into the hammock and turned to where I'd left off.

A morning phone call the Saturday before Easter had cut the vacation short. Our house had been robbed, the dogs poisoned while the guard slept.

We left the beach in a hurry.

It hadn't taken long for the news to create a big stir in town. We arrived to find two local policemen as well as a group of curious neighbors at the house, discussing and speculating about the break-in.

Dad, barely in control of his anger, sized up the situation and took a deep breath. He moved to the center of the crowd and said, "Thank you all for your concern. But please return to your homes while we investigate. I'll be sure to inform you as soon as we learn anything."

He shook hands with everyone and gently guided them back to their cars. Then he called the guard. "Cruz, come here. I need you to explain exactly what happened."

"Don Quique, everything was fine and in order last night when I went to sleep. When I woke up this morning, Noche was lying here whimpering and Zorro was dead. I tried to help Noche but she had a seizure and died. I think they were poisoned."

"Go on, Cruz. What happened next?"

"I went over to check the house. The kitchen door had been forced and the door handle tossed on the ground. When I went down the hill to check the gate, it was wide open."

"And the lock?"

"The chain and padlock were thrown in the gravel. That's when I went back to the house and called the police. Then I called you."

"What time was that? Did you get up late this morning? Do you have a hangover?"

"Sure, I had a few drinks last night. But I didn't get drunk."

Dad, seething, turned on his heels and went back inside, where the police were looking around. I took one look at him and decided to stay out of his way.

"Keep an eye on the police," he whispered to Mom.

The two uniformed men poked around, more interested in items still in the house than in what might have been stolen. They wore no gloves and collected no evidence. They ran their hands over tables and stared curiously at our belongings. Mom followed them around, on the lookout for light fingers. When the two officers split up, she said under her breath, "Vero, follow that other policeman."

He looked back at me three or four times as we went through the rooms. After a while they both left.

Mom checked to see what was missing. The only items unaccounted for were a pair of gold earrings and a small amount of cash.

A son of one of the workers came running in. "*Señor Quique, hacen falta tres caballos y seis vacas.*" Dad took this in—three horses and six cows gone. This was more disturbing than a little cash and jewelry.

Dad made his promised phone calls to the neighbors. In no time, the phone began ringing. Several people promised to inquire around, using their connections, to find the thief. Retaliation was inevitable.

Later that afternoon Dad called the guard again. "Cruz, I need to speak with you."

"*Si, don Quique?*"

"The worst thing you could have done was call the police. Why did you do that?"

Cruz hung his head. "My wife's brother is one of the officers and he always complains that no one notifies them." He stared at the ground. "I thought they could help."

"Well, you thought wrong. Do you know of a single incident around here where police intervention solved a crime?"

Cruz looked sheepish, "Well…no."

"Cruz, you were drinking last night. I smelled booze on you this morning. You're fired. Pack your things and leave."

Dad turned and walked away.

"But don Quique," Cruz pleaded to his back, "I didn't want this to happen. I didn't help the thief. I'm a victim as well. What about my family? Where will we live?"

"You should have thought of that before getting sloshed last night."

Dad was on the phone all evening trying to find out where the animals might have been taken. He notified the border stations in case the animals crossed into El Salvador in the next few days.

The other thing he did was send Mom and me to the city. "Go ahead and do some shopping. I'll let you know when it's safe to come home."

*Safe?* I thought. I hadn't known we were threatened. We left, glad to have an excuse to spend some time away from home. It was Easter weekend, and we could go to the American Club for the festivities and attend the Union Church. There were always things to do in the capital.

It was a week later when we returned to the farm. Our first night back, I was curled up in the big easy chair in the living room, reading. Mom and Dad were in the kitchen talking.

"Quique, I saw some animals in the corral. Are those the ones you recovered?" Mom asked.

"Yes, we managed to get most of them back. A neighbor found them in a stable in Aldea Las Cabezas, just north of Jalpatagua. Daisy is gone. Sold, I assume. It's too bad about her. She was our best dairy cow. She must have fetched a good price."

"Who was the thief?"

"Remember Ricky R.?" Mom shook her head. "He was a guard I fired a couple years back," Dad explained. "I saw him in church on Palm Sunday."

"He did it? How did you figure that out?"

"What tipped me off was that the gate padlock had been opened, not forced or cut. Any of the former guards could have had an extra key. I started by investigating people who had worked for us during the past three years.

"That *serote* had a real aversion to work. He had an attitude and didn't like to take orders. He was eager for his paycheck, though, always asking for money in advance. It's a wonder he wasn't stealing while he worked here. Maybe he was and I just didn't notice."

"Well, if he wanted the job, he should have put more effort into it."

"Yeah, there are plenty of people willing to work. I can't be coddling my employees. Stealing is easier than working. They all think they're too smart to get caught. Ricky got what was coming to him. He was found murdered in his house a few days back."

"That's terrible."

"He'd been thieving a while. Both don Chepe and don Arturo lost cattle last month. Don Pedro lost three horses a few months ago."

"I don't approve of vigilantes, Quique. You know that."

"I agree. It's not the ideal situation. But we don't live in an ideal world." Mom sighed. "How was he killed?"

"Someone threw a hand grenade into his house while he slept. He never knew what hit him."

"A hand grenade? Where did that come from?"

"Lots of people have them—leftovers from the civil war."

"I don't want to know if you had something to do with this, even if it was only condoning it. Please don't mention it to Vero." I saw Dad nodding his head.

"Did he have a family?" Mom asked.

"His wife left him several years back and took the two daughters. He was a mean bastard—knocked her around. I think he gave them money, though. The older boy took after his father. He stayed behind and Ricky raised him alone. Jaime must be about seventeen now. I wouldn't be surprised if he was involved as well."

"He wasn't in his father's house when it happened?"

"No one saw him around."

"What about the police?"

"The police filled out the usual papers informing their superiors of the murder. I managed to get a copy of what was written. The report didn't connect the stolen animals to the murder. No arrests will ever be made. No inquiries, either. You know how things are here."

I closed the diary and lay back on the bed. Revenge was justice in these parts. With the authorities unable or unwilling to cope with problems, vigilantes did the community a service and most people were grateful for it. Perhaps Jaime considered my father responsible for his father's murder. Was that what was behind all of this?

Maybe. But he hated us before any of that happened. The break-in happened later, after the processions and the market. I was missing something.

I looked out at the empty expanse of sand. An hour had passed since Santiago left. I wondered where he'd gone.

María Santos was patting tortillas in the outdoor kitchen. I got up and wandered over to their cottage. "*Buenas tardes.*" I lifted the cloth covering the tortillas. "They look yummy. Can I have one?"

"Of course, Veronica. Help yourself." I took one off the top of the pile and replaced the cloth.

"Did you notice what was going on last night?" I asked her.

"You mean out in the water?"

"Yes, with the airplane and the boats."

"Veronica, don't discuss it." Her eyes darted from side to side, as if looking for someone lurking around, possibly eavesdropping. "Loose tongues are dangerous."

I didn't say anything more. I gazed around their small dwelling. Poured concrete floors and cement block walls matched the grey metal front door. The only other door in the home was the white metal bathroom door. Colorful curtains separated the children's sleeping area. The roof was thatched, palm fronds visible, expertly woven in and out and evenly spaced on a mangrove pole frame. Among his other talents, Julián knew the art of weaving palm and helped others install their roofs.

An aged sofa, cast off from our home many years ago, took up most of the living room. It faced a small television, the focal point of the room. Dishes, pots, and pans overflowed the simple pine standup kitchen cabinet. Baskets of food hung from ceiling poles on heavy fishing line. A four-burner tabletop stove sat on a stand near a dining table. Several out-of-date calendars decorated the walls.

"Do you remember Santiago?" I asked.

"Santiago Godoy?"

"Yes. He and his sister, Ana, were childhood friends of mine."

"They have a weekend house nearby. I do housework for them from time to time."

"Oh," I said, surprised. "He's bringing food for our lunch, I mean for the two of us. Would you mind preparing it? After your family has finished eating, of course."

"You don't even need to ask, Veronica. We're at your service."

When I went outside, I saw Santiago sauntering along the water's edge, shoes in one hand and a bag in the other. Instantly I felt my body respond to him and a smile crossed my face.

"You were gone a long time," I said when he got closer.

"Sorry about that. I ran into someone."

"What's in the bag?"

"I got *camarones* from a shrimp farm a kilometer up the road. I couldn't find any fish. Apparently fishing is no longer a priority in these parts."

"Julián told me the same thing."

We took the shrimp in to María Santos and climbed over the porch railing to the hammocks. Santiago picked the biggest one. "Come here, Vero," he said. "There's room for both of us."

We lay together, head to feet, the hammock swaying slightly under our weight, the ocean breeze cooling us.

"*Seño Vero*," María Santos called after a little while, breaking the spell. We walked over and she handed us garlic fried shrimp on thick plastic plates, along with tortillas and plastic glasses of lemonade.

"This is heaven," I said as we sat on the steps and looked out toward the water.

When we finished eating, Santiago said, "I didn't want to spoil your lunch, but when I went to the *aldea* to look for fish, I ran into Mayor Jaime. His black Land Rover was parked behind the local *tienda*. He was sitting at a table drinking beer with three other men. 'Look who's here,' he said. 'If it isn't Santiago Godoy, my rival.'"

"Why did he call you his rival, Santiago?"

"I didn't know, so I asked. He said we are both after the same thing—you."

I frowned. "Why is Mayor Jaime after me? I thought he was after the farms."

"Apparently there is more here than meets the eye. I asked him why he thought I was after you, since we're old friends." He hesitated for a moment. "I don't know if I should tell you this part."

"Go ahead. I need to know what I'm up against."

"Okay. He said he'd like to be on such friendly terms with that hot piece of ass. He meant you."

His eyes met mine in apology.

"And?"

"He asked how it was."

"What'd you say?"

"I told him I didn't know what he was talking about. He told me not to play stupid, that he knew we were together on the beach and that I slept here last night."

Horrified, I exclaimed, "That was him on the beach during the drop, wasn't it."

Santiago nodded. "He knew we were there and let us watch."

"What are we going to do?"

"Nothing. I asked him if he came down to talk and he said no, he had come for business. The conversation was to be continued on Thursday with you, alone."

"Can't you come with me, Santiago? He knows we're a couple now."

"I'd like to, but I don't think it's a good idea. You have to make this decision yourself. I don't want to be the one to influence you." He looked out at the water. "At least you're meeting at city hall. He wouldn't dare hurt you in a public place."

My hopes were dashed. I'd hoped Santiago would at least try to be there for me. I'd begun to depend on him. "What if I didn't go? What if I left the country before anything was settled?"

"He'd probably take over the farms, fudge the paperwork and say you'd signed. There's no one who would dare oppose him."

"What about my family?"

"They don't live in Moyuta. They never even visit. Tio Carlos is the only one who is faintly interested in the farms, but he has little backbone. He's a weak man."

I thought for a moment. "I guess I'd better go and see what I can do. Maybe there's still a way to keep the farms."

"You won't know until you try. He hasn't harmed you and he's had plenty of chances." I could feel his eyes on me. "Once you've worked it out with him, I can help you get the farms back in order."

"How long have you known Jaime?" I asked, changing the subject.

"Since grade school. We were in the same class until sixth grade, when he dropped out. I didn't see him again until his father was killed."

"Were you friends?"

"Not by a long shot. Jaime was mean, a bully. He hated Ana and me because we lived in town in a decent house with both parents. He saw us as rich, even though we weren't."

I remembered what I'd read earlier in the diary and said, "His father broke into our farm and stole some cattle and horses just days before he was killed. Do you think Dad had anything to do with his father's death?"

"I don't know, Vero. But the only thing that matters is whether Jaime *thinks* Quique did. Even if it were true, your father probably didn't act alone. Likely several people got the money together and hired the hit."

"Do you think he blamed Dad?"

"Possibly."

"I'm glad we're going to Guatemala City in the morning."

# CHAPTER SEVENTEEN

"Santiago, please stop soon, I have to pee!" I crossed my legs and unbuckled my seatbelt.

He glanced over at me. "Okay, don't worry. We're getting close to Barberena. I'll stop at a restaurant and order something while you use the bathroom."

"Thanks," I said, much relieved. A liquid breakfast didn't do well before a road trip; there are no rest stops on Guatemalan highways.

We pulled into the café and Santiago waited for me in a booth. Then we continued on toward the city.

Traffic was light. Everything outside of Guatemala City looked as it had ten or even twenty years ago. Coffee, corn, and sugarcane fields flanked the two-lane highway. The road widened into four lanes as we approached the capital. Thriving new communities had sprouted where cattle once grazed.

I stared at the upper-middle class homes interspersed with mansions. Wealth hadn't been so obvious when I left. "Do you know where Juan José lives?"

"*Zona 14*. I was there once, just after he moved, to drop off some things as a favor. It's easy to find."

"Thanks for bringing me. Juan-Jo sounded happy about my visit when I called. I haven't spent time with him in years."

"You sound a little nervous, Vero. Are you?"

"Maybe. Juan José is great. He was always a sweet brother. It's not like

I'm nervous about seeing him or Ita. It's just that there's so much about the past I don't like to think about. When I see him, the memories come rushing in."

"He was an innocent. No one can blame him for what happened. He's just the product of your father's infidelity."

"I know. But it took me so long to accept it. I can't help but remember those times when I see him. His arrival ruined my relationship with my father."

"It was the realization of what your father did. But you can't just blame Quique. It's more complicated than that."

"What do you mean?" I asked. It seemed simple enough to me. "Dad was the one who got that woman pregnant."

"In Guatemala lots of men have affairs and illegitimate children. Society accepts it. Your family was just a victim of Guatemalan culture."

"Are you justifying it? Mom is American, not Guatemalan. She sure didn't think it was okay."

Santiago sighed. "No, Veronica, I'm not justifying it. I know what this did to you when you were growing up. It scarred you. I would never do something like that to my own family."

I calmed down. "It's the reason I left Guatemala, or one of them, anyway."

"I'm sorry. I know it's a sensitive subject."

We rode in silence after that. I braced myself to face a different kind of enemy, my own inner demons.

My stomach fluttered slightly as we turned onto *Avenida de las Americas*. The family apartment we used when I was a child was on this street, now rented out to strangers. It was my mother's property, part of her inheritance from my father. She collected rent from this apartment and several others through an agency.

We stopped in front of a two-story, brown-and-white stucco townhouse in a small gated community. A red sedan was parked in the garage at the side. I buzzed the intercom.

"*Sí?*" said a woman's voice.

"It's me. Veronica."

"I'll be right there."

Santiago got out of the car and embraced me. "Are you sure you wouldn't rather stay with me? I have to get to work quickly, but you could hang out at the university." He glanced at his watch. "I'll be free by four."

"No, I'm fine. I'll call you tonight or tomorrow."

Ita opened the door. "Veronica!" she greeted me. "Come in, come in."

I waved goodbye to Santiago and watched him leave before following Ita into the living room. Though the house was small, the furniture was large. A beige leather sofa and loveseat faced a heavy mahogany coffee table. Overstuffed pillows dominated the sofa; I had to move a few in order to sit down. Persian rugs warmed cool tile floors, and heavily framed paintings of barns, snowy mountains, and leafy forests hung on the walls.

"Juan-Jo is at the hospital. He won't be back until late afternoon."

"You don't mind me coming so early, do you?"

"Of course not. I'm delighted. Oh, Aunt Antonia called. She's having a dinner for you tomorrow."

I wondered what I would wear; Santiago and I had driven straight to the city from the beach. "Can we do some shopping later, Ita? I need to pick up a few things."

"Of course. And your car, Vero?"

"I left it in Moyuta with Tio Carlos. Santiago brought me. I'll be going back with him Thursday morning."

Her blank expression made me realize that she had no idea who Santiago was. "I'm sorry. I should have introduced you, but he was late for work."

After a quick breakfast, I called Mom and updated her on the family. "I'm at Juan-Jo's. We're having a family reunion at Aunt Antonia's tomorrow night."

"Make sure you tell everyone hello for me. Oh, and when is your next meeting with the mayor?"

I told her I had definitely decided to keep the farms. "Maybe you should leave town quickly after you tell him. Better yet, leave the country. Men like the mayor don't live long anyway."

I tossed the thought around in my head.

"No, on second thought," she said, "don't tell him yet. Buy yourself some time. I'm going to get the first flight down I can. If you're in danger, I'd rather be with you than worry about you from far away."

"You don't have to do that, Mom. In fact, I'd rather you didn't come. I don't want you in danger, too. I can take care of myself."

"That's what your father thought."

We said our goodbyes and I promised to call her in a few days. I had mixed feelings about her coming. Though confident I could handle things on my own, I longed for her support.

"Ready now, Vero?" Ita poked her head into the guest room, keys in hand. "It's eleven. We can eat at one of the malls and come back later."

Guatemala City had changed. Clean streets, landscaped parks, and new brick-lined sidewalks surprised me. Merchandise was displayed in tantalizing ways in new stores.

"Wait until you see the malls," Ita said. "No more flying to Miami to shop."

At the end of the afternoon, we returned to the house loaded down and exhausted.

Ita changed into blue sweat pants and a grey numbered sweatshirt, the baggy outfit accentuating her petite figure.

"Would you like a glass of wine, Vero?" She set out two glasses and a bottle.

I poured some for myself. "I'm so glad we have time to get to know each other. Did you grow up in Guatemala City?"

"My family is all from here. Juan José and I met at a university party. We hit it off right away."

"I don't recall him having other girlfriends before you."

"No. He was really shy. It took him a long time to work up the courage just to ask me out. You can imagine how hard it was for him to ask my hand in marriage."

"What did your family think of him?"

"I was so nervous the night Juan-Jo came to ask my father's permission. I was afraid he wouldn't give it, and without my father's blessing, my family wouldn't support me."

"Juan José has money. You didn't need support."

"Emotional support and family support are important, too."

Family support? I sure hadn't provided any for Juan José during the past ten years. "Why were you worried? Surely they loved Juan José. Everyone does."

"Don't think my family hasn't taken to him. He adores them and they love him. In fact, I sometimes think he married me for my relatives. But he hadn't graduated yet. After we started seeing each other steadily, my parents told me we should wait to marry until he was out of school. But medical school takes forever and we just didn't want to wait that long. Since Juan-Jo already had a house and some income from rentals, he convinced my father."

"Are you done with school? Are you planning to work?" I asked.

"I graduated before we married, but haven't looked for a job because we're hoping to start a family. Juan-Jo is really thrilled with the idea of a family of his own."

"He must have felt really alone here after Dad died and Mom and I left."

Ita nodded in agreement.

I couldn't help thinking about how I'd abandoned my little brother. Ita noticed my expression and continued, "He doesn't talk about what happened. He told me his mother died and his grandmother dumped him on your doorstep. I've always wanted to hear more about it. Can you tell me what happened?"

"I'll try."


It was July, 1991. Mom, Dad and I were sleeping late after coming back from a wake in Jutiapa.

*Knock, knock, knock.*

The noise at the door woke us. I was surprised the guard had let anyone through the gate, but Juan José's grandmother was a persistent woman.

Mom was the first one up. She grabbed her bathrobe, still tying it as she hastened to the door.

An elderly lady and a little boy stood outside. The woman was a peasant, a *campesina,* her long grey hair knotted up in a bun on her head. A thin cotton dress clung to her stocky frame. She looked worn, as if worry and hard work had prematurely aged her.

The boy was small, about nine years old, clean and carefully dressed. He had a knapsack on his back.

"*Buenos dias,*" Mom said. "*En que les puedo servir?*"

"Señora Villagrán, I'm here to bring my grandson to live with you," the woman said in a matter-of-fact tone. "His mother passed away a few weeks ago and I can't raise him alone. He needs to be with his father."

"Take him to his father then," Mom said.

"That's why we're here."

Mom was slow to understand. When she did, she turned abruptly and stormed back to her room, passing Dad in the hallway. "What is it, Liz?"

"Your problem, that's what it is! You deal with it." She slammed the bedroom door behind her.

I stepped back out of sight so he wouldn't see me as he passed my room. I knew I shouldn't eavesdrop, but didn't want to miss whatever was going on.

Dad went to the front door. "Yes, can I help you?"

By this time, the woman was angry. "This is your son. Take him and raise him. Thanks to you, Silvia had to leave town. She died a few weeks ago, away from family and friends."

"*Señora*, please come in and sit down. Let's talk about this calmly." He ushered them into the living room. "Can I get you something to drink?"

He went into the kitchen and brought her back a tall glass of water. "Please tell me your story."

Once they were in the living room, I couldn't hear them, so I slipped down the hallway and into the bathroom to be closer.

"Silvia died of cancer a few weeks ago and left this boy orphaned." The elderly woman turned to the child and rested her hand on his shoulder. "I never wanted her to get schooling, a girl doesn't need it, but my late husband insisted. He wanted more for his children. He sacrificed everything for them, even his life."

Dad nodded to the woman and encouraged her to continue.

"When Silvia finished her education, she became a teacher. She thought herself too good for her family, made new friends. Even rented a room in town.

"Then she met you. She thought her life would be different, that you would leave your family for her. Stupid girl." She glared at him. "When she got pregnant, she left Moyuta. That was probably your idea."

I didn't hear my father's words, so I peeked out from my hiding place. His body language expressed denial.

"She was alone when she died, except for the boy. A fellow teacher knew she was from Moyuta and brought the boy to us. I have discussed this with my daughter Claudia. She's the sensible one—didn't waste her time on schooling. We both agree it's better for him to be with you."

Dad spoke softly to the woman. Then the conversation became louder as the woman got angry.

"I'm widowed. I have no way to care for him." When Dad said something quietly to her, she retorted, "I don't want your money. You think you can fix anything by just throwing money at it. He's *your* son. *You* take responsibility for him. Why should I? I've already raised three children."

"You're right," Dad told her. "The boy will stay here."

Juan-Jo's grandmother gave him a quick hug, told him he'd be better off with us, and left. Juan José hadn't spoken a word.

Ita was transfixed by my story. "What happened then?"

"Mom blew up, throwing things and yelling. It was scary. My mother generally whispers when she's angry, but this was much more than anger: she was deeply hurt. In the end, we left the country for five months. We went to my grandparents' house in California. It was a rough time for both of us—all of us, I guess. I started high school in San Diego as a Latin American, feeling really out of place. I didn't have any guidelines or rules. No one was there to help me adjust." I took another sip of wine. "You see, I'd been homeschooled at our farm. I was completely unprepared for the drastic change.

"Mom got really depressed. Dad was frantic, being so far away when Mom was ill. Juan José just retreated further into his shell. It was weeks before he started talking, and even then he didn't say much."

Ita interrupted, "I didn't realize what a trauma it had been. I mean, I should have known. It's such a difficult thing to happen to a family, but I only heard about it briefly from Juan José."

"I'm afraid I never forgave my father. I thought I had, but it's still painful to think about."

"Juan-Jo loves you and your mother. You were always there for him when he was young. The rest of the family never truly accepted him."

I remembered the conversation with Aunt Antonia. "It was hard for everyone. I think the other relatives sympathized with Mom and blamed Juan-Jo somehow for bringing this on us. It wasn't his fault, of course, but he was easier to blame than Dad."

Juan José came in a while later. He smiled with pleasure when he saw us engaged in conversation.

"How did it go today, ladies?"

"We didn't miss you at all," Ita said, winking at me.

"Look at us now." I held up a wineglass. "We shopped and explored the city."

He sat down between us and put his arms around our shoulders affectionately. "I'm so happy to have my two favorite people with me. Do you have plans for tomorrow?"

I shook my head. "No plans. I thought perhaps we could decide in the morning. Do you have any suggestions?"

"I have to work, but Ita can take you anywhere you wish." I looked over at her; she smiled her consent and nodded slightly.

"Thanks so much. Juan-Jo, I know I've said it before, but I'm so sorry I didn't come down for your wedding. I should have been able to, somehow."

"It doesn't matter, Vero. It was only a small family gathering. You were busy. Would you like to look at the photos?"

"I'd love to."

Ita got up and brought back a white, cloth-covered wedding album. "I could look at these pictures all the time," she said. "It was the happiest day of my life."

I saw from the pictures it was a small wedding indeed, at least by Guatemalan standards. There looked to be no more than fifty people. "Where are all our relatives?" I asked.

"Most of them weren't there. Mario and Antonio came with their wives and Melinda came with her husband. Karla was at a photo shoot out of the country."

"What about our aunts and uncle—Antonia, Marielos and Herman?"

"They couldn't make it. They sent gifts."

As I looked at the photos, I felt even worse that I hadn't come. I saw Mom, tall and slim in her blue suit. She had flown down for four days to attend.

I should have done that.

Then my eyes shifted to a photo of people I didn't know. "Who are these people, Juan-Jo?"

"They're from Moyuta, my mother's family. This is my grandmother, my aunt Claudia, her husband and kids, and Uncle Jaime."

"I didn't know you were in touch with them."

"After Dad's murder, my uncle came to find me. He took me to Moyuta and introduced me to the rest of my family. I hadn't even known they existed."

I squinted at the picture. The figures were small and hard to make out. *No it can't be.* Suddenly I understood. There in front of me, narrow-eyed with acne scars, was the key to everything: Juan José was Mayor Jaime's nephew.

# CHAPTER EIGHTEEN

I GOT TO MY FEET. "WHY DIDN'T YOU TELL ME THE MAYOR WAS YOUR UNCLE?"

"Wait a sec, Vero. Why the big deal? Does it make a difference?"

"As a matter of fact, it does. I need all the information I can get to make a decision about what to do."

"What do you mean 'what to do'? You either sell or you don't," Juan José said. "It's not that complicated. When was the last time we talked, Veronica? You arrived late Saturday night, left early Sunday morning, and haven't called us except to say you'd be back in the city for two days. When was I supposed to tell you?"

"You weren't hiding it?"

"Of course not. Why would I do that? Half the people in Moyuta already know."

"Why didn't I?"

"Because you don't live there, I guess. You're an outsider. You've been away too long."

"I'm sure Mom didn't know, either, or she would have told me."

"Mom lived in her own world on the farm and she wasn't privy to town gossip because she was different, an American. Her only source of information was Dad, and he didn't provide much. Now that she lives in California, she's even less likely to hear."

"Didn't she meet Mayor Jaime at your wedding?"

"Sure, along with all the other relatives. But I didn't introduce him as the mayor of Moyuta, just as my uncle."

I sat back down again, pulled a pillow onto my lap, and twirled the tassels absently. "What has your uncle said to you?"

Juan José tensed. I could see he really didn't know what I was asking.

"I mean about the farm. Why is he so interested in buying it?"

"Didn't he tell you? He wants to build low-income housing there." Juan José's foot tapped anxiously and he leaned forward to straighten some magazines on the coffee table. "Veronica, it isn't a crime to develop property. Besides, it'll be a boon to the local economy."

"Well, yes, he told me that. I mean, what's his real reason?" I couldn't believe that Juan José wasn't hiding something.

"*Qué te pasa, Veronica*? Why must he have another reason? Why are you so suspicious? Suddenly, I'm on the defensive with you. Can't you take it at face value?" He stood up to leave the room. "I don't want to argue. We haven't seen each other in ages."

I pursed my lips, then forced a smile. It was obvious Juan José didn't know. "Sit back down. Forget it. I'm just being paranoid. Guatemala does that to a person."

He took a deep breath and sat stiffly. "It's okay. I understand."

I hadn't noticed Ita leave, and was surprised when she came into the room with another wineglass. She poured some for Juan José. "Here," she said. "It's cool, the way you like it."

He took the glass by the stem, drained half of it then wiped his face with his sleeve.

I got up from the sofa. "I'm a little tired. I'm going to rest for a while and make some phone calls."

I went into the guest room and closed the door.

My first call was to Santiago.

"I was just thinking about you," he said.

I plunged in. "Santiago, did you know my half-brother is Mayor Jaime's nephew?"

He hesitated. "I think I did know that, but I'd forgotten. That all happened so long ago."

"After Dad's murder, when Mom and I were gone, Mayor Jaime looked up Juan José and formed a relationship with him."

"Hmm."

"Do you think it's connected somehow to his wanting to buy the farms?"

"It could be. I don't know, Vero. Keep your eyes and ears open. Like I said before, don't trust anyone."

Great. If you can't trust your own family, who can you trust?

"I'll let you go, Santiago. I just wanted to touch base. I'll see you Thursday morning early."

"I'll be there at seven."

I put away the clothes I had purchased. *The Coffee Diary* was underneath my pajamas in the overnight bag. I picked it up. Why hadn't I realized the truth about Juan José sooner? The young man who argued with his sister at the big party following completion of the *bodega* had definitely been Jaime.

Thinking the diary might hold the answer, I opened it to another entry. This one was from the months we spent in San Diego.

> *August 3, 1991*
> *Dear Diary,*
> *I hate it here. I hate both of my parents. Why did Dad have to fool around with a girl from town? Wasn't Mom good enough for him? Why did Mom bring me to San Diego? Grandma and Grandpa are trying, but Mom doesn't do anything. She stays in her pajamas all day and even forgets to shower. I told her to wash her hair or do something with it. I'm really getting frustrated with her.*
>
> *She's gotten really thin. Sometimes I hear her sobbing through the wall dividing our rooms. She needs to be stronger. At least for my sake.*

At the end of the third week, I overheard Grandma say, "I told you, Liz, a long time ago, you never should have married that man. Latins are all the same. A bunch of skirt-chasing drinkers."

"Stay out of it, Mother. You don't know what you're talking about. It's none of your business anyway."

"It is my business when you and Veronica come back to live with us because of him."

"If that's how you feel, we'll leave. I hate to impose." Mom turned, stormed back to her room, and slammed the door.

Grandma was a small woman, but her character was reflected in the steel blue-grey of her eyes. She butted into other people's business, organized church bazaars, presided over the local chapter of the League of Women Voters, and volunteered at a homeless shelter. She was confident she could get us back on our feet.

I tried not to create problems for my grandparents, but it was difficult for me, too. I missed home; I missed my friends. I anxiously awaited the nightly calls from Dad. But if my grandmother answered the phone, she always made some excuse and wouldn't let us talk to him. Mom didn't care, but I did. "Why won't you let me talk to him?" I asked, tears welling in my eyes.

Her mouth was set in a straight thin line. "Your father doesn't deserve to speak to you."

I knew there was no arguing with her. The next night I was prepared. When the phone rang, I quickly picked it up. "Hello?"

"Vero, honey. It's so good to hear your voice."

"Dad. I miss you."

"I miss you, too. How are things going?"

"I want to come home."

"I need you to be strong for your mother. How is she? Do you think she will talk to me, Vero?"

"No, Dad. She isn't doing very well. She hardly speaks at all. How is everything there?"

"Juan José is quiet, too. It sounds like he'd get along great with your mother right now. I've been trying to get him interested in the coffee farms."

My stomach churned and I felt nauseous. Was I getting edged out by my newly acquired brother? "Dad, you've been teaching me about coffee farming all year. I'm the one who is supposed to inherit the property. Has that changed?"

"Vero, nothing has changed. Juan José is too young to know what he wants. I have two children and two farms. Besides, Juan José may not be interested in coffee in the end."

The next morning, I was up early. Juan José had left and Ita sat at the kitchen table sipping coffee. A newspaper was spread out in front of her.

"Good morning. Anything interesting?" I asked. The headlines blared out murders, corruption, drug trafficking, and child theft.

"Are you serious? Only bad news. I don't know why I read the paper at all. It's so depressing."

I poured a mug of coffee from the pot on the stove and sat down across from her.

"What shall we do today?" she said. "Is there any place you'd like to go?"

"Maybe I should just stay here and think things over."

"A change of scenery would be better for you. Let's go to Antigua for lunch."

"Good idea. I haven't been there for years."

The morning was warm and clear; we ate breakfast on the patio deck. The smell of freshly mown grass filled the air. In the distance, steam rose from the Pacaya Volcano.

"It's a gorgeous day," Ita said. "We'll be able to see all the volcanoes. Pacaya's been active lately and may be due for another eruption."

It was a forty-five minute drive across the mountain to Antigua, the former capital of Central America and one of the best-preserved colonial cities in Spanish America. As the road wound down the final steep section, Ita shifted to a lower gear. Both sides of the road were peppered with iron and wooden crosses, memorials to those killed on this dangerous stretch.

Coffee plantations surrounded the base of the valley, and the Volcán de Agua towered above. The sky was clear and bright. We could see the twin volcanoes of Acatenango and Fuego ahead of us.

We entered town with a bump as the paved road changed to cobblestones. Interspersed between shops, hotels and restaurants were the ruins of ancient monasteries, convents, and churches. Red, orange, purple, and yellow flowering bougainvillea spilled over the walls, coloring the picturesque scene. People of many nationalities strolled over stone slab sidewalks worn and shiny from nearly five hundred years of use.

"Antigua looks almost the same as it did last time I was here." I glanced again at the variety of people on the street. "Well, maybe more touristy."

"We come here every weekend for lunch. Lots of our friends do too. We've even considered buying a weekend house in Antigua, but property here is expensive."

We walked toward the fountain in the center of the park. It was built in 1739, inspired by the Neptune Fountain in Bologna, Italy. Mermaids looked out on each of the four sides, water streaming out of the held breast of each nymph. Groups of tourists were lined up in front of the fountain taking photographs.

"That fountain embarrassed me so much when I was young," Ita told me. "My mother used to laugh at me. She told me I was silly, that it represents female fertility."

At one corner of the park, three men in native hand-woven costumes played the marimba, a xylophone-like instrument.

As we strolled, a tall, suntanned, athletic-looking man approached me. "Veronica? Veronica Villagrán?" he asked. His eyes were an unusual shade of green, accentuated by his dark hair. I remembered only one person who had eyes like that.

"Pablo? Is that you?" I glanced around and saw immaculately dressed men standing nearby, talking in low tones over their radios. I knew for certain then it was him.

"It's been a long time," he said, oblivious of his bodyguards. "I lost track of you after high school. Didn't you move to the U.S.?"

"I've only recently returned. This is my sister-in-law, Margarita. What are you doing now?"

"I came over for the day." He gestured toward a woman on the bench with a toddler.

"Your wife?" I asked.

"No," he said. "I'm not married. I'm here with my sister and niece. I run one of the family's companies in the city. Here's my card." He took a business card from his wallet and handed it to me.

I noticed him glancing at my left hand.

"Give me a call when you're in the city. We can go for dinner or something. I'd love to catch up on the past."

"I'd like that," I said. I looked down at the business card and slipped it into my purse.

"Good to see you again, Veronica. Be sure to call."

He went back to his bench and we moved on.

Ita glanced back over her shoulder. "How do you know him?"

"We dated in high school."

"Are you planning on going out with him?"

"It'd be fun to catch up."

Back when we'd dated, Pablo always arrived in a big car with two bodyguards in front. Usually there was an escort vehicle following, with more bodyguards.

Dad hadn't like me going out with him. "His family is too wealthy. You could be a target just being near him."

"I thought you'd like that he has all these bodyguards. You don't have to worry about me. Geez, Dad, you can always find something wrong with anyone I date."

Pablo's family was rich and powerful. In addition to a beautiful home on a family-owned mountain, they had vacation houses in other parts of the country and kept a house in Miami, right on the water. His family owned clothing factories, beverage industries, and a chain of fast food restaurants.

I had visited Pablo's home on the night of *Luces Campero*, the annual holiday fireworks show. He arrived to pick me up in a Mercedes sports car driven by a burly chauffeur who doubled as a bodyguard.

Surveillance cameras dotted the way as we raced up their long driveway, passing through three different guard stations. The house was situated a thousand feet above Guatemala City, a stunning place from which to watch the display. I tried not to look overly impressed, since after all, we also owned a small forested mountain and a home overlooking a town. But this, of course, was on a whole different scale.

Virgin forest surrounded the Georgian style mansion. Pablo showed me around. Outbuildings in the back housed a staff of sixty: cooks, maids, gardeners, maintenance men, and security. A fleet of cars parked in the garage area was ready to take any member of the family wherever they might need to go. Our home at *Las Marías* was beautiful, but this house was ten times the size, even boasting a helipad. Pablo's father kept a car at the airport, in the hangar with the family's private jet, and used the helicopter to avoid traffic.

It was a chilly December night. Pablo slipped his arm around me as we sat on the balcony of the family room, sipping cocoa and watching the magic of the brilliant colors as they lit up the sky. I admired his lifestyle as much as I liked him.

"Can you come up to Miami with us next weekend?" he asked. "We're taking the jet. We have plenty of room at our house."

"I'd love to," I said, thrilled at the idea. "I'll ask my parents."

Dad had flipped. "I'm sorry, Vero. You are not allowed to be hopping from country to country with boys you date. Absolutely not."

Our relationship fizzled out after that.

I thought back to what a nightmare it had been every time someone asked me out and I had to ask Dad for permission.

"What are you thinking about, Vero?" Ita asked.

"About when I dated Pablo. He's from the Santos family, Santos Escobar."

"Oh," she said, knowingly. The name was familiar to anyone who lived in Guatemala.

But it wasn't just him. Dad hassled me about every boy I wanted to date. When we got back from California, Mom, Juan José, and I moved to the apartment in the city so we could attend school. Dad arrived Friday afternoon, just in time to give the weekend permissions. That's when I began to wish he would just stay at the farm.

The conversation would go like this: "Dad, Daniel asked me to go to the movies tonight."

"Vero, are you asking my permission or informing me?"

"I can go, can't I?"

"Vero, I don't know David..."

"It's Daniel, Daddy."

"Does the boy have a last name, Vero?"

"Daaaad..." I would say in frustration.

"I don't know Daniel, so how can I let you get into a car with a boy I don't know?

My face would fall with disappointment. Then he would say, "Fine, I'll take you and pick you up afterwards. You can meet David or Daniel, or whomever, at the movie theatre."

So I tried another technique. I began bringing boys home before I would go out with them. "Daddy, this is Michael."

My father would shake his hand. "Nice to meet you, sir," the boy would say.

Dad would take a seat across from him. "Have a seat, Michael. What's your family name, son?"

"Sanchez, sir. Sanchez Enriquez."

"Are you related to Pancho Sanchez?"

"No, sir."

"To Mario Enriquez?"

"He's my uncle. My mother's brother."

Satisfied at last with the boy's lineage, Dad would then begin his lecture, telling the boy that I was a princess and I needed to be treated as such. If he would be dating me he had to obey and respect the rules of the house.

Typically, I'd be sitting next to the boy. His foot would be tapping and hands sweating. I would turn several shades of scarlet, first from embarrassment, then from anger at my father for putting us through this.

I shook away the memories. Ita and I sat down on a bench to people-watch. Young Indian girls wearing traditional dress circulated through the park selling jewelry and little purses to tourists.

"Pretty, for you?" one of them asked, unfolding a piece of fabric to show me several pairs of earrings.

"*No, gracias,*" I answered. She and her friend giggled and moved away.

"Where would you like to have lunch?" Ita asked.

"Anywhere is fine. But let's walk around a little more first."

We wandered over to the cathedral. Originally built in 1680, an earthquake had destroyed it, but it was rebuilt in 1773. Stepping into its cool gloom transported me to another time. Four-foot-thick stone walls insulated us from the warmth of the street. Candles cast shadows on the walls and lights shone over works of art and images of saints. I sat down on a plain wooden bench to pray while Ita walked over to look at the side chapels.

*Lord,* I prayed silently, *give me insight and wisdom, courage and safety. Help me make the right decision.*

Ita sat down beside me. "Can we go now, Vero?" she asked softly.

We found a quiet restaurant on a side street that offered Guatemalan specialty cooking. I ordered *hilachas,* a highly spiced stew, and Ita ordered fish. We chatted as we waited for our meals.

"So, Veronica," Ita asked. "What do you think you'll do about the farm?"

"I didn't tell Juan José, but Mayor Jaime wants both farms. I'd be left with nothing."

She raised her head. "Would that matter? Aren't you settled in California? Juan-Jo has given up on you coming back."

I hesitated and looked over toward the cement fountain that graced the center of the indoor patio. "Once I got here, I felt I'd come home. I'm not sure I want to return to California. I don't know."

"I wonder why he wants both farms."

"I think he's trying to prove a point."

"What point? It's not like he isn't going to pay you."

"I just get a bad feeling from him."

"Then tell him you won't sell."

"It isn't that simple. Have you met Juan-Jo's uncle?"

"Yes, he came to our wedding, remember? He's been good to Juan José these past two years."

"I can't see that, Ita. He's a scary guy. Not only have I heard bad things about him, but I've seen some of them with my own eyes."

I thought about the activity on the beach a few nights ago. Santiago had confirmed it was the mayor.

"Are you sure about that?" Ita asked, doubtfully.

I took a deep breath and nodded.

She looked down at her plate and pursed her lips. "I don't think Juan-Jo knows. He trusts the people he cares for."

"Why would he care for Mayor Jaime? He didn't even know him during his childhood." The bitter words came out before I knew what I was saying.

Ita looked up as if searching for the right thing to say. "He wanted family."

"Did his uncle say why he waited so long to look for him?"

"He said when Silvia died and Juan José came to Moyuta, he wasn't in touch with his mother or any of his Moyuta relatives. He didn't learn until some years later that Juan José was living with your family."

The waiter brought clay bowls full of steaming food. "*Muchas gracias*," I said. We put our napkins on our laps.

"Don't you think it was too convenient, the way the mayor looked up Juan José after we had all left?"

"What do you mean?" Ita looked at me intently. "I agree with Juan-Jo. You're awfully paranoid, Vero. You probably think it's all some plot to get back at your family for something."

She was right. I did.

# CHAPTER NINETEEN

"HURRY, JUAN-JO," ITA CALLED. HE WAS LATE GETTING HOME FROM THE hospital and had just stepped out of the shower.

"I'm coming!" He entered the living room still buttoning his shirt. We grabbed our purses and the car keys. Juan José slipped into the driver's seat and we were on our way.

Rush hour traffic was terrible on *Avenida de las Americas,* the main thoroughfare between Zones 13 and 14. Red buses, sides adorned with bright ads for toothpaste, shampoo, and makeup, jammed the streets, swaying ponderously, overloaded with passengers that bus assistants pushed in so tightly little breathing space was left. Black smoke poured from the exhaust pipes, coating everything in grime. Delivery motorcycles with colorful boxes fastened behind them weaved in and out of traffic, hurrying to unload their deliveries of pizza, burgers, or Chinese food. Other motorcycles carried entire families—dad, mom, and up to three small children. Cars of all sizes, models, and makes jammed the avenue. No one who could afford a vehicle took public transportation.

Forty minutes later, we arrived at a residential neighborhood in Zone 15. Aunt Antonia's house was hidden inside an eight-foot brick wall topped with double layers of razor ribbon. We parked on the street in front along with several other cars.

I pressed the buzzer. A voice answered through the intercom. I looked up and waved at the security camera.

My cousin Mario, as jolly and smiling as I remembered, opened the door and greeted us enthusiastically. He had the same twinkle in his brown eyes but was heavier than when I had last seen him. He wore an untucked polo shirt in an attempt to cover his growing midsection.

In the familiar living room, my aunts, uncle, and cousins waited to greet me. Aunt Antonia came out of the kitchen. "Look who the cat dragged in! Veronica, if I hadn't talked to you myself, I wouldn't have believed you were here."

I smiled sheepishly. She hadn't changed a bit.

"I should be angry with you for not keeping in touch."

"I've come to apologize."

"Apologies are only accepted if they come from the heart. You never once called in all these years. Are we so unimportant to you?"

"No," I said, the years melting away. "I got involved in my new life and just put Guatemala behind me."

"Not only your country, but everyone in your family."

I knew I had it coming, but surprisingly hadn't expected it. "You're right, of course. I hope it's not too late to make amends."

"It's never too late. Come here." She opened her arms and embraced me. Aunt Antonia always knew how to put me in my place.

"Juan José, Margarita, how are you?" she said, and put her cheek out for them to kiss. I gave her a second glance until I remembered that Ita was short for Margarita. Of course, my aunt wouldn't use the more familiar term with Juan-Jo's wife.

Antonio and Sara, his wife, greeted me from the living room. Sara held their two-year-old son and Antonio was listening to his five-year-old daughter as she breathlessly exclaimed, "Is that her, Daddy? Is that my Auntie Vero?"

"Hi there," I said to the saucy, bright-eyed girl. "Let's see now. You must be Natalie."

She giggled, "No, I'm not Natalie."

"Jane?" She shook her head. "Oh, I've got it! You're María Sara."

She ran to me and hugged my waist.

"Have a seat, Veronica," Uncle Herman said as he entered the room. Aunt Marielos' husband had kindly eyes and a hairline receding halfway back on his shiny head. He had been attractive in his youth before my aunt's cooking got the best of him. Now his roundness made him look shorter than his five-foot-seven frame.

I gave him a quick hug and looked around. "Where is Aunt Marielos?"

"She's in the kitchen helping Antonia. She'll be right out." He held a drink in his hand and asked, "What can I get you? We have *rosa de Jamaica, horchata, Cuba Libra,* and *Cerveza Gallo.*"

"It's been years since I've had *horchata,* thanks."

He stirred the pitcher of the opaque rice beverage and poured me a glass. "Can't get this outside of Guate, can you?"

"I've never seen it."

Mario brought over a young woman with a big smile and small, even, white teeth. Her shoulder-length hair was pulled back into a ponytail. "Veronica, this is my wife, Terry."

"Nice to meet you." I kissed her on the cheek.

Aunt Marielos came out of the kitchen. She was the taller of my two aunts, with a fair complexion and hazel eyes. "Vero!" She embraced me. "We're so thrilled you're here. Did you hear I'm a grandmother? By Melinda, of course. Karla says she'll never have kids. She's afraid bearing children might ruin her figure."

Melinda and Marcos arrived next. I peeked inside the blue blanket at the infant Melinda cradled in her arms. "And this must be little Brad." The two-month-old baby slept soundly.

Before we got the door closed, another car pulled up. "I think it's Karla," Melinda said. "I'm amazed she was able to come, Vero. She's on the road a lot and is hardly ever around."

I watched as a more elegant version of the Karla I remembered got out of the car wearing a short fuchsia dress and matching pumps. She waved at me. "Is that you, Veronica?" she asked.

"Karla! How are you?"

"Oh, I'm still the same snotty girl that I've always been!" she laughed.

"Where's Paul?"

"He couldn't make it. He flew down to Sao Paulo for a week of shooting." Karla's boyfriend, Paul, was a fashion photographer she'd met during a photo shoot in Jamaica. Karla looked almost as good as her pictures, tall and slim with sleek brown hair falling halfway down her back. Her face appeared in magazines all over Latin America.

"Remember the last time we were all together at the beach house? Was it fourteen years ago?" Mario said. "And Karla, you spent your time under the umbrella reading *Vogue.*"

"Cousin, it paid off for me. It wasn't for nothing I worried about pre-mature aging and the latest styles."

We laughed.

Just as we were settled onto chairs and sofas, Aunt Antonia announced, "The food is ready. Come get a plate and serve yourselves."

Everyone was reluctant to start. "Veronica, as the guest of honor, you go first," Uncle Herman said.

I helped myself to tamales wrapped in banana leaves. "These look delicious," I said to my aunt. "Did you make them?"

Making tamales takes days of work and preparation or lots of assistants. "Of course not," Aunt Antonia said. "You're special, but not that special. I ordered these."

I smiled at her frankness. Then I served myself black beans mashed into a paste, fried plantains, and rice cooked in coconut water, a specialty from the Caribbean coast.

Mario and Terry settled in next to me on the sofa. They'd only been married a year and a half, and I asked how things were going for them.

"We're expecting," Mario announced. Terry blushed modestly.

I congratulated them, thinking how most everyone in my family seemed either to have young children or be working at it.

"I hear life has been treating you well," Mario said. "When are you going back to California?"

"You know, Mario. I'm not sure I am going back."

"Mother told us you had an offer for the farm. I thought you would jump at the chance to sell. I mean, you have an enviable life in the U.S. and a good job."

I wondered how enviable a life I really had. It seemed so ordinary to me. I went to work every morning, enjoyed drinks with a few friends on occasion, but my time wasn't really my own.

When we finished our meal, Aunt Antonia tapped her glass with a fork. "Can I please have everyone's attention?" The conversation ceased and all heads turned. "Veronica, we want to know if you have come to a decision."

It was just like my aunt to put me on the spot. I stood up and gazed around the room filled with family, people who loved me and had known me since childhood.

"I guess you all know I've had an offer to sell the farm," I began. "I thought it'd be an easy decision, but it's more difficult than I expected."

Several people looked up in surprise and a buzz of conversation interrupted me. My aunt stood up. "Hush, everyone. Let her continue."

"Well, being home has been wonderful and I've missed you all so much. I'm deeply sorry I didn't keep in touch. I just hope you've remembered me as fondly as I have you." I looked around at my relatives. "If I do stay, I hope you will visit me in Moyuta. Maybe we could meet at the beach house like we used to. You are my family, the only family I have here. You are all very important to me." I hesitated.

"If I keep the farms, I'll do my best to bring them back to the shape they were in when Mom and Dad were here." I felt a pang in my heart at the mention of my father. "With any luck, even better. But no matter what happens, I promise to let you know."

"It sounds as though you want to keep the farms," Mario said. "Why don't you?"

"I'm under a lot of pressure to sell."

"What do you mean? What kind of pressure?" Aunt Marielos asked.

"Well, I've been threatened verbally and I've been followed, not here in the city, but in Moyuta. Someone took a shot at me one day while I was at *Las Marías*."

"What?" exclaimed Juan José. "And you didn't leave town right away? Are you crazy, *hermana*? You didn't tell me any of this."

"Veronica, how can you even think of staying in Moyuta facing that kind of danger?" Aunt Antonia scolded. "Don't forget how your father met his end. Violence is rampant in that part of the country." Making sure she had everyone's attention, she said, "I heard Arturo Buencamino was killed a few days ago for not selling some land to the mayor."

I watched my brother's face register surprise and shock at the mention of the murder.

"I honestly haven't considered I was in much danger while still deciding. But I haven't known who to trust."

"You're staying with Carlos, aren't you?" asked Aunt Antonia.

"Yes. I've been staying with Tio Carlos and María Celia. But I think one of them, Tio Carlos, I suspect, has been tipping someone off about where I go every time I leave the house."

"Tio Carlos? That's hard to believe," Aunt Marielos said.

I shrugged. "It's really just a hunch."

"If you can't trust family, who can you trust?" Uncle Herman said, echoing my earlier thoughts.

Melinda's forehead creased. "Maybe you should hire bodyguards."

"Can't you go to the authorities or to the police?" Antonio suggested.

"Bro, don't you get it? The mayor is the authority in town," Mario said. "The police are probably on the take. Besides, in a small town, they wouldn't go against the mayor."

"What about the governor?"

"No way," Uncle Herman said, shaking his head. "Fernando Prieto, the governor of Jutiapa, is one of the most corrupt in the country."

"The president?" Karla offered.

"They're friends," I said. "I saw their picture together in the mayor's office."

"That figures. These people think they can become respectable by going into politics. It's just another kind of crime, fleecing the public," Uncle Herman said.

"See, there is no easy solution. Not only does he want *Las Marías*, but now he wants me to throw in *Ojo de Agua*."

"Then there would be nothing left in Moyuta," Aunt Marielos said. "None of us would have ties there anymore."

"Would that matter? We haven't been there for years," Antonio said.

"And good riddance, anyway," Karla interjected. "I never liked Moyuta."

"Speak for yourselves," Mario said. "I like that town."

"What's the mayor's name?" my aunt asked.

"Jaime Ramírez."

Suddenly the questioning eyes of my relatives fell on Juan José. "Isn't that your second last name? Your mother's maiden name?" Uncle Herman asked.

Juan José nodded.

"Any relation of yours?" Antonia asked.

"He's…my uncle."

An awkward silence reigned in the room. "Well, then," Uncle Herman said, breaking the quiet. "That's lucky. There's your solution. Juan José can speak to him for you."

Juan José and Ita sat on the couch. She reached over to take his hand. He was pale. "You didn't tell me any of this, Vero," he said. "Why?"

"I was too shocked, Juan-Jo. When you told me he was your uncle, I didn't know what to think, especially after seeing those family pictures. It made me question where your loyalties lie."

"I can't believe you don't trust me." He got up to leave, trembling with anger and hurt. "Stay here tonight. You can pick up your bag at my house in the morning on your way out of town. Come on, Ita." He pulled her to her feet. "We aren't wanted here."

"Wait, Juan-Jo," I called after him. But they were already out the door.

"Let him go, Veronica," Aunt Antonia said. "How do you know he isn't involved in this somehow? I always figured he had to covet those farms. At least your father had sense enough not to leave them to him."

"How can you say that? Juan José would never hurt me. I'm going after him."

I ran out of the house without saying goodbye. Juan José and Ita were in the car buckling up when I got there. "Let me in," I said, knocking on the window. "I'm leaving, too."

"Stay with the rest of them, Vero. Don't pretend you trust me. It's obvious you don't."

"Please unlock the door. I'll be devastated if we can't straighten this out, Juan-Jo."

"I'm already devastated. I never expected this from you."

I took a deep breath. "Please, little brother. Hear me out."

Reluctantly he leaned over and unlocked the rear door. I slipped in. "Let's go somewhere we can talk." Juan José started the car. We drove down *Boulevard Vista Hermosa* in silence.

"Where are we going?" I asked.

"Home. I don't want to be anywhere else."

We arrived and Juan José unlocked the front door. "After you," he said formally.

We sat stiffly in the living room. Then Ita jumped up and said, "I'll get some drinks."

"Why didn't you tell me what was going on, Vero?" Juan José asked after his wife left the room.

"It's been so difficult. I haven't known who to trust. Look what happened with Tio Carlos, and I trusted him completely."

"That is hard to believe."

"I also found out he's been stealing from me."

Juan José looked shocked. "Are you serious?"

I nodded. "I never would have believed any of this just a week ago."

"Tell me about Uncle Jaime. I'm not convinced by what you said."

"It's true, Juan-Jo. I think he may have used you to get to me."

"That doesn't make sense, Vero. He's been so supportive. He's had nothing but good things to say about our family."

Ita came back and put two glasses of wine on the table. Then she sat down next to Juan José.

"You went to Moyuta with him, presumably to meet the rest of the family," I said. "What else did you do there?"

"I visited Tio Carlos and he gave me the extra keys to the farms, the ones I gave you."

"Did you go out to see the farms?"

"Tio Jaime wanted to see them. I didn't think it was a big deal. He told me about the development project he had in mind. Honestly, Veronica, I thought I was doing you a favor. I had no idea you might consider coming back to Guatemala to run them."

"Why *Ojo de Agua*?"

Juan José paused as he gathered his thoughts. "He never said he might want that farm. He just told me he'd heard a lot about it and wanted to see it. It's well-known as one of the original coffee farms. I didn't think there was any harm in showing it to him. I guess I should have mentioned it, but how could I know there might be an ulterior motive?"

I sighed. He couldn't have known.

"I wish I didn't have to choose my loyalties" he said. "But if I must, you will always be number one with me. Remember when you and Mom came back from San Diego? I'll never forget that."

I remembered. It was November, 1991. Mom and I were anxious to be home again, but nervous at the same time after those months in California.

Dad was waiting for us with a big smile and open arms as we came out of the airport terminal. Aunt Antonia and her two sons greeted us with banners that read, "Welcome Home Liz and Vero." Aunt Marielos and her daughters had bouquets that shouted "Welcome Back" from silver globes.

We hugged and kissed each one of them. Juan José was standing to one side, looking forlorn, unsure what to do. I recognized him by his small, thin frame and unimposing stature.

I put my bag down, jostled my way over to my half brother, then knelt down to be at his level. "*Hola, hermanito. Cómo has estado?*"

"*Bien,*" he'd replied in his tiny voice.

"*Venga, Juan José.*" I grabbed his hand and led him to the rest of the group. "Stay with me."

After our return, Mom and I accepted this small boy into our family unconditionally and quickly learned to love him.

As I looked at Juan José, I could still see traces of that little nine-year-old boy in his face. "You were my hero then, Vero. You'll always be my hero."

I smiled tightly. Many things still needed airing. Perhaps together we could make sense of it after all.

# CHAPTER TWENTY

SANTIAGO ARRIVED AT SEVEN SHARP. WHEN HE RANG THE BELL, I OPENED the door and hugged him, reveling in that safe feeling. Santiago returned my embrace, then backed off a bit to look at me. His eyes showed concern. "Whoa, Vero. Are you okay?"

"I missed you."

"I missed you, too. Come on. We'd better be going." He gently pushed me aside, put my bag in the trunk and opened the car door for me. Then he slid into the driver's seat and fastened his seatbelt. "How was your time in the city?"

I shook my head. "It all seemed so simple before, when the mayor was the bad guy. I just had to figure out how to keep myself safe. Now Juan José tells me I've got Mayor Jaime all wrong. It doesn't add up. Why would he tell me that? Do you think Juan José fits into the equation somehow?"

"It's hard to say."

"I thought the mayor was evil, but he evidently has some redeeming qualities, at least according to Juan José. What do you think?"

He shrugged, listening but apparently not ready to commit himself to any theory.

I bit my lip. "I still think it was easier before."

"Look at me, look at you," Santiago offered. "Neither of us is perfect."

"But Mayor Jaime?" I said. "I don't think you can put us in the same category. I don't recall anything good about him. Do you?"

We stopped at a traffic light, and he turned to look at me. "No one is totally good or evil, but I have yet to see Jaime Ramirez's good side."

"Thanks. I guess I'm not so far off."

"You're reading *The Coffee Diary*, aren't you?" he said.

*Why would he ask that?* My face must have expressed the question in my mind.

"I saw it near the bed the other day at the beach."

I looked at his profile. He was deep in thought. Suddenly I was defensive. "Did you read any of it?"

"How far have you gotten?" he said, not denying it.

"I've skimmed over most of it. I just have some later entries to look at."

"Keep reading. There are other memories from that year that might be useful."

"What do you mean? Which ones? Did you read it?"

"Of course not." He was quiet. "Okay," he admitted. "Perhaps I picked it up and glanced through it."

"You did what? You read my diary?"

"Why the fuss?"

I threw myself back against the seat and turned away. He had looked through the book without my consent. How could he? "It's private. You should have asked me before you picked it up."

"It was your journal fourteen years ago, Veronica. There's nothing new in it. I just wanted to see if it could help me remember anything significant."

"Help *you* remember?"

I tried to wrap my mind around this. *Was Santiago manipulating me, too?* I stared out the window, my hands clenched.

When Santiago reached for me, I brushed him away. I leaned against the door and answered in monosyllables. I was fuming: how could he not realize I'd be angry?

The two-hour drive seemed to take twice as long with no conversation. When we reached Moyuta, Santiago stopped the car in front of Tio Carlos' clinic. "Are you sure you want to go in?"

"What do you think?" My voice had turned cold. "All my things and my car are here."

"Hey, Veronica," he pleaded. "I'm sorry. I should have thought first. I didn't know it would upset you so much. Forgive me."

I turned toward him. His face was filled with remorse and I softened slightly. "I need to tell Tio Carlos I'm leaving. I've learned my lesson. I can't let people take advantage of me, and I need to rethink some of my relationships."

As I reached for the door handle, Santiago touched my arm gently. "Hey, you. You're forgetting something." He leaned over and kissed me on the mouth before I could turn away. He smiled. I could tell he hoped everything was forgiven. "Now you can go. Come by the house after you've met with the mayor. Bring your things and stay with us."

I hesitated before I got out. "Thanks for the ride."

I grabbed my bag from the trunk, slammed the lid down, and went into my uncle's house. María Celia was sweeping the patio and looked up as I entered.

"Good morning, Vero. Where've you been? I was just thinking about you."

"Sorry I didn't let you know where I was."

"I was worried. We called and Julián said you'd left the beach Tuesday morning. You should have let us know."

"Don't you have my cell phone number?"

"No. I didn't think to get it before you left."

I walked over to a corner table where a pad and pencil lay next to the phone. I scribbled my number. "Here," I said. "I trust *you* with it." She nodded her understanding.

"I won't give it away."

"Not even to Tio Carlos." She didn't say anything, but her face showed surprise. "I went to the city with Santiago and stayed with Juan José and Ita."

"How was the beach?"

"Wonderful, as always. I've missed it. We watched the *arribada* at night." I didn't mention the other things we'd seen.

"I saw it once, many years ago. The poor turtles. They work so hard just to have their eggs dug up later by poachers."

"We didn't see any poachers."

"And how was your time in the city?"

"Interesting," I said. "Did you know Juan José is the mayor's nephew?"

"Didn't you? I thought everyone knew. Juan José was here a few months back with the mayor. He borrowed Carlos' spare keys to show him the farms, the ones he gave you. Didn't you wonder why he had them?"

"I never thought about it."

My face must have registered surprise, because she quickly added, "I would have told you if I thought you didn't already know. Really, Veronica, your mother was my friend and I don't want to see you hurt in any way."

I didn't say anything. Instead of the pieces falling into place, the more I learned, the more I realized I didn't understand.

I changed the subject. "How have things been here?"

"Not good. Your uncle started drinking again after you left. The murder and everything else have really gotten to him."

I watched her carefully as she spoke. Tears formed in her eyes. I put my arms around her and she clung to me, silent sobs racking her thin body. "I told him he shouldn't see patients in his state, but when he's like this he doesn't listen to anyone. He opens the clinic at odd hours, then abruptly closes and goes back to drinking."

"Oh, dear," I said. "I'm sorry."

She dried her eyes with a tissue she found in her pocket. "Don't mind me. I know you have plenty of problems of your own."

"María Celia, I'm going to pack my things and go stay with Santiago and his parents. I feel safer there."

"What do you mean? You don't feel safe here?"

"It's not you. You've been great."

She studied the ground, a frown on her face. "It's your uncle, isn't it? I don't know what's gotten into him. He's changed lately."

I looked out toward my car in the parking area. "I wish things were different, but they aren't. I'll be back to pick up my things after I meet with Mayor Jaime."

"I feel terrible about this. I've tried to make you comfortable. I don't know what else I can do."

There wasn't anything I could say to her. I excused myself, went into the guest room, and changed into some clean clothes. In the mirror I looked pale and drawn. I applied makeup to give myself some color and hoped it would boost my confidence.

Finished, I stood in front of the full-length mirror. I looked better and felt revived. My jeans fit tightly across my rear, and my red V-neck sweater not only flattered my coloring, it showed the slightest bit of cleavage. Perhaps it wasn't a great idea going to see the mayor looking so good, but at this point I didn't care. Sometimes a girl needs to dress up to feel better.

I slipped *The Coffee Diary* into my purse along with my wallet, sunglasses, cell phone, and gun. I went out to the kitchen to sit with María Celia for a few minutes before leaving.

"It's strange the mayor called you in today," she said as she poured me a cup of coffee.

"Why is that?"

"Doña Julieta works as the treasurer's assistant. She told me Mayor Jaime gave everyone the day off."

"Any particular reason?"

"Building maintenance, he said."

"I'm positive he told me today at ten." I wondered what I should do. I looked at my watch. "It's already ten twenty. I'm late. With everything else, I don't want to risk missing my appointment."

"Do you want me to go with you?" she offered.

I took a deep breath and remembered what Juan José had said. Maybe the mayor had been bluffing. Maybe he wasn't as bad as we all thought. "He told me to come alone. If I don't come back soon, let someone know and come looking for me."

The sun was bright, and I slipped on my dark glasses as I stepped into the street. Businesses were open; people were sweeping sidewalks and the areas in front of their stores.

I walked slowly, uneasy about this meeting. I wanted people to know where I'd gone. "*Buenos días*," I said several times in greeting.

Two black Land Rovers were parked in front of the town hall. I saw movement out of the corner of my eye and turned. The dog from the cemetery limped towards me, looking even worse now than he had last week; his mottled fur was thin with patches of skin showing.

"Centinela," I called. "Come here."

He looked up and continued approaching.

"Come on, boy." His ears perked up as he heard me, but he stopped about ten feet away. When I took a few steps in his direction, he backed up. I turned around and kept walking. When I glanced back again, he still followed.

Two men leaned against the *municipalidad*. Mayor Jaime's henchmen.

The driver-side door of the other Land Rover opened and a pair of ostrich-leather cowboy boots appeared and slid to the ground. Mayor Jaime stepped out.

"Miss Veronica. I knew you wouldn't keep me waiting long." He glanced at his watch.

"Mayor Jaime." I nodded. "I heard the office is closed today. I thought you might cancel our appointment. I almost didn't come at all."

"On the contrary. I thought it better no one was around to hear our business."

When I raised my eyes, my reflection showed in his silver-tinted Ray-Bans.

"Introduce us, boss. She knows us, but we've never been formally presented," Chico Negro said, as he looked me up and down. "Ain't that right, kitten?"

I glanced at him and shivered. His shirt was unbuttoned halfway down, exposing a hairy chest with numerous gold chains sparkling in the sun. He grinned, flashing two gold teeth, a diamond set into one. A pair of holstered guns, a cell phone, a sunglasses case, several clips of ammunition, and a sheathed knife hung from his belt. He probably had a small weapon stashed in his boot, just in case.

"Shut up, Chico," Jaime retorted. Then he thought better of it and said, "Veronica, Chico Negro and Montaña Ocho." I glanced over at them again. Chico Negro tipped his hat and Montaña Ocho just leered.

Montaña, fair skinned and sinewy, crouched near the wall, close to the open door. "She's hotter than I remember. But that was a long time ago."

"Shut up, Montaña. It ain't polite to talk that way in front of a lady," Chico said.

"I don't know no ladies."

"With your manners, it ain't no wonder." The men looked at me like ranchers appraising a mare for sale.

A low throaty rumble sounded. The cemetery dog had circled around behind the men and crouched, teeth bared, hackles raised.

"I thought you got rid of this dog, Chico," Montaña said uneasily.

"It wasn't me. Lalo shot him. But if it's the same one, he's got more lives than a cat," Chico commented. "He was shot a couple o' times."

The dog crept towards Chico Negro, snarling. Mayor Jaime drew back his leg to kick it with his metal tipped boot.

"Step aside, *compadre*," Chico said, drawing one of his guns. "I'll get him good this time."

I screamed. "Don't do it!"

"Don't push your luck, sweetheart," he said as he pointed his gun at the dog. "When I shoot, I don't miss. Unless I ain't aimin' to kill."

Mayor Jaime reached for me, and I slipped away, out of his grasp. I kept my eyes on Chico Negro as he pulled the trigger. His aim was good. The dog yipped, then collapsed.

Alerted by my scream, several people came out on the street. Townspeople drifted toward us cautiously.

"Stay back," Jaime said to the gathering crowd. "There's nothing to worry about. The cemetery dog gave us a scare. I think he was rabid, bitten by bats or rodents. We put him out of his misery. He won't be a threat anymore."

The metallic scent of fresh blood reached me and I felt sick. I leaned against the cool aqua-colored cement building, trying to overcome my nausea. My eyes focused on Chico Negro, refusing to look at the dead animal. "Why did you do that?" I asked.

"I was only doing my job," Chico drawled. "After all, witnesses ain't never allowed to live."

# CHAPTER TWENTY-ONE

I STARED AT CHICO NEGRO, HARDLY BELIEVING WHAT I'D JUST SEEN AND stunned by the implications of what he'd said. The mayor took my arm. "Come with me, Veronica. I need to talk to you in private." Still in shock, I let him usher me into the *municipalidad*.

The room was cavernous, devoid of people and activity. The lights were off, but daylight seeped through the gap between the top of the wall and the corrugated metal roof. Chain link mesh covered the separation, protection against thieves and bats.

"Why?" I whispered, still in a daze. "Just tell me why you did it."

"Did what? Killed the dog? He was just a nuisance anyway." He jangled keys in his hands and searched for the one he needed. "Besides, that was Chico's doing. I only calmed down the people who came to see what happened. It seems like folks had a soft spot for that flea-bitten mongrel."

"It's easy to put the blame on Chico, isn't it? That was my father's dog. Chico killed him in front of me to prove a point." I hesitated. "But that's not what I meant."

The clinking of keys brought me back to my senses. Suddenly I realized how foolish I was to be in here alone with him. "You know what, Mayor Jaime? I think I'd better leave."

He held my arm a little tighter as I tried to pull away. His fingers made indentations in my flesh.

"You're hurting me."

He loosened his grip slightly. "Veronica, I must speak to you in private. My boys are loyal, at least I think they are, but I don't like doing business on the street. No one can be completely trusted these days."

I continued my train of thought. "My father. You were there."

"What are you talking about? Are you accusing me of murder?"

"Why are you after us? It's been coming back to me in pieces. Just tell me, so I can understand."

He stood in front of his office and inserted the key in the lock. I watched him, transfixed. Perhaps I would hear the answer now. The question had plagued me since I arrived.

"You don't understand. Our lives are forever intertwined, my dear Veronica. My sister was with your father; my nephew is your brother; your father fired mine, who later stole from him. My father was murdered. Your father was murdered. Now, there is you and me. Doesn't it make sense to you?"

"No. And what about the part where you kill my father?"

"Believe me. I didn't kill him and I never wanted him dead."

He kicked the door open and followed me in, flicking on the lights. I slid into the chair, expecting him to sit down, too. Instead he locked the door. A chill ran through me.

"Just give me what I want," he said simply, still standing at the door.

"And what is that? My life?"

"I have no intention of killing you, Veronica. I've had opportunities."

"The shot at the farm. You were behind that, weren't you?"

"If I had meant for you to be harmed, you wouldn't be sitting here. No, believe it or not, that isn't my intention."

I laughed. "That's a good one." I looked at him, ready to call his bluff. "Do you expect to convince me?"

"I don't need to. It's the truth."

"Why should I believe you? You've never given me any reason."

"Believe what you want."

He swung himself into the swivel chair behind the desk, reminding me of our first meeting. Despite having many reasons to fear him, I no longer felt intimidated. He didn't exude the same confidence I'd first observed. He looked weary. Fine lines showed around his eyes. He picked up a pen and idly drew circles on a blank paper.

"What do you need to talk to me about?"

"A lot has come up lately." He turned toward the far wall and I followed his gaze. His eyes rested on the photograph where he and President Porta were shaking hands. Each had his other arm in a half embrace.

"I'm seeking respectability. Perhaps I'll continue in politics." He paused. "I need to leave my past behind and look towards the future. I want to get out of the dirty business I've been in. I need to have the right person beside me."

I shrugged, not sure how this revelation related to me. Politics was just as dirty as illicit business. Worse, in fact, because it wore the veneer of honor.

"Honestly, Veronica. It never occurred to me you might want to keep the farms. Even Juan José was certain you'd never return."

"Why didn't you tell me he's your nephew?" I asked, glad he had broached the subject. "I can't believe he discussed this with you, that the two of you hatched this plan to take the properties away from me."

He chuckled. "To take the properties away? You know I could seize them if I desired. I've offered to buy them, and for an excellent price at that. You don't get it. I'm trying to do things lawfully."

"And what about Juan José? Why didn't you tell me about your relationship?" I repeated.

"You were the only one in town who didn't know. When I realized that, I thought it might be advantageous."

"Why would you think that?"

"I'm not as scary now, am I?"

I looked at him again. He wasn't.

"You're scary enough," I said, with a hint of sarcasm and a smirk.

He laughed. "Thank you. I've got a reputation to keep."

A glimmer of hope reached me. Did this mean I could say no to selling the farms? My expression must have given me away, because he continued, "Too bad I already have so much invested. I couldn't just scrap it. But I've given a lot of thought to how this issue can be resolved and I have come up with a solution." He looked at me intently, waiting for a response.

"If you didn't kill my father, who did?"

"Why are you so obsessed about that? It won't get you anywhere. I'm not pointing fingers in regards to my father's death. Why should you?"

"You admit to extorting money, right?"

"That's a far cry from murder. Anyway, why would I want Quique dead?

He was an outstanding citizen, a good father to my nephew and to you, though you didn't think so at the time—a good coffee farmer and husband. If he was dead, I couldn't expect to get any money."

"It was Chico, wasn't it? The cemetery dog knew."

The mayor looked up at the ceiling. "I'm not at liberty to say. All I can tell you is that I didn't want it to happen."

"My father took part in your father's murder, didn't he?"

"I never found proof, but it's likely." He studied his hands for a moment. "I don't think my father's murder was personal. It was home-grown justice. That's the way things go around here. I've accepted it."

"Did my father know the connection between you? That his son was your father's grandson?"

"He must have. It's a small town. But I doubt it mattered to him. Silvia and Juan José meant nothing to him until my mother showed up at your door and foisted off Juan José on your family." He looked at me intently, as if the force of his stare could convince me. "Have you considered the possibility that someone besides me might have wanted your father dead?"

"What do you mean?" My mind raced. "You can't mean Juan José. Are you saying he might want have wanted revenge for his grandfather's murder? He doesn't even know." I discounted that idea completely. "You know my brother. He wouldn't hurt a fly."

"That wasn't what I meant. You don't give me much credit." He leaned back in his chair, analyzing me. "I guess that means you probably won't agree to my proposal."

"Which is?"

"First let me tell you this. Your life may be in danger and I've thought of a way to keep you safe."

"Why would my life be in danger? And why would you want me safe?"

I was becoming increasingly angry and confused. I tried unsuccessfully to stay calm and keep my voice even.

"Oh, Veronica, don't listen to what everyone would have you believe. I'm not as bad as people say."

"Tell me, then, why were you so resentful of me when we were younger?"

"I wasn't the only one. Perhaps the only one you noticed. Those of us who struggle from day to day just to have enough food to eat naturally resent the rich. You had plenty and your family lived thoughtlessly, taking what they needed from others."

"What do you mean by that?"

"My sister, for example. Your father never cared for her. Then your father fired mine with no warning, leaving us kids to deal with the consequences. My father had his faults. He was a lousy husband, perhaps a poor employee. But he loved his children and did his best for us. He wanted us to do better, to be educated, to have enough to eat. Your father never gave him a second chance. He didn't care about any of us. It was then I decided to change my life and never be poor again."

My cell phone rang, interrupting our conversation. I took it out of my purse and looked at the caller number. It was Juan José. The mayor indicated I should answer. "Hello?"

"Veronica, it's me. I thought about our conversation last night. I'm taking time off to come to Moyuta. I'll be there tomorrow afternoon, spend the weekend and go back on Tuesday. Maybe I can help you."

"Stay in Guatemala City, Juan José. No need for you to be involved," I said.

"But I want to be. You'll be in less danger with me there. Your final day to make the decision is Sunday, and I want to be there with you."

"If you think you could help, I'll be at the..." I hesitated, remembering who was in front of me. "You know what, Juan-Jo, I'll call you back later." I put the phone back in my purse.

Mayor Jaime was looking at me. "My nephew, I take it."

"He's coming tomorrow."

"I sincerely wish he wasn't."

"Why is that? You don't want to disillusion him?"

"No, dear. Because I'll have to keep him out of harm's way. Like I said, things have come up."

"You'd better see that he doesn't get hurt. He's my brother and I love him."

"Hmm. And who has been here for him when he needed family?" I ignored the question. "Thanks to your father, my sister left town and died alone, away from family and friends."

"My father paid for his sins. What's your proposal?"

He rested his elbows on the desktop calendar, then looked over at me. "You are young and attractive, Veronica. Don't think I haven't noticed. I've always had my eye on you."

I waited for him to continue.

"I would like someone to share my life with. I have money and possibilities. I'm looking for someone special, a partner, an arrangement of mutual benefit."

My eyes opened wide with incredulity. He couldn't mean this.

"Be my wife. We can share the farms. Your family, they're like royalty in these parts." He paused for effect. I was glued to my seat, stunned into silence. "I know I should have brought a ring. But we are practical people and the details can be worked out later."

I was aghast. "You can't be serious."

"Why not? We're both of marriageable age. I have plenty of money. You're from a prominent family and have two of the best farms in the area. It sounds like an ideal match."

"What about love?" I asked.

"Ha! What is love? It's a chemical attraction that fades with time. Arranged marriages work so much better."

"I'm floored, Mayor Jaime. I don't know what to say."

"Call me Jaime. I've proposed marriage, so drop the title. I'll give you some time to think about it. Sunday is decision-day anyway. Tell me then."

I was horrified, but tried hard not to show it. I could already see his anger rising at my lack of enthusiasm.

"Is this any different from what Santiago wants?" he challenged.

"What are you talking about?"

He squinted. "He isn't worthy of you. At least I'm honest and upfront about what I want."

I'd heard enough. The chair scraped the floor as I pushed it out of my way and stood. "Are we finished for now, Mayor Jaime? I need to get back."

For a large man he moved fast. By the time I grabbed my purse off the back of the chair, he was standing in front me. I waited for him to unlock the door and move out of my way. "No, Veronica. I'm not quite finished." He crossed his arms and stood between me and the door.

"Please let me leave now, Jaime."

"See, it wasn't so hard to call me by my first name." His mouth stretched into an unnatural smile. "Come here." He grabbed my arm and I tried to pull away. "You're a feisty one, are you? I like a woman who takes it rough."

My heart beat rapidly and my mind raced. What could I do to get out of here? If I screamed, would anyone hear?

"Don't be so frightened. All I want is a little taste. I know you fucked Santiago. He already got to sample the wares. All I'm asking for is a kiss."

I pulled back. "You were at the beach that night."

"What night? The night you were with Santiago? Which one? I heard you were together two nights."

"Santiago saw you Sunday morning. He told me what you'd said to him about being rivals."

"He's dreaming. I was in Jutiapa. The governor had a mayor's retreat that weekend. Ask around, you'll see."

"Why should I believe you?"

"Why should you believe him?"

I hesitated for a moment, confused. He grabbed me while I was off guard and pulled me close. "I've wanted you for years, Veronica. But I wouldn't take you by force. You remember."

I looked at him blankly.

"Just ask Chico."

He brought my body tight against him and I could feel his erection. "I want you to give in to me."

"Let me go!"

"You turn me on, Veronica. If I had you, I'd have everything. You know how persistent I am." His hands roamed up and down my back and he squeezed my ass. "Kiss me," he demanded in my ear. "Kiss me and I'll let you leave."

I felt nauseated.

What choice did I have? I had to get out of there. I took a deep breath before relenting and offered my mouth, lips tightly closed. Seconds later his tongue came through, searching. He repulsed me and I was sickened by my lack of resistance. I pulled away. "Can I go now?"

"Please, just one more." He reached for me and I eluded his grasp.

"No, you said I could leave."

"Fine. I'm a man of my word. But you leave me longing for more."

He unlocked the door and I slipped out without another word, anxious to be gone. Leaving, I saw the two goons still there, leaning against the wall, chewing tobacco.

"Hey, sweetheart. How was the mayor? You had a nice long chat alone with him. Sounds fun." Montaña Ocho drawled out his taunts.

"He slip it in you? I'm bigger and better than he is," Chico said, leering. "I'd like to do it, too. We've got unfinished business, you and I. You're such a hot piece of ass."

Those were the words Santiago had used. It was Chico at the beach, not the mayor.

# CHAPTER TWENTY-TWO

THE STREET BLURRED PAST ME AS I RAN TO MY GREAT-UNCLE'S. TOWNSPEOPLE must have wondered what had happened. I didn't care. I breathed a sigh of relief when I reached the quiet house and collapsed on the hallway bench to catch my breath. Elbows on my knees, I rested my head in my hands. The adrenaline slowly wore off and tears of anger and frustration welled in my eyes.

"Vero, is that you?" María Celia called. "I was getting worried."

She came out from the kitchen and sat down beside me, tucking her skirt under her. "Are you all right?"

I stifled the silent sobs rising in me and composed myself. I took a tissue out of my pocket and dabbed at my eyes and nose. I nodded, not trusting my voice.

She reached into a pocket of her apron, retrieved another tissue, and handed it to me. "You don't look all right. What happened? I heard a shot from the direction of the park and raced over there. Men were throwing the corpse of the cemetery dog into the back of a truck. They said he had rabies. I looked for you everywhere, but I didn't see you."

"It was horrible. He wasn't rabid at all, the major just said that. Chico Negro killed the dog right in front of me."

"Why did he do that?"

I wiped my face with my hands and stared out toward the patio garden. "I was standing outside the *municipalidad* with the mayor, Chico, and

Montaña when the cemetery dog came up behind them. He was snarling and looked like he might attack Chico."

"Chico's evil. He must have done something to the dog. I can't think of any other explanation."

"Chico said that the dog was a witness. He couldn't allow him to live."

"A witness? To what?"

"He didn't say. But I think it was to my father's murder. I think Chico is one of the men who killed Dad, and the dog was after revenge."

"He could have been a witness to other things, too. Don Arturo's body was thrown out of his car near the cemetery. Several other hits have taken place near there."

"Maybe. But I felt sure Chico was talking directly to me, telling me he killed my father."

She gazed at the far wall as if searching for words in the cracked plaster. "I've heard rumors."

"What kind of rumors? I thought after Dad's murder, the suspects were hunted down and dealt with."

"Yes, that's what happened."

"What about the mayor and his two buddies?"

"No one directly implicated them but they disappeared for six months. Many of us in town found their leaving suspicious. When they returned, Jaime ran for mayor and became invincible. The rest is history."

"It was Chico and Montaña who attacked me when I was fourteen. Mom told you about that, didn't she?"

She nodded. "Those two have always been bad news."

"They think they're above the law."

"They have been. Look at don Arturo. Nothing will be done about his murder. Who is the law in this town? The mayor. The police don't take a step without his approval."

"That's what I hate about Guatemala."

"You take the bad with the good." She shrugged. "*Así es la vida.* Anyway, where were you?"

"In the mayor's office. He wanted to speak privately."

"What?" She looked at me in surprise. "With the *municipalidad* closed today, you shouldn't have gone in there with him."

"No, I shouldn't have. I was in shock after seeing Chico kill the dog and I let the mayor lead me in. I just wanted to get away from that scene." I shook my head. "I wasn't thinking clearly."

I felt better once I'd talked about it. But as for the mayor's proposal, I couldn't bring myself to mention it.

"Did he threaten you?"

I shook my head. "He expects me to sell and I don't want to."

"What are you planning to do?"

"Juan José is coming tomorrow. He thinks he'll be able to convince his uncle to let me keep the farms."

"Good luck with that," she said. It was obvious she didn't believe it would do any good. "Will you be taking your things over to Alba's? Would you like some help?"

"I'd like to stay here another night, if you don't mind. I don't have the energy to move. I just want to hang out in the guest room alone. I need to mull things over."

"You know you're more than welcome to stay for as long as you want."

I retreated to my room, shut the door, and collapsed onto the bed. With so much happening so fast, my head was spinning. I wanted to rest and relax, take my mind off my troubles, and gain some perspective.

I took out *The Coffee Diary* and flipped to the last half of the book. It was after we returned from San Diego. What had it been like to suddenly have a new brother in the family? I almost couldn't remember.

I settled on the entry from Thanksgiving.


We had been back for several weeks. Though Juan José was welcomed into our family, Mom and I couldn't get accustomed to having a constant reminder of Dad's betrayal around. Juan José, too, was having a difficult time. He hungered for affection and followed us around the house hopefully. I felt sorry for him and would sometimes read to him from a children's storybook[TK], then, in turn, let him read to me so I could correct his pronunciation. He was struggling to learn English; it wasn't easy for him.

On Thanksgiving Day, kitchen activities began early. We cooked all morning and into the early afternoon. All the food preparation puzzled Juan José. "Mom," I heard him ask. "Why we fix so much food?"

"Thanksgiving reminds us of harvests when we settled in America, and God's love for us. We celebrate by cooking a special meal and sharing it with family and friends."

He looked at her intently. "But we not have coffee harvest yet, do we?"

"Harvest season in the United States is in the summer and fall, during Guatemala's rainy season. Here, it's later because our biggest crop is coffee," she told him. "The coffee harvest will begin in January."

The turkey cooked all day and filled the house with mouthwatering smells. At three o'clock, Mom put the pies in the oven.

A car drove up. "They're here," I called, and went out to greet our friends. Tio Carlos had come with the Godoy family. I was especially excited that Santiago had come, as I hadn't seen him since we returned from San Diego.

"Happy Thanksgiving!" I said and gave everyone a quick hug. "Come in."

"*Buenas tardes,* Liz." Guillermo kissed my mother on the cheek. "The turkey smells delicious!"

"I love this U.S. holiday!" Santiago said.

"You just love to eat," Ana retorted.

Our formal dining table was set for nine people. Juan José helped Mom bring in the food. When we were all seated, Dad announced, "Today is the day we share our abundance and thank God for our blessings. I will start the prayer and anyone who wants to add something, please do."

"Thank you, Lord, for bringing this family back together safely. Thank you for the new addition to our family," he said.

"Thank you Lord, for all your many blessings," said Tio Carlos gravely. "Help us to be continually grateful for what we have and not to covet those things we don't have."

"Thank you for health and enough food," said Guillermo, falteringly in his poor English.

"Thank you for our home and children," added Alba.

"Thank you for friends," I said, looking across the table at Ana and Santiago.

Ana and Santiago were quiet, embarrassed to say anything.

"Thank you for all your blessings, Lord," Mom said. "Thank you for helping us decide to come back home and reunite our family."

"Thank you, Jesus, for answer my prayers," piped up a tiny voice. "Thank you for bring me a family."

That was the moment Mom and I both fell in love with Juan José.

My cell phone rang. It was Mom. She asked about my meeting with the mayor.

"Interesting," I told her and changed the subject. "Centinela survived you know."

"Who?" The phone was quiet for a moment. "Oh, you mean the dog. I never told you because you didn't know him. He was Cacique's pup." She hesitated. "Did Carlos tell you about him? When I heard what happened to your father at the farm, I raced back to Moyuta. By then, Quique was already at the *funeraria*. Alba and Guillermo were preparing his body and getting the casket ready. I couldn't face that.

"I went to the farm to see what'd happened and found Centinela, also shot. The guard had wrapped him in a blanket and was trying to give him water. He was badly injured, so I put him in the car and took him to Carlos. I figured since there was nothing I could do for your father, I could try to help the dog.

"We didn't expect him to live, but Carlos worked on him and kept him for several weeks while I got things packed and ready to leave. When Centinela was out of danger and recovering, I tried to get Alba or Carlos to adopt him, but he chose to live at the cemetery, to be near Quique, I guess. I even thought about bringing him back to California, but I didn't think he'd be happy here. I set out blankets for a bed at the mausoleum before I left. I never knew what happened to him."

"I saw him when I went to put flowers on Dad's grave. The townsfolk fed him."

"I'm glad to hear that. Why'd you bring it up?"

"He was killed today. Chico Negro shot him right in front of me."

"Oh, sweetheart, I'm so sorry. What a shocking thing to see. He was such a nice dog." After a moment, she added, "Chico Negro...that name rings a bell."

I was quiet on my end, thinking about the scene.

"Did you come to an agreement with the mayor?" Mom asked, breaking the silence.

"He wants me to sell, but he did give me another option."

"What was that?"

"To marry him."

Mom tried to smother a laugh and it came out as a snort. "I don't expect there's any chance of that."

"No way."

"What do you think you'll do? Give up and come back to California?"

"Mayor Jaime happens to be Juan José's uncle. Did you know that?"

"No, of course I didn't." She paused. "Why didn't anyone tell me?"

"Shocking, isn't it? I found out a few days ago. Juan-Jo's coming tomorrow to try and help me."

"I guess that's good news." She sounded uncertain. "Be careful. I can't stress that enough. I know you aren't cautious. You never were. I hope you haven't forgotten how dangerous it is there."

I changed the subject. "Are you still planning to come?"

"It's up in the air. I'm trying to get a few days off."

"Take care, Mom. Love you."

"Goodbye, honey. Love you, too."

I looked down at the cell phone, thinking I needed to talk to Juan José to let him know what was happening. I dialed his number.

"Vero, is that you?"

"*Hola hermanito!* Sorry I had to cut short our earlier conversation. I was talking with your uncle."

He laughed. "What timing."

"I didn't want to discuss where I'd meet you tomorrow. I wasn't sure. I'll still be here at Tio Carlos'. Perhaps I was hasty to think of moving so quickly."

"It sounds like you're having a hard time figuring out who to trust."

"That's putting it mildly. At least now I know I can't trust Tio Carlos."

"I'll be there tomorrow after lunch."

"Okay. Call me before you leave the city." I put the phone back in my bag. Someone rapped on the door.

"Yes?" I asked.

"Vero, can I come in?" It was Santiago.

"Just a minute."

I started to the door, then changed my mind, went back and slipped *The Coffee Diary* inside my bag. No more taking chances. I didn't want anyone reading my diary, no matter how dated it was. I paused in front of the mirror and smoothed out my clothes.

"I'll be out in a second."

"I came to help you move to our house."

I hesitated at the door. What was I going to say?

# CHAPTER TWENTY-THREE

I LEANED AGAINST THE WALL OUTSIDE MY ROOM, ARMS FOLDED, AND GAZED at him.

"Hey, have you got your stuff ready?" he asked. "I'm here to take you to your new home."

"I've decided not to move just yet, Santiago. It's been a long morning and I just want to hang out."

His eyes searched mine. "Why don't you hang out at my place?"

I shook my head. "I'll just stay."

"Are you sure? Everything is set. Mom fixed up the guest room for you. Her idea. I'd rather have you stay in my room with me. We're all looking forward to you coming."

"I'm sorry."

"Okay, whatever you say. Is everything all right? I hope you aren't still mad at me."

I consciously unfolded my arms and assumed an open stance. "I'm okay. Just tired."

"How'd it go? Come on. You want to take a walk? Let's get out of here."

"I don't want to go anywhere. I'm recovering from my meeting."

"Okay," he said. "Let's just sit down for a while, then."

We walked over to a bench facing the patio garden. "What happened with Mayor Jaime? I expected you to come by the house afterward." He put his hand on my thigh. It burned my skin through the fabric of my pants.

I inched away, ignoring his question. "Did you hear the gunshot?"

"I heard it was the cemetery dog gone rabid."

"It could have been me."

"Don't be so dramatic, Vero." He looked annoyed. "No one would murder you in the center of town."

"I'm not so sure. When Chico shot Centinela, I was right there. I thought you'd at least be concerned." I brushed his hand off my leg.

"Come on, why are you so sensitive?"

"I could have used your support. I feel like you let me down." I gazed toward the garden, where a myriad of colored flowers bloomed: orange and purple birds-of-paradise, orange, red, and fuchsia impatiens. "It doesn't matter."

"Let me start over. How'd it go with Mayor Jaime?"

I shrugged.

"Talk to me, Vero. I can't read your mind. Are you still mad about the diary? I said I was sorry."

"It's not just that. I need space. I've got a lot on my mind."

"What did Jaime tell you?"

"Nothing."

He got up. "I can see you don't want talk about this—or maybe just not with me. I'll be home if you need anything."

My heart ached as I watched him walk out the door and into the street. Was he walking out of my life as well?

I went back to my room. The door closed sharply behind me. Loneliness swept over me. I wanted him to be the one, yet he'd lied to me and invaded my privacy. Even though I desperately wanted things to work out with him, I knew I'd have to let him go. Why had I been so sure he was the right one? What was I expecting anyway? I threw myself down on the bed and wept.

Did I even want to be here anymore? Maybe I should leave. I could get my money, go back to my life in California, and forget this place all over again.

After I returned from San Diego I never spent time with Santiago again. We attended the same parties in Guatemala City, but he never singled me out for more than a dance or two. He had slipped through my fingers.

The thought of letting him slip away again pulled my head up from the pillow. I got to my feet and went to find him. If nothing else, we needed to finish our conversation.

Out on the street, the sunshine was blinding. I slipped on my sunglasses and headed towards the park. I stopped in front of *Funeraria Godoy* and hesitated.

Chepito waved at me from the corner. "*Hola, señorita Vero.*"

I waved back and rang the bell.

Doña Alba came to the door. "Vero, we've been waiting for you."

We embraced. "I'm here to see Santiago."

"Come in, come in." She ushered me into the kitchen. "I'm making hot chocolate. Would you like some?"

"Thank you." The smell of cinnamon and cocoa rose from the cup she handed me.

"Santiago will be right back. He went to doña Violeta's." I must have looked blank, because she clarified, "Don Arturo's widow. I sent her some tamales."

She turned back to the stove to tend to her cooking. "I'm glad you came. I got the guest bedroom ready. You know you're always welcome."

"I told Santiago I wouldn't be moving over here yet. I'm staying with Tio Carlos for a while longer."

"He didn't say anything."

"What I really want to do is fix up the house at *Las Marías* and stay there. I'll be glad to have my own place again."

She turned towards me. "Are you really going to defy the mayor and keep the properties?"

"That's my hope."

"Those men are ruthless. Don't think being a woman makes you any safer. We'll help however we can, Vero. But I just don't know how much help we can be."

"Juan José comes tomorrow. He and Jaime have gotten to know each other over the past two years. Juan-Jo feels pretty sure he can talk his uncle into giving up on the farms."

"Good luck, but don't get your hopes up too high. Remember, the mayor has Chico Negro and Montaña Ocho to deal with. Who knows what deal he's made to keep them in hand. As your mother's friend, I have to advise you to leave town. I don't think you're safe here."

I sipped the thick dark chocolate. "Thanks for the advice. I hope you're wrong."

I heard the lock click as someone opened the door. Santiago.

"You came after all," he said as he walked through the doorway. "Did you change your mind about moving today?"

"No. But I changed my mind about talking."

Santiago sat down with us.

"Did Vero tell you she plans to keep the farms?" doña Alba asked.

"How could she not? She's her father's daughter."

"Don't take it lightly, son. It's no joke. I'm telling her to leave. I don't want her to end up like Quique."

"Hey, Santiago," I said. "How about that walk?"

We got up and he took my hand. He looked over at his mother. "Excuse us."

We strolled in the direction of the cemetery. His hand felt warm and dry. Mine was cold and clammy. We sat down on a cement bench under a large *ceiba* tree. Exposed tree roots lifted the cement paving stones and wildflowers struggled to come up between the cracks.

"What's the problem, Veronica?"

"You should know what my problem is. I trusted you. Now I wonder if you have ulterior motives."

"What do you mean by that?"

"Are you just another guy interested in my coffee farms?"

"Another guy?"

"Like the mayor."

"Very nice. I'm flattered," he said sarcastically. "Is that what you believe? Who told you that? Our friend Mayor Jaime, I presume."

"He said you haven't been entirely honest with me. I'm wondering about that myself."

"I haven't been honest? Who is he to say that? Why are you even listening to him, Veronica?"

"It wasn't him at the beach, was it?"

"It was Chico. Okay? What's the difference? He speaks for the mayor."

I looked down. "This isn't easy for me to say, believe me. But you have told me several times you'd be happy to help me with the farms."

"And I would."

"You even knew how much I should be earning from a harvest."

"I was trying to be helpful. Instead of a simple 'thank you,' I get suspicion thrown at me."

My face grew hot. "I'm sorry."

He lifted a stone from the ground and threw it down in the brush. "I've thought about a lot of things. I was engaged to be married while I was in Davis, you know."

"Ana told me."

He picked up another stone and tossed it in the air. "I wanted to spend my life with her."

I nodded. "I'm sorry."

"I didn't think I'd find anyone else. Then you showed up."

My stomach turned. What was he going to say? I held my breath in anticipation.

"I realized we could have something together. I like you, Vero. You like me. We could combine our farms. You and I would be a great team."

Disappointment filled me. I shook my head. "I want to marry for love, not convenience. It isn't enough that we like each other. The sex is fantastic, but I want you to love me for myself, not for what I would bring into the marriage."

"I care for you, we have a history, common interests, and we'd make good life partners—but I won't lie to you. It's a different kind of caring than what I had for Cindy."

"I could never be happy knowing I was playing second fiddle to a memory."

"You expect too much."

"Besides, I may not have any farms if Mayor Jaime has his way."

"I'm sure you'll be able to work it out with him."

"You never wanted me to give in, did you? You always had this in the back of your mind. Tell me, would you still be interested in me without the farms?"

He ignored my question. "I loved Cindy. I can love you. We'll make it work."

"I don't think so." I got up and brushed the seat of my pants. "I have to go."

"Wait, Veronica!"

I didn't turn back.

# CHAPTER TWENTY-FOUR

THE AROMAS OF COOKING DREW ME INTO THE KITCHEN WHERE MARÍA Celia was preparing lunch. "You're just in time," she said. She piled food onto two plates and set them on the patio table.

I sat down across from her. "Where's Tio Carlos?"

Her face fell. "He's on a drinking binge. I haven't seen him since he went out this morning. He started the day with a Bloody Mary, followed by three turtle eggs with orange juice and vodka for his hangover."

I remembered those pliable leathery eggs we'd seen at the beach and wrinkled my nose.

"This is the third day he hasn't opened the clinic," she continued. "I don't know what to do. He's been drinking steadily for the last four days. Night before last, it was nearly dawn when he staggered in."

She had dark circles under her eyes. She wasn't wearing her usual makeup or her constant smile. She seemed to have aged ten years since I last saw her.

I got up, went around the table, and put my arms around her. Her frail frame shook as she fought back sobs.

"I'm so sorry," I said. "I've been wrapped up in my own problems. Has he done this before?"

"Lots of times over the years, but not since I've been living here. I told him when I moved in that I'd leave if he did."

"I wouldn't blame you."

We ate in silence. After lunch she fixed coffee and set a mug in front of me. "This coffee is delicious. Is it from my farms?" I asked.

"No, Alba gave me a few pounds from their last crop. We didn't get any of your farms' coffee this year. Too bad, because it's even better. It was sold right on the bushes. The buyers brought their own pickers in to harvest it."

"I can hardly wait to get back into the coffee business." I stared toward the garden, daydreaming. I told her about wanting to move back to the farm.

A smile appeared on her face for a second, then she bit her lip. "What about the mayor? I trust you're not being too optimistic. Do you really think Juan José can convince him?"

I didn't reply. Hadn't the mayor proposed marriage? I was hoping he'd at least hesitate before ordering my murder. He could easily kill me just the same, a voice in the back of my head assured me. But now that I had decided to keep the farms, I wasn't going to back down.

"I'll continue praying for you, Vero. I pray every night for your safety. If you have to leave, I'll miss you." She put her hand over mine.

"I don't expect to be going anywhere. But thanks. I hope things work out here for you. The house looks great, and you and Tío Carlos have seemed so happy."

"Not happy enough," she sniffed, "or he wouldn't be drinking. Oh, well. With the grace of God anything can happen."

She sighed and began stacking the dishes. I got up and helped her take them to the kitchen. The liquor cabinet above the sink was open. The rum bottle was almost empty. The other bottles were gone.

I returned to my room, thinking about my uncle and his drinking problem. Sober he had been a loving, jolly uncle. When he drank, my parents had kept me away from him, and I remembered why.

I was thirteen when I was left alone for the first time at night. Mom and Dad had left for Guatemala City early that morning, expecting to return in the afternoon. It was rainy season, and that particular week the rains were especially heavy.

"Are you sure you don't mind staying here?" Mom said. "I hate to leave you alone, but we have things to take care of in the city."

"I'd rather stay. Besides, I have homework I can catch up on. Don't worry. Juanita will be here with me."

"Okay," she said, still looking a bit doubtful. "We'll call you."

Dad phoned late that afternoon. "Veronica, how is everything in Moyuta? How's the weather?"

I glanced out the window. "It's windy and raining, but I'm okay."

"Sweetheart, there was flooding in the mountains and a mudslide blocked the road near Oratorio. It won't be cleared until tomorrow morning. Will you be okay there by yourself?"

"I'll be fine, Daddy. Don't worry."

"I'll call Tio Carlos and have him look in on you."

The house felt big and empty; I was uneasy. I'd never been home alone at night. I would have asked Juanita to stay but she had already left.

Afternoon turned to dusk; the rain continued to fall. The usual noises began to spook me. Trees groaned and scraped against each other in the wind. A chorus of frogs croaked, competing with the crickets. Water dripped on the roof and in the drainpipes.

I called Ana's house. The telephone rang and rang. Then I remembered Ana telling me they were going to the beach for a long weekend.

The rain came down in sheets. I went through the house and turned on lights in every room, drew the curtains, pulled down the shades and locked the doors. I tuned the radio station to *Musica Tropical* and turned up the volume. Satisfied, I went to the kitchen to fix a sandwich.

I heard a car on the driveway and ran to the window. Perhaps Mom and Dad had made it through after all. I breathed a sigh of relief. As the car came around the last bend and pulled up in front, I saw that it was Tio Carlos' white sedan.

I thought he'd wait in the car for the rain to let up some, but he got out, staggered to the door, knocked hard, and slurred, "Vero, are you there?"

He had been drinking. I opened the door cautiously.

He burst into the room. "Quique told me to look in on you." Seeing my uneasy expression, he added, "I've had a few drinks, but not too much."

He was dripping water all over the floor. "Don't just stand there looking at me! Get me a towel. I'm wet."

I ran to the linen closet for a towel and handed it to him. Then I went to the kitchen to make coffee. As I readied the coffeemaker and turned it on, he called, "Vero, can you put my clothes in the dryer?"

Tio Carlos stood in his underwear in the center of the living room, a soggy pile of clothes at his feet. Horrified, I ran to get Dad's bathrobe and handed it to him, my eyes averted.

"Thanks, dear," he slurred. "So thoughtful, so thoughtful. You are the best niece ever. Thank you for the robe."

The white terrycloth robe didn't reach completely around his pudgy body, and gapped open in front. He staggered to the couch and fell onto the cushion. The sofa creaked in protest.

I picked his wet clothes off the floor and carried them to the laundry room. When the humming of the dryer began, I took a deep breath and went back.

He had a drink in his hand and Dad's liquor cabinet was open. He put down his glass. "Can I get you a drink, sweetie?"

"No!" I didn't understand why he would even offer. "I'm too young to drink."

He turned his head from side to side, taking in the room. "What a lovely home my nephew has. I wonder why he doesn't invite me here more often." He saw my blank look. "Never mind. Come sit by me, dear, while my clothes dry." He patted the cushion next to him.

I started for the kitchen. "I'll get you that coffee."

"I don't need coffee. Sit down!"

Afraid of angering him, but frightened, I sat down cautiously at the other end of the sofa. He reached over for me.

I leaped up, ran to my room, slammed the door, and quickly shoved my bed against it. My heart pounded from effort and fright.

"Vero! Vero!" he called. "Come back!"

Shuffling sounds came from the living room. A dish broke from the direction of the kitchen. Then all was quiet except for the radio. After a while I put on my pajamas and went to sleep.

In the morning, I woke to a rapping on my door. "Vero, where are my clothes?"

"In the dryer," I answered.

A few minutes later, the dryer door slammed shut.

"I'm leaving now," he shouted. I got up when I heard his car start down the driveway.

The smell of vomit was overpowering in the bathroom. Tio Carlos had thrown up all over the floor. Every light in the house was still on and music blared from the radio. I turned off the lights, the music, and the coffee-maker. Then, covering my nose as best I could, I mopped the bathroom with disinfectant and swept up the broken shards in the kitchen. A little while later my parents arrived.

"Hi!" Mom said brightly. "How did it go? I hope you weren't afraid."

"No, Mom, everything was fine. Tio Carlos came over and slept on the sofa. But if this ever happens again, please don't have him check in on me. I'd rather be alone." I didn't know how to tell them about his behavior. I was embarrassed for Tio Carlos, and confused about my role in the mess. Had I somehow brought it on?

The next time I saw my uncle it was as if nothing had happened. I wondered if he even remembered.


I rolled over and stared at the ceiling. The memories from back then mingled with the present. What a big disappointment Tio Carlos had turned out to be. First he stole from me, and if that wasn't enough, he was spying on me for someone. He'd always had a drinking problem, but I'd never taken him for either a thief or a snitch.

The front door slammed, interrupting my thoughts. "Where's my niece?" My uncle's voice was loud and demanding.

"She's resting in her room," María Celia said. "You leave her alone."

"I need to speak with her. It's urgent."

The voices got quieter, but the arguing continued.

"Vero! Vero!" Tio Carlos called, his voice slurred. "I have to talk to you."

I decided to face my drunken uncle.

"*Si, Tio*?" I went out of the room and into the corridor.

He plopped down on a bench and I dragged a chair over to sit in front of him. María Celia stayed close enough to hear the conversation.

"You guessed right," he said. He stared straight ahead. "I'm not going to lie anymore. You need to know the whole truth."

"About...?"

"I have been reporting to Chico Negro."

I gasped.

"He told me he'd see that *Ojo de Agua* was mine if I kept an eye on you and let him know where you went."

Horrified, I stared at him, mouth agape.

He held up his hand before I could say anything. "Wait—hear me out. You see, I expected you to sell. I didn't see the harm. I never wanted to see you hurt. When someone shot at you that day at the farm, I realized things were out of control, but he wouldn't let me out of it. Don Arturo was murdered after that."

My mind raced. It wasn't the mayor after all—or was it? "You were reporting to Chico Negro?"

"I'm going to make it up to you."

I sat still, waiting for him to continue. I couldn't think of anything to say.

"Why wouldn't you sell? You haven't lived here for years. Why come back to Moyuta? I was sure you wouldn't."

"You were wrong." I started pacing the floor. "Why did you encourage me to stay in the first place?"

"It was just talk." He showed his empty hands as if to say he was no longer hiding anything. "I'm a weak man, Vero. *Soy una mierda.*"

"You endangered my life. You stole from me. I thought the world of you. How could you stoop so low?"

He stared at the floor. "The farm should have been mine, not yours. I only took the earnings from *Ojo de Agua.* Quique knew his grandfather would have left that farm to me. You got both farms and you don't even live here. It wasn't fair."

María Celia got up and went into the back bedroom.

"I can make it up to you now. I have some information."

"What information? What can you possibly say to make amends?"

"I was at the bar earlier. The one around the corner from here," he continued. "Chico and Montaña were at the table behind me. They didn't see me, but I overheard them talking. They plan to kidnap you, Veronica, after the mayor pays you off. They didn't say they'd kill you, but they probably will. Then they'll have the money and the farm. Jaime wouldn't dare oppose them. They'll kill anyone who gets in their way."

"I guess it's not a problem, then, because I won't have the money. I'm not going to sell."

"Even if you don't sell, you'd better leave town. They'll come after you. They kept talking about 'unfinished business.' I wish I could help you. I was wrong. Forgive me."

María Celia walked out with a small bag of her things and turned to Tio Carlos. "I'll be back tomorrow for the rest. I don't want to hear anything more. You no longer exist for me."

He buried his face in his hands.

She nodded towards the door. "Vero, let's go. I have a place on the other side of town where we can stay."

# CHAPTER TWENTY-FIVE

"I can't believe it, Vero," María Celia said as we drove toward her small house. "I would never have expected that from Carlos. I always knew about the farm and his slighted inheritance, but after more than forty years, you'd think he'd put it behind him and get on with his life."

"I guess it's been festering all this time. He confessed when he realized Chico had no intention of giving him *Ojo de Agua*." I thought about it for a second. "I bet that's why the mayor added *Ojo de Agua* to the package. It was for Chico and Montaña. They're rough guys. They must have given him an ultimatum. He probably didn't have much choice."

"Don't make excuses for him. Jaime's no saint. Those two have been running his illegal businesses for years. Carlos was naive to think the farm would be handed over to him, a valuable property like that. I really thought he had more integrity, or at least more smarts. Chico and Montaña would be thrilled to have *Ojo de Agua*. They probably think it would give them better standing in the community. As if anything could." She threw her head back to show how ludicrous she found the idea.

We bumped down the uneven paving-stone road. Was Chico Negro the true villain, along with Montaña? Or was it Mayor Jaime? Or all of them?

"Carlos was cutting his losses." She sounded disgusted. I glanced over at her. She gazed out the window. "He must have thought if he confessed and exposed their plan, we would forgive him. You've suspected him for some time, haven't you?"

I nodded. "I hated to believe it. It's always worse when someone from your family betrays you."

"I've only allowed myself to see his good qualities. He's impossible when he's drinking. We've been together a long time, but I refused to move in with him until he stayed sober a year. He's done so well until now. You never really know a person, do you?"

"No, you never do." I thought about Santiago. I had expected him to care about me for myself, not me as part of a package that included my inheritance. Was that unreasonable?

She must have read my thoughts. "Has anything happened between you and Santiago? Are you still an item?"

"I don't know. When we talked about our relationship earlier today, it all sounded so businesslike. I can't imagine marrying someone who's looking for a business partnership, rather than a soul mate. Am I expecting too much?"

"You're still young. Things will look different when you are a little older. Maybe you aren't soul mates, but that doesn't mean you don't make a good couple. You're obviously attracted to each other.

"Oh! Turn right here, Veronica," she said. The narrow unpaved alleyway was difficult to see in the late afternoon light and we almost missed it. "Just park on the street in front. I don't have a garage." I hesitated, looking at the five other houses. "Don't worry. None of my neighbors own a car."

A six-foot fence of iron bars topped with barbed wire separated her house from the street. "I added the wire just recently." She unlocked the gate. "I seldom come here and I didn't want anyone to break in."

The yard was overgrown with grass and dandelions. Roses grew on gangly stems in front of the window.

"It's nice," I said.

"It's cozy, but a little run-down. It's been empty for the five months I've been living with Carlos. Occasionally, the neighbors throw water on my plants." She picked up some litter, plastic bags and advertising flyers, from the yard. "This little house suits me. I don't *need* Carlos in order to be happy."

A cement fountain, dry and dusty, nestled under a scrub oak in one corner of the yard. Leaves had settled inside and stained it. We picked our way up the short gravel path to the steps. She opened the door, flipped on the light, and I stepped into her humble abode. The granite floor needed sweeping and grit covered the simple wooden end tables. She turned to me, slightly embarrassed by the state of her house. "I hope you don't mind. I know you're accustomed to better accommodations."

I waved her apology away. "I'm not accustomed to anything. Thank you for your hospitality. I'm more comfortable here with you than in the fanciest place in town."

She smiled. We both knew there were no fancy places in town, but that wasn't the point. She showed me to the tiny spare bedroom and sat down on the bare mattress. "Carlos began fixing up his house when I moved in. Come to think of it, it was right around the time he sold the coffee crop. I never questioned where the money came from. I figured he was doing well as a doctor. I hate to think he started stealing from the farm to impress me."

"It's not your fault."

She sighed. "Men. You can't live with them and you hate to live without them."

She got out sheets and blankets and made the bed. I picked up a broom and swept the floor. After the house was moderately clean, I called Juan José and told him where I would be the next day. He planned to arrive around three.

I gazed out the window. This part of town was dark, lit only by the scattered light of neighboring houses and the haunting glow of the moon.

The refrigerator turned on in the kitchen and cabinet doors opened and closed. Five minutes later, María Celia came in brandishing a bottle. "I don't have much in the way of food here, but I found this." She held out an almost empty whisky bottle. "It's very old. Carlos brought it over years ago. I'd almost forgotten I had it. How about a nightcap, Vero? I believe we both deserve one."

She poured; we raised our glasses and clinked them.

"*Salud*. To a new beginning."

The whisky warmed me as it went down.

The next morning I awoke to the smell of coffee and the sounds of María Celia busy in the kitchen. Plastic bags with eggs, beans, rice, and other staples lined the counter. "It looks like you've been to the *tienda*."

"I was up early. I didn't sleep well last night."

Soon, smells of breakfast filled the little house.

"What will you do this morning, Vero?" María Celia asked as she set the plates on the table.

"I want to go to *Las Marías* to look around. I haven't been back to the house since I arrived. Juan José will be here this afternoon and I told him to meet me there."

A glint of mischief passed over María Celia's face, followed by a smile.

I looked at her, hoping she'd explain.

"I'm not going to say. It's a surprise."

I took my coffee back to the bedroom and picked up *The Coffee Diary*. Then I laid it back down. There was still one entry I hadn't read. It was written hastily, angrily even. When I had put down the words, I let go of the memory, and ever since I'd tried not to think about it.

The sky was vivid blue when I left the house. Near the center of town I stopped at a *tienda*. "*Seño Vero*? Is that you?" the woman behind the counter asked.

I recognized doña Conchita. The narrow glasses perched on her nose partially covered her honey-colored eyes. Her light brown hair was drawn up in a bun; grey showed around the edges and in the part. "*Sí, soy yo,*" I said. She clasped my forearm, as townswomen did, in greeting.

"I've wanted to talk to you since you arrived in town. I miss your family so much." She paused for a moment. "My husband, Mario, passed away last year." Her eyes glistened with tears.

"I'm so sorry to hear that."

"There are too many widows in this country, my dear. I was very depressed for a while, but I've decided to take a stand. We need to take the leadership away from men—too much violence, too many murders, too little justice."

"What are you planning to do?"

"I'm running for mayor in the next election. The situation has gone from bad to worse with Mayor Jaime. Chico Negro and that Montaña fellow keep the townspeople terrified. No one is brave enough to stand up to them. For my part...since Mario's murder, my own life means little to me. I hope I can make a difference—for my grandchildren, anyway."

"He was murdered?"

She moved her head slightly. "He was investigating his brother's death and must have learned something. He was shot as he left Jutiapa."

"*Mis condolencias.* And your children?"

"María Elena and her husband are in New York with their kids. Juan Manuel lives in the capital with his new wife, and Titi moved to

Suchitepequez with her family to be near her husband's parents. They seldom visit. This is all I have now." She waved her arms to indicate her small store.

I waited for her to continue.

"You may wonder why I'm telling you this." She hesitated again, searching my face. "I will need some money to compete with candidates who are funded by illegal businesses. Yours is the wealthiest family in town. Always has been. I hope you're interested."

"Doña Conchita, I think that's a wonderful idea. I would love to help you. Please let me get back to you in a few days. First, I have to deal with my own problems."

"I've heard. I'm sorry to bring this up now, but I felt sure you'd be sympathetic. Your family has been touched by violence, too."

Her words resonated with me. I knew what she meant, what she wanted. A better Guatemala. A safe place to raise a family.

With my purchases hanging from my arm in a black plastic bag, I returned to María Celia's, fixed myself a snack to take with me, and left for *Las Marías*.

When I arrived at the farm, I was astonished to hear salsa music blaring. A handyman was fixing outside rockwork, and through the window I saw several ladies working. It sounded like someone was having a party. *What is going on?*

"*Buenos días*," I called when I opened the door, although it was closer to noon.

María Celia greeted me laughing, a wet rag in her hand. "Surprise! I organized this when I learned you meant to stay. The electricity and water have been connected. Your home is almost ready to move into."

The floors shone; cobwebs had been swept from walls and ceilings. One woman vacuumed, another cleaned tiles in a bathroom, and yet another mopped. The furniture was uncovered and the dust had been beaten out. The kitchen sparkled. The master bedroom was ready for use.

"Thank you so much," I said. "But this is premature. I haven't talked to Mayor Jaime yet."

"I know. But I thought you'd want to spend a few nights here, even if you do have to give up your home. You won't want to stay with Carlos."

She turned to a nearby woman. "Doña Florecita, let's liven up this party!"

Her feet tapped out the music and she raised her hands in the air, shaking her hips. She grabbed doña Flor's hands and twirled her.

"This is more like it." She grabbed my hand and pulled me over. "Come on, Vero. Let's dance."

The women came out from where they were working. One of them, in a purple cotton dress, grabbed the mop and twirled it like a dancing partner. The others danced in time to the music, their bright clothing a blur of color. After a while, I plopped down on the couch. "You ladies are a blast!" I laughed.

"It's the men who bring us down," María Celia said.

By two o'clock, the party was over and most of the work was done. "Vero, I'm going home for lunch," María Celia said. "Would you like to come?"

"No thanks. I'll stay here. I ate before I left and brought a snack with me. Juan José should be here shortly."

After María Celia was gone, I had the house to myself. The empty halls and rooms echoed with memories.

Yes. I'll fight to keep this place. I can't bear the thought of losing it.

I went back to my old bedroom. The closet hadn't been touched in the frantic cleaning of the last two days. Thick layers of dust and dirt, along with several faded papers, an empty box, and a hanger, lay on the floor.

I got a broom and garbage bag from the kitchen and started to sweep. I saw the envelope that had fallen from the diary the day I arrived. It was wedged between the box and the wall. It was addressed to me in Dad's handwriting, and dated just a few days before his murder. I sat down on the floor, cross-legged, opened the envelope, and began to read.

My father's voice spoke to me in his firm, strong handwriting.

*Wednesday, August 6, 2003*
*Dearest Vero,*

*I can only hope you find this letter. I am leaving it in the old diary in your closet, since I think you would be the only one to look here.*

*I am having a difficult time and I know that I may not get through this alive. There is so much I want to share with you. You are the apple of my eye, my reason for living, my pride and joy. Vero, please know that you have never disappointed me. I admire you and am amazed to have been blessed with a daughter like you. Your courage has inspired me.*

*There are some men in town who are threatening me. They want money in exchange for my life. I refuse to pay them. This extortion must stop somewhere. If I pay them now, it will never end. In the future they will do the same to others—perhaps even to you.*

*Sometimes, Veronica, we must stand up for what we believe. It is the only way to combat violence and corruption. If I live or die, it will be with integrity. Know that whatever happens, they can never hurt my soul, only my body.*

*Your mother doesn't understand. She thinks I am betraying her by not giving in and paying, or not running away to save myself. Even paying will not guarantee my life. I know you can understand because we are alike, you and I. A long time ago I promised myself I would never give in to extortion, and I will not go back on that.*

*No matter what terrible things may happen, know, my lovely daughter, that my soul is free, my mind far away from whatever ugliness may occur.*

*Your loving father*


I wiped my eyes with my sleeve. *Dad, I do understand. I, too, will fight if it becomes necessary.*

I heard someone enter the house. My heart pounded. I hadn't thought to lock the door.

"Vero! Are you there?"

"Juan José? Is that you? I'm in the back bedroom."

Another voice joined his. "Vero, honey?"

"Mom?"

# CHAPTER TWENTY-SIX

THE BEDROOM DOOR SWUNG OPEN AS I REACHED FOR THE KNOB. WE ALMOST collided.

"Surprise!" Mom and Juan José simultaneously exclaimed. I hugged her tightly then greeted my half-brother.

"You're here! Why didn't you tell me you were coming?" I took Mom's hands. "When did you get in?"

"Early this morning. I took the red-eye from L.A."

I couldn't stop smiling. Though I had told her not to come, at the same time I'd longed for her. Pragmatic Mom didn't hide her thoughts, a refreshing change from the deception around me.

I hadn't seen her since Christmas. I studied her tired but happy face, eyes slightly swollen from the overnight travel. Her platinum hair was shoulder-length and her fair skin flushed. "You've been out in the sun and you styled your hair."

"You like it?" she asked and turned around to model. She wore blue jeans that reached halfway down her calf, and her tee-shirt said, "Healthy Bodies = Healthy Minds: Sammie's Gym and Spa."

"You are beautiful as always. Have you been working out?"

"I started at the beginning of the year. I feel so much better about myself now."

I remembered the depressions Mom had suffered: first when Juan José showed up, then when my father was murdered. I was glad to see her feeling better. "I can't imagine you'll stay single long."

"Quique was the love of my life. I could never replace him. But I am still seeing that teacher I told you about."

"You deserve a life, Mom. Don't feel guilty for enjoying yourself. You can't replace someone special, but you can let another person into your life and have something different. Come on into the living room where we can sit down. María Celia and her friends cleaned the house as a surprise. They finished today."

"You've had your share of surprises lately, haven't you?"

I rolled my eyes for emphasis. "You have no idea."

Mom paused in front of the bay window. "This view looks even better to me now than it did before I left. I've missed the quiet of the farm."

"I didn't think you'd ever want to come back."

"To visit, yes, but not to live here again. Not without Quique."

Mom and Juan-Jo settled on the couch and I pulled up a chair. "What exactly is going on, Vero?" Mom asked.

"I've decided to stay."

"You said that on the phone. But can you do that safely?"

"Juan José thinks he can work things out with his uncle, Mayor Jaime."

"You are so like your father, Vero." She gazed out the window. "He didn't let me help him when he started having problems with extortionists. I've always felt badly about that."

"He was protecting you."

"But no one protected him, did they?"

"Mom, I think I know who killed him."

"Why are you bringing that up now?" She looked distressed. "Those men received Moyuta-style justice. They're all dead."

"Not all of them. Chico Negro was there. Centinela was trying to let me know, just before Chico shot him. Chico said the dog was a witness and had to be killed."

Juan José cleared his throat. "Let's not get off the track here. We have to come up with a good plan, one that minimizes danger. I'm sure I can figure something out with Tío Jaime. Tell me about your last conversation with him."

"Well, he knows I don't want to sell, yet he can't give up the idea of owning the farms. He even said I should marry him, so we could both have the farms. He wants to become respectable and continue his career in politics. He thinks marriage into our family would help him."

"That doesn't seem likely to happen," Juan José said. "But it's an interesting idea." His eyes twinkled with amusement. "You could be my aunt, as well as my sister. Your children would be nieces and nephews and also cousins."

I made a wry face. "Sorry, kiddo. It was hard enough to get used to the sister part. Being your aunt is definitely out of the question."

I turned to Mom. "You heard about Tio Carlos?"

"I never would have guessed he was capable of something like this."

"He confessed last night. He's been on a binge, and when he was in the bar, he overheard Chico Negro and Montaña Ocho talking. They're planning to kidnap me and take the money after the mayor pays me for the farms. Then they'd have *Ojo de Agua* as well as the two million from the sale."

Mom gasped. "They're planning to kidnap you?"

I waved my hand in dismissal. "Don't worry. I'm not selling, so there won't be any money for them to take."

"That doesn't mean they won't kidnap you out of spite and ask for a ransom. There's no telling what those men might do."

"I'll be careful. Besides, I'm hopeful that something can be worked out."

"What did María Celia think of all this?"

"She was really upset. She moved out of his house. We both stayed in her little house last night. She doesn't want anything more to do with him and I can't blame her. We had a higher opinion of him than he has of himself. He always did say he was a *mierda*. I guess he was right."

"Poor Celia. I'm glad she left him, but she must be pretty broken up about it."

"She's strong. She'll be fine. A weaker woman would have stayed."

Juan José interrupted. "Let's get back to our plan. I'm meeting Tio Jaime for dinner and I'll stay the night at his house."

"What will Chico think of that? Won't he be suspicious of you staying with Jaime?" Mom asked. "It sounds like Chico's the one to fear."

"I had a long talk with Jaime last night and he told me everything. He said he'd tell those two that I'm here to convince Veronica to sell."

"I don't understand the relationship," I said. "I thought they worked for Jaime."

"Technically, they do. The three of them grew up together. Jaime was always the leader, ever since they were young. But Chico's a mean guy and Montaña always sides with him. Jaime wants to change, put his past behind him, and make a fresh start without them."

"Good luck, *hermanito*." I turned to Mom. "We can stay here for a few days."

She looked around. "It's not a good idea, Vero. I wouldn't feel safe here. And you aren't safe here either. You're only safe as long as Chico Negro and Montaña Ocho don't suspect you want to keep the farms."

I hadn't thought of that. "You're right. We can stay with María Celia and doña Alba. Where would you prefer to be?"

"I'd love to stay with María Celia. You stay with Alba. Besides, you'll be close to Santiago that way. Aren't you seeing him?"

"I'm not sure." She looked at me, a question in her eyes. I shrugged. "It's a long story and I don't want to think about it right now."

Mom put her things in my car and we followed Juan José back to town. When he turned toward Jaime's house, we continued on to Alba's.

I couldn't get used to the idea of Jaime not being the evil villain. I wondered if he planned to give up his criminal activities entirely, or if he was just seeking a slightly easier road. Regardless, politics was just another way to get rich. Corruption was inevitable.

Mom interrupted my thoughts. "I'm glad to see Juan José gave you the car." She looked through the glove box. "All my old papers and receipts are still here. Look! My sunglasses! I thought they were lost." She slipped them on.

We pulled up in front of the *funeraria*. Mom hesitated for a moment before getting out. "This is where I last saw your father." Moisture gathered in her eyes.

The door was ajar. We walked past the caskets to the living quarters. "*Buenas tardes.* Doña Alba, are you here?"

"Vero?" Santiago stepped out of his room. "I'm so glad to see you." He kissed me on the cheek, and then greeted Mom. "Liz, I didn't know you were coming."

"It was a surprise."

"I—I'm taking you up on the offer to stay," I said, feeling self-conscious. "I'll be back in a while with my things." I couldn't help wondering if I'd be able to handle being so close to him.

"I'll let my mother know."

"Alba's not here?" Mom asked.

"She'll be right back. Please have a seat." He pulled up two chairs. I fidgeted. I was drawn to him against my will. Maybe it would be better if Mom slept here and I stayed with María Celia. I focused on the garden, not listening to the conversation until it was brought back to me.

"Isn't that right, Vero?" Mom asked.

I looked up blankly.

"You didn't hear a word of what we said, did you?" Santiago asked.

I shook my head. "Sorry."

"Can I get you something to drink?" he offered, getting up. "Coffee, tea, fresh milk, lemonade, or perhaps something stronger?"

"Water's fine." I said.

"Coffee, please. It's been a very long day," Mom responded. He nodded and walked to the kitchen.

"Santiago always was a handsome young man, and charming too," Mom whispered. "How you can resist him?"

I watched him through the screen door. "Not easily."

A parrot called out, "*Albita, Albita, mi amor,*" announcing Alba's arrival. She greeted the green bird, "You're my love, too, Pepito." Then she saw us. "Liz! *Cielos*! I didn't expect to see you!" She dropped her things on a chair and rushed over. They embraced. "What a surprise. Why didn't you tell us she was coming, Vero?"

"I didn't know. I was as surprised as you."

"Can you stay tonight? We've got an extra room."

"I'm staying with María Celia. Vero's staying with you."

"At least have dinner with us. I've invited a few people from town. It's just a small thing I'm doing for doña Conchita. She wants to launch a career in politics." She glanced at the packages she'd left on the chair. "I just picked up some things at the store."

Mom looked at me. "We'd love to."

"And bring Celia with you."

Santiago came in from the kitchen. "Here's your coffee, Liz. And Vero, can't I get you something stronger than this glass of water?" He winked as he handed it to me. My heart beat quickly. *Damn him, why does he have to be so attractive?*

"Where's Guillermo? Off at the farm?" Mom asked, sipping her coffee.

"Santiago looks after the farm now. Guillermo's in bed. He's been ill for some time and mostly rests and watches television. Would you like to see him? I know he'd love to see you."

She led us through a door in the corner of the patio. The light was dim and the room windowless and stuffy. "*Memo*, you have visitors."

He was sprawled on the bed, a television in front of him. He squinted. "Liz, is that you?"

She sat down on the edge of the bed. "Guillermo, it's good to see you. I'm sorry you haven't been well."

"It's my own fault. I should have paid attention to the warnings on the cigarette labels."

"I thought you quit years ago," Mom said.

"The damage was done. I came down with pneumonia a few months ago. X-rays showed several lumps in my lungs."

"What are you doing for it?"

"I take medication. They wanted to operate on me, but I refused. It's not like it would do me any good, anyway. I can't go out much, especially if there's any breeze. Drafts don't do me any good and I don't want to chance another bout of pneumonia."

"I'm so sorry."

"Life—if it doesn't get you one way, it gets you another. At least I've had time to catch up on all the latest soaps." He gestured toward the television, then began coughing. Alba handed him a tissue. "I'm home with family and friends. That's all I want. Thanks for stopping by. It means a lot to me." He extended his frail hand for us to take. When I kissed him goodbye, he whispered in my ear, "I think Santiago is a good match for you. I approve."

"I...I..." I couldn't bring myself to say anything.

Santiago opened the door for us as we left. I turned to him. "Why didn't you tell me your father was so ill?"

"You didn't ask. You've been pretty involved in your own problems."

I looked down. "I'm sorry. That was inexcusable."

"I'm sorry, too. I wish I could make things right."

"I'll be back later," I said and gave him a quick hug.

I was pensive as I got into the car.

Mom studied me for a minute before speaking. "You and Santiago don't seem that comfortable together, Vero. Has something happened between you?"

I shook my head. "I don't know. Yes, I do know." I told her about him reading my diary, then about our conversation and Santiago's description of marriage as a partnership, rather than a love match. "What happened to getting down on one knee in a romantic, candlelit restaurant and proposing with a ring?"

"Would it have made a difference?"

I thought about the mayor, then about Santiago and his dead fiancée. "I don't know. Maybe." I hesitated. "Okay, yes, it would have. Jaime was right. Santiago sees our relationship as a business alliance. How different are the two of them? Santiago just wasn't as honest about it."

"Would you prefer I stay with the Godoys tonight? You could stay with María Celia again."

I knew she didn't want to be near the funeral caskets, a reminder of Dad's death. "Thanks, but I'll be fine."

We left and got Mom settled at María Celia's house. I gathered my things together to take to Alba's when we went for dinner. A few hours later, the three of us piled into the car.

We parked in front of the *funeraria*. I hopped out, reached into the back seat to grab my overnight bag, and turned to look around. Behind some scraggly trees in the nearly deserted park, Chico Negro and Montaña Ocho leaned against a black Toyota Land Cruiser. Chico saluted me military-style. Anger seeped into me. I knew he was trying to intimidate me. I ignored him and turned away.

Even though the late afternoon air was warm, I shivered. Mom shut the car door with a bang. "What is it, Vero?"

María Celia gave me a knowing glance.

"Let's go in." I turned my back on the park and locked the car.

"Alba, we're here," María Celia called.

Alba came out of the kitchen to greet us. A mid-length black-fringed skirt swirled about her, and a green knit sweater outlined the soft bulges in her midsection. She wore eyeliner, mascara, and had unsuccessfully attempted to lighten the dark smudges under her eyes. "Liz! Vero! Celia! *Pasen adelante.* I'm so glad you could come!" she said as she hugged each of us.

Then she turned to Mom. "Liz, how wonderful you look! I love your hair." She reached out to touch it. "You just don't see this kind of hair around here. You're so lucky. Instead of graying, it's turning white." She stepped back to admire her again, then motioned with her head toward the kitchen. "Come in."

She took us into the dining room, the focal point of their house, and we sat down. "The other guests will be here soon. Excuse me for a moment." She stepped outside to add wood to the outdoor stove and stir something in a large pot.

"Santiago, can you take Vero's bag?" she called.

Santiago greeted us and flashed me a quick smile before taking my bag to the guest room. When he returned, he offered us beverages. He was subdued. I wondered if he was upset about our talk, or if it was his father's health.

Mom noticed the empty chair at the head of the table. "Don Guillermo? Will he be eating with us?"

Santiago placed our drinks on the table. "Papá took a turn for the worse after you left this afternoon."

Doña Alba came in breathless. "Sorry, the woman who works for me took the evening off." Seeing Santiago's expression, she stopped. "Oh, you're discussing Memo. I had hoped he'd be able to have dinner with us, but he had a coughing attack earlier and I gave him a shot of morphine. He's been asleep ever since."

I shook my head sadly. I felt terrible about don Guillermo.

"He was happy to see you both today. Thank you for the visit."

"He looked much better last week, at your luncheon," I said. "I didn't realize he was in such poor health."

"He's taken a turn for the worse and is going downhill fast." She sighed. "I fear he may not last more than a few days. The doctors didn't expect him to live this long. I know it isn't a good time to have a dinner party with this hanging over us, but it had been planned and he insisted. 'Please,' he told me, 'have your friends over and enjoy yourselves. You need a break'".

I glanced at Santiago. His expression revealed nothing. He stared at the wall where the family photos hung, as if he hadn't heard the conversation.

Doña Alba, putting on a brave front, continued, "doña Conchita is coming, and so is doña Meches and her husband, don Filadelfo." She looked at her son. "Doña Conchita promised not to completely monopolize the conversation with politics, but we may need to remind her. That is really all that's on her mind lately."

"Have you seen her since you've been back, Vero?" Santiago asked.

I nodded.

"Then you know what I mean," doña Alba said.

Mom turned to me. "It's been so long, I wasn't sure you'd remember these people."

"Let me see," I said. "Doña Conchita has the store near María Celia's. I saw her this morning. Doña Meches has the *tienda* on the way out of town, and her husband…I don't know what he does."

"He owns the taxi service," Santiago said. "You've seen the little three-wheeled tuk-tuks around town." They were more like covered motorcycles with seats in back than taxicabs.

"Is Juan José here?" doña Alba asked. "I remember you said he'd be coming to Moyuta,"

Mom and I exchanged looks. "He's staying with his relatives."

The doorbell rang. "Maybe our other guests have arrived," Alba said.

Santiago stood up. "I'll get it. You stay here."

A moment later, doña Conchita breezed into the dining room in a wave of color. Her bright fuchsia blouse matched her lip color; crystal earrings dangled like chandeliers from her large ears. Worn black boots peeked out from underneath the flowered skirt that reached her ankles. She kissed everyone in the room, leaving lipstick smears on their cheeks. "Liz, I saw Veronica this morning and she didn't mention you were coming."

"It was a surprise."

Doña Alba put corn chips, hot tortillas, and a bowl of guacamole on the table. "How does it feel to be back, Liz?"

"I wouldn't be here if it wasn't for Veronica." She nodded toward me. "I came to protect her from herself. She's as stubborn as her father."

Doña Alba flashed a look at me, reminding me with her eyes of our earlier conversation.

Someone banged on the outer door. "It must be don Fila." In a lower voice, Alba confided, "He never uses the bell. I think he secretly despises modern technology."

Santiago went to the door again. He returned with don Fila, a short, balding man. His wife, doña Meches, clung to his arm for support, staggering in three-inch spike heels.

We stood to greet them then situated ourselves at the table, scooting over to make room for everyone. Doña Alba passed enchiladas around. I took one and bit into the crisp shell. It was filled with ground meat, vegetables, and capers, and topped with sliced hard-boiled eggs, tomato sauce, onion, and beets, all of which kept sliding off.

"I'm serving *tipica* food, in honor of my two California, formerly Moyuta, guests."

"Don't forget I'm hoping to return," I reminded her between bites.

"Speaking of that," doña Meches said, "why on earth would you want to come back? This is hardly the land of opportunity, unless of course you wish to make money illegally." She glanced around to make sure her joke was understood. "Everyone I know wishes they could leave. My god, Veronica, you have a great job in California. Why Moyuta?"

"My roots are here. I love the town, the coffee farms, the warm evenings, and seeing all these people I care about. Dad had a strong connection to the land, and I feel it, too. I don't feel that sense of land or community elsewhere."

"Strange you would say that after staying away for the past ten years," Santiago said.

I shrugged. "It took me a while to figure it out."

"Sense of community?" Doña Conchita spit out the words with disgust. "We haven't had community since Jaime Ramírez took over, since President Porta has been in power. Community means nothing now. Our neighbors are too afraid to take a stand, too fearful to help when their neighbors are victimized. Corrupt politicians have made the country a place where no one wants to live."

"Now, now. You promised you wouldn't get political tonight," doña Alba reminded her.

"It's the only way we can get our country back. Veronica understands what I mean. She has a vision of what life should be here. That's why she wants to stay. The vision her father had that night at *Las Marías*. He stood up to the extortionists as an example to us all. The vision don Arturo had when he said, 'No, I won't sell my land.' How can we not get political? It's the only way to fight the violence."

"Politicians don't try to curb violence," don Fila said quietly.

"Politics! It's been the ruin of this country," doña Meches exclaimed. "After thirty-five years of brutal civil war, the people are trained not to speak out, not to challenge the status quo. It was that or join the ranks of the disappeared."

"The war made weapons so commonplace, violence was bound to

follow," Mom pointed out. "The Mayans were never a peace-loving people, their leaders were bloodthirsty. The Spanish *conquistadores* were just as savage as those they conquered. It's only fitting that the descendants of such a racial mix have inherited their cruelty."

Doña Alba sighed and passed the black beans, blended and fried into a paste. "I seem to have no say in my own home. Please help yourselves to the cream and cheese. They're from today's milk." The table was quiet for a moment. Then she passed us small dishes of stewed red *majunches*, a native banana, cooked with cinnamon sticks. "It's just a simple meal."

"I couldn't ask for a better one," I said. "It's delicious."

The conversation turned again to politics when Arturo Buencamino's fate came into discussion. "Are we going to have to go after the criminals ourselves?

"Look what happened to Quique when he tried to do the right thing." Doña Meches glanced at Mom and tried to hush her husband, but he was too worked up. "Justice, law? Aren't we all law abiding citizens?" don Fila exclaimed, his face reddening. "We shouldn't have to fight crime ourselves. The problem is the politicians who hold out their hands and get them filled by violent criminals."

"Yes, dear, we all know there is little law or justice in Guatemala," doña Meches said, patting her husband's hand.

"It's sad, but true," doña Conchita said. "Violence is accepted. Even our president openly brags about committing two murders. What kind of role model is that?"

"What do *you* think is the solution?" don Fila asked.

"Women! If more women are empowered, violence will be reduced. Women see the effects of things on their children, in their families and communities. They are eager to make an impact," doña Conchita replied.

Rap. Rap. Rap.

"Who do you suppose that is?" Doña Alba walked across the courtyard to the door. "More people who don't use doorbells," she muttered.

Wishing to escape the political discussion, I feigned curiosity and followed her.

Rap. Rap. Rap.

"*Un momento*," she called out.

Outside stood a *campesino* family, the father dark and wizened from the sun, bent and careworn from work. Behind him stood his wife in a thin cotton dress, colorless from years of washing and drying in the sun. She held an infant, wrapped in a shawl. Other children, ranging from three to about twelve and dressed in clean, starched rags stood in the background. "*Seño, muy buenas noches.*"

"What can I do for you?"

The man gazed toward the ground, too humble to look at Alba directly. "My family, we walked here from San Antonio. We left our home at two o'clock."

I glanced at my watch. It was past seven.

"My youngest," he gestured to the babe in his wife's arms, "has a fever. Is there something, anything, we can do for you to earn a few quetzals to buy ourselves some tortillas and an aspirin for the baby?"

Doña Alba's face filled with compassion. "Please come in."

The family filed into the waiting room, filled as it was by reminders of death. A crucifix hung high on one wall. The mother looked up and made the sign of the cross.

The babe in her arms made a squeaking noise. She unbuttoned the top of her dress, pulled out a dark, shriveled breast and pushed it into the child's mouth. He squirmed feebly and wouldn't take it. She saw me watching her. "He doesn't want the *chichi*. I'm afraid my milk has soured."

"Let me bring a doctor." I stood up to go.

Alba's hand stopped me. "Come here, Veronica." She took me outside, so the family couldn't hear. "Go back and finish your meal. They can wait. This child has been ill for many weeks. I'll bring the family some food. Then I'll make sure they're taken care of."

"*Permíteme, señores.* I'll see what I can do for you," she said when we returned. She went back into the kitchen.

"Would you like to come into the house?" I asked.

Startled at the thought of interrupting our meal, the mother emphatically said, "No, *seño*. We will wait here for the *señora*."

I went into the courtyard and brought back chairs for them. The oldest girl smiled at me. "What's your name?" I said.

She looked down at the ground, clearly embarrassed. "María del Rosario López Crispín."

She said it softly and quickly. I barely understood. "María?"

"*Sí.*"

"How old are you?"

"*Trece.*"

She looked closer to ten than thirteen. Dusky, gangly legs shot out from under her pale green dress: scratches and white scars spoke of an outdoor life. Her hands were large and calloused. She probably worked with her father in the fields. Her large black eyes spoke of suffering beyond her years. "Do you go to school?"

"I've gone already. I know my letters and numbers," she said proudly. "I made it to second grade. My brother still goes. He's in fourth."

"Why don't you continue?"

"I'm just a girl. I stay home to help my parents." She looked down at her dusty bare feet. "My mother needs help with the younger children, and my father with the field work."

My heart went out to the child. She seemed bright, but hers would be the story of so many girls in the countryside. In a year or two she would find a young man, and they would start their own family and repeat their parents' lives.

Doña Alba came in with plates of food for the family and set them down on a small table. The mother looked at her, not comprehending.

"Please eat," doña Alba said.

"*Seño*, we can't take this food. We have no way to pay you." She looked at her older daughter. "Do you need a *muchacha*? María del Rosario can help you around the house. She even knows a little cooking."

Alba looked at the desperate people. "She can help me with the dishes tonight. I have guests. Please take the food. It isn't charity. Rather, it's a sin to waste. I made much more food than I need."

The woman glanced toward the dining room. After confirming there were guests at the table, she nodded. "*Muchas gracias.*"

I stayed a moment longer and then, sensing their discomfort, started off to the dining room. When I glanced back, the younger children were tearing into the meal with their fingers like half-starved animals.

At the table, Mom was telling doña Meches about her job and new life in California.

"Do you ever miss it here?" doña Meches asked.

"When I think about Moyuta I long for the beauty and peace of the farm, for friends and laughter, and I miss Quique so much. I try not to dwell on it. It's still too fresh. I hope I can get past the horror."

"Do you think you'll ever remarry, Liz?"

"Never. Love is too painful. Too much can go wrong."

I looked over at Santiago. His thoughts seemed distant.

"Is everything okay?" I asked.

He looked up. "No. I'm sorry."

I didn't know what I could say and he didn't wait for my answer. He turned back to his food and continued eating.

When he finished, he pushed back his chair. "*Muchas gracias y buen provecho.*"

"*Buen provecho,*" the rest of us echoed.

# CHAPTER TWENTY-SEVEN

THE GODOYS WERE MIDDLE CLASS, NEITHER POOR LIKE THE VILLAGERS, nor upper middle class like our family. The guest bedroom was simple: a plain wooden chair and table; the mattress firm and practical, like life in Moyuta. Warm, scratchy woolen blankets from Momostenango in the Guatemalan highlands, covered the bed. I slipped between the sheets, and brought out *The Coffee Diary*—ready at last to read the entry from December 13, 1991. The hard-to-decipher notes brought back that awful day.

I had raced home, leaves and dirt clinging to my damp clothing, my legs scratched from brush and stones, my wrists red where rough hands had held them, and chafed where the twine had bitten into them. I trembled feverishly, my teeth chattering despite the heat.

"Veronica, what happened to you?" my mother cried when she saw me. I was too upset to reply. She was taking clothes off the line. She wrapped a warm, clean towel around me and took me into the house.

"Quique, Quique!" she called. When he didn't answer, she paged him on his radio phone and told him to come immediately. Then she sat with me until my shaking eased.

My father burst through the door. "Sweetheart, *qué pasó?*"

The concern in his voice threw me into sobs. Only when I recovered from these could I tell my story.

"Who were they?"

"One was Chico and the other Mickey. A third boy made them let me go. I don't know who he was."

Dad jumped to his feet, grabbed another clip of ammunition, and headed for the door.

"Quique, stop," Mom said. "Nothing happened in the end."

"It doesn't matter. The point is what could have happened. I'll see that they won't be doing anything like this ever again." He left, heading toward the *laguna*.

It was a warm December afternoon, a day like any other day. Juan José was outside with Cacique, throwing a stick for him to retrieve when I set out on a walk. It was one of the last idyllic days at the farm. Juan José and I would be starting at the Colonial School in Guatemala City in January, staying at our apartment in the city with Mom. Dad planned to visit on weekends.

Rainy season had ended a few months earlier. Gone were the afternoon thundershowers; the parched land had drunk its fill. Already the winds of November had dried the earth and covered everything with dust. December, sandwiched between the windy months of November and January, restored a temporary quiet.

I strolled out the gate toward the community pond, *La Laguna de San Juan*, adjacent to *Las Marías*. Water hyacinth choked the surface, making a green garden with purple flowers.

It was a twenty-minute walk around the small lake on a hard-packed trail—a path much traveled by riders on horseback on their way to town, range animals led to drink, and people going to bathe.

I wore Bermuda shorts and a thin T-shirt. A hat protected my face from sunburn. I walked quickly as though I had a purpose more pressing than exercise.

Out of the silence a kitten squealed in terror. I heard voices from among the reeds near the edge of the water.

"Throw it in."

"Do you think it can swim? I never seen a cat swim."

"Let's find out. Just do it."

"It's clinging to me."

Splash.

"Don't let it get back up."

The kitten thrashed in the water and I raced over to rescue it. "What do you think you're doing?" I scolded.

Two young men crouched near large boulders, hidden from view. They turned in surprise. One of them was heavy-set and sullen. Peach fuzz had sprouted on the other, a lanky boy. Freckled legs poked out of his cut-off pants, and his feet dangled in the water where the hyacinth was cleared away.

"Well, look who's here," the first boy said, sizing me up.

I ignored them, knelt down and reached for the terrified animal. They pushed me in. I went under, breathing in the murky water, too surprised to hold my breath. After a moment I thrust myself back to the surface, sputtering and indignant.

"Look, now there are two kittens!" They laughed.

I could barely touch the muddy bottom on my tiptoes, but managed to push the kitten to the edge. It scrambled up and raced off. The lanky boy started after it, but the other boy stopped him. "We don't need it anymore. We got something more interesting to play with now."

I looked for a place to pull myself out of the water. The edges on this side of the pond were steep. The other side was shallow, but swimming over there would be impossible; the hyacinth was too thick. There was only one easy place to get out of the pond: next to the boys. "Come on, little kitten," one invited. "Don't be afraid."

An edge of cruelty tinged his voice, and I held back when he offered his hand, preferring the water. "What's your name?" he asked.

"Veronica." I glared at him defiantly.

"Veronica, Veronica. I like that," he said. "Veronica Villagrán."

"How do you know my last name?"

"How would I *not* know the name of the most important family in town?"

I waited for him to do something. "Are you going to let me get out?"

The heavyset boy stretched out his hand again and this time I took it. I felt the water sliding off me as he pulled me out. My clothing clung to me, a dingy brown second skin.

I tried to get free, prepared to run. "Where do you think you're going?" he asked, tightening his hold on my wrist.

"Let me go. I want to go home."

"I don't think so," he said. He turned to the lanky boy. "What shall we do with her?"

"Why, Veronica, you can't go home like that," the second boy jeered. "What would don Quique think?"

I jerked my wrist, trying to wrench away. The lanky boy caught my free arm and the two forced me to the ground.

"How old are you, Veronica?"

"What do you care?"

"You have the figure of a woman. Look at those tits."

I looked down and much to my chagrin, the T-shirt had turned transparent and my nipples stood out through my bra. I drew up my legs, trying to hide myself.

"We ain't gonna hurt you, sweetheart. I'm real happy you came by. This is much more fun than drownin' a kitten."

In spite of my struggles, the bigger boy had his hands on me. "These tits look like they need to be played with."

"Stop, leave me alone!" I yelled, hoping someone would hear me. "*Auxilio.*"

The lanky boy peeled a sweaty red bandana from his neck and rolled it into a ball. "Open wide, kitten."

My teeth clenched shut and I turned my head from side to side. The stronger boy forced my mouth open and pushed the smelly bandana in. I gagged when my mouth filled with the sour cloth.

"Sorry 'bout that. If you'd cooperated, we wouldn't have had to do that." He eyed me with fake compassion. "It also keeps you from biting."

"You got rope, Mickey?" the husky boy asked. "I got some plastic cord. You want to tie her up?"

My eyes widened as he took out a ball of yellow twine.

"What do you keep that around for?" Mickey asked.

"You never know. Maybe a nice horse, cow, or pig might look homeless. Or you might need to tie up a pretty girl and have your way with her."

I kicked and tried to make noise with my throat as he tied my hands together. "God, you make me horny when you struggle. Keep it up and I'll be sure to fuck you all afternoon."

The other boy unsheathed a fishing knife and held it to my throat. "Don't fight us. We can do this just as easy with you dead."

"Hey, Chico. Mickey. Where are you guys?" I heard someone call.

"Over here. We fished ourselves a real catch."

The reeds parted. Another boy stood facing us. His face oozed with acne, and his eyes, masked by dark glasses, darted between the two of them and me.

"What the hell?"

"She's a beauty, ain't she? Best catch I've ever got out of this damned fish pond."

The third boy looked at his friends. When he looked at me, his tongue passed over his lips. He hesitated, then seemed to make a decision. "Let her go."

"What? What are you saying? Are you crazy? Do you have any idea what we could do to her?"

"I said let her go. It's not worth it. Do you ninnies have any idea what her father would do to us?" He pulled out a gun and pointed it at the other two. "Let her go."

"You wouldn't," one of them said uncertainly.

"Oh, yes, I would. That man killed my father for less than this. At the very least he'd castrate us and throw us to the dogs. Most likely he'd kill all three of us and ask questions later. I can guarantee he'll be coming after us with a gun. Let's get the hell out of here before he shows up."

"Let's have fun first. Besides, don't you want to get back at him for your father's murder?"

"I'm not seeking revenge. I have other plans for my life."

"Yeah, right. Like what?"

"I'm gonna be somebody."

"Maybe you don't want revenge. But I'd love to kill the bastard. Just to know that I could. Maybe not now, but eventually," Chico said.

In spite of Chico's words, the two boys backed off, and the third lowered his gun, took the bandana out of my mouth, and untied me. As soon as I was free, eyes blurred with tears of fright, I raced home, stumbling and hysterical.

The third boy had been right. Dad would have shot them, but they had a head start. They escaped, and weren't seen again in Moyuta for several years. By the time they returned, the incident was mostly forgotten.

The third boy, I now realized—the one with heavy acne and dark glasses, the one who didn't want revenge—was the future mayor of Moyuta, the ringleader of the three, Jaime Ramírez.

## CHAPTER TWENTY-EIGHT

ANXIETY BROUGHT ME OUT OF BED. I THOUGHT ABOUT PHONING MOM—though here in Moyuta, she seemed far away. The memories from that last scene in my diary were so disturbing that I wanted the comfort of hearing her voice. I dumped out the contents of my purse looking for María Celia's number.

Pablo's card landed next to my cell phone like some kind of sign. I stared at it. He had said to call, so I punched in his numbers.

"Pablo? Is that you?"

"Veronica? I hoped you would contact me." After we chatted for a few minutes, he asked, "Are you in the city?"

"No, I'm in Moyuta."

"When you come into the city, be sure to call. We'll go out."

I finished the conversation and put the phone down. I wondered about rekindling a relationship with Pablo. I wasn't too interested earlier when I thought things were going well with Santiago. But so far, my relationship with Santiago was going nowhere. Pablo was a wild card—something to think about.

I heard a tapping at the door and glanced over. The handle turned, but I had locked it from the inside.

"Veronica, can I talk to you?" Santiago said softly.

I let him in. When he saw the diary next to my bed, he asked, "Did you finish it?"

"Yes, finally."

"Jaime was one of them, wasn't he? You wrote about three boys."

"He saved me. He made the other two let me go."

Santiago looked doubtful. "After it happened, don Eliseo saw the three of them come running out from the edge of the *laguna*. He told my father about it."

"The diary isn't a detailed account of how things went, Santiago. It just holds reminders for me. It wasn't for anyone else to read—it wouldn't make sense."

"Oh, I'm sorry...again." He looked down and shook his head. "What's wrong with me? I've been saying that too often with you lately. Can we be friends? I really care for you."

I studied his face, open with grief. Was it for his dying father, his dead fiancée, or for the chance we might have had together?

Santiago had disappointed me. He wasn't the man of my dreams I'd imagined him to be. I attempted a smile. "Of course we can be friends. I value your friendship."

"My father's illness has me preoccupied. Please give me another chance."

I didn't make any promises. We said goodnight and he left.

I looked at my watch and remembered Mom had flown in on the red-eye. It was too late to call.

I crawled between the sheets once more, slept soundly, and dreamt of Moyuta where flowering trees shade fields of coffee, where bananas grow in variety and abundance, where butterflies and biting gnats flutter and buzz through plantations, and common people laugh and cry, tired of violence, yet optimistic about a better future.

Early the next morning the cell phone's ring broke through my dream. I leaned over and took it from the bag beside my bed. Juan Jose's number showed up on the small LCD screen.

"Juan-Jo?"

"Vero, I need to talk to you as soon as possible. Jaime thinks we should meet in his office. It's the safest place. The walls are soundproofed."

I remembered the last time I was with Jaime in his office and shuddered. I didn't want another scene like that. "Are you sure that's the best place?"

"Of course. And it won't cause suspicion. Everyone thinks I've come to act as an intermediary. I hope you haven't told anyone you aren't going to sell."

My eyes drifted to a small tapestry on the wall. "Well." I hesitated. "Sort of."

"Chico Negro and Montaña can't suspect. Don't leak it. I'll meet you at Tio Jaime's office in half an hour."

*Dang.* I wished I'd kept my mouth shut.

I pulled on jeans and a top, slipped into my Birkenstocks, and joined doña Alba in the kitchen for coffee. "Guillermo had a bad night," she told me. Her eyes were puffy from lack of sleep.

"I'm so sorry," I said, wishing I could say something to ease her pain. "I hope he feels better this morning. I'm going out for a quick walk." I gulped down the brew, excused myself, and hurried down the street to city hall.

Outside, women with baskets headed to the *tienda* to buy eggs, bread, or tortillas. Men strode toward the fields to work. Several stray dogs sniffed at pieces of garbage left in the park the evening before.

I reached the *municipalidad* just as Juan José appeared. He carried a ring of keys, his head down, deep in thought.

"Tio Jaime will be here in half an hour," he said, eyes red-rimmed. "Meanwhile, I'll fill you in on what we worked out." He put a key into the padlock that secured the entrance. "*Pasa,*" he said and held the door open for me.

We walked past desks where silent manual typewriters conjured tapping noises in my imagination, past empty chairs awaiting the crush of Monday morning, past Mayor Jaime's personal secretary's desk. I stopped in front of the door marked *Alcalde* and waited for my brother to unlock it.

"You seem to know your way around," he said.

"I've been here more than enough times. I can't say I've been looking forward to another visit."

He opened the door and I sat down in the familiar seat. He brought in another chair. "Jaime and I talked most of the night, and we came up with what we think is a perfect plan."

"There's no such thing as perfect," I said. "But let's hear it."

"Tio Jaime..." He looked at me and corrected himself. "Mayor Jaime told me he wants to pursue a career in politics."

I nodded and gestured toward the photo with President Porta. It wasn't surprising that a small town crook would get involved in politics. It happened all the time.

"He wants to clean up his reputation, disassociate himself from Chico Negro and Montaña Ocho. They're murderous, power-hungry, and have begun to rebel against Jaime. They think he's too cautious. With the plan we came up with, you'll be able to keep the farms and he'll be rid of his accomplices."

"Why can't he just fire them?" I asked. This question had been hounding me for days. Why all the fuss if they were his employees?

"It isn't as easy as that, he tells me. They're on the payroll, but they don't really work for him. They're like his partners, and they know too much about each other. We were up late last night and he told me a lot of things. You were right about him, Veronica. He isn't the nice guy I thought he was. He confessed to trying to extort money from Dad."

I nodded. "He told me as much, but wouldn't confess to Dad's murder."

"He didn't do it. He sent Chico and a group of thugs as a scare tactic. When Dad killed two of them, Chico retaliated."

"That's Jaime's version," I said. "I bet Chico had the murder planned from the beginning."

"Maybe. But when Jaime learned what had happened, it was too late. He never meant for Dad to be killed."

I thought for a moment. "Why do *you* think Chico did it?"

Juan José turned away and looked at the wall. "I don't know, Veronica. Because he could? To prove a point with Jaime? It must have made him feel powerful. How can you know what goes on in the mind of a scumbag like Chico?"

I sighed. Any of those reasons were enough. "Okay. Where is Jaime?"

"He's on the phone with the U.S. Embassy. He's talking to the man from the Drug Enforcement Agency. They're getting the details together."

Juan José explained the plan. After spending most of the night working on it, they would spend a good amount of time that day setting it up.

Just then Jaime entered. "Veronica," he said. He reached for me and kissed my cheek. I would have preferred a handshake, however painful. "I hope you have good news for me."

At first I didn't know what he meant. Surely he didn't think I'd sell him the farm after all this. Then I remembered his marriage proposal.

"I'm still considering."

He smiled, satisfied with my answer. "Juan José explained everything?"

Jaime wore his usual outfit of jeans and cowboy boots. He took his .45

Magnum out of the holster and laid it on the desk in front of him before he sat down.

"Yes, I think so, but what about your development project?"

"Pancho Bocanegro offered to sell me his farm. Fortunately, it also has a small well, which can be expanded. Like *Las Marías*, the land lends itself to development. Perhaps it will be a blessing in the end.

"I'm going all out for you, Vero. I let the DEA agent know you're coming to my house. Chico and Montaña expect you to be there. You never know, they might call and want to talk to you. The three of us are driving to the coast first. I have the money stashed in a bank in Ciudad Pedro de Alvarado."

I must have had a questioning look on my face, because he added, "It was easier to keep it there. An arrangement with the bank manager. Traveling with large amounts of cash isn't a great idea."

"What time should I be at your house?"

"Eleven o'clock tomorrow morning. Jake from the DEA plans to arrive at ten through the back entrance. He's going to put microphones on me and give me instructions. He's coming with military reinforcements. Chico and Montaña won't go quietly." He explained the timing and I listened, amazed at the plan they had worked out.

"Perhaps I was wrong about you, Jaime. I'm sorry." I stood up to leave, gave him a handshake and a smile. "Good luck."

Santiago was waiting for me on the sidewalk outside the *funeraria*. "Veronica, where were you? I called you for breakfast, but my mother said you'd gone out."

I shrugged. "I'm here now, and I'm hungry."

I followed him back to the kitchen and let him fix breakfast for me. He broke two eggs into a cast-iron skillet and turned the fire on under the black beans. I studied the family pictures on the wall. Doña Alba and don Guillermo smiled back from a portrait taken ten years ago.

"How's your father today?" I asked.

"Not good." He turned to me. "After he regained consciousness last night, he started wheezing. He's been hooked up to oxygen since then. I'm afraid another shot of painkiller would be the end of him. I called Ana. She and Oscar are on their way."

"Had I known, I would have sat up with doña Alba last night."

"I didn't want to worry you further. He's not your responsibility. You have enough on your mind. If it was up to me, he'd be in a hospital, but he wants to die at home."

"Doña Alba?"

"She's with him now. The priest is administering the last rites."

We sat quietly while I ate my breakfast. On the patio, a village girl swept up leaves. The parrot squawked, and I could hear the Jacuzzi humming in its outdoor enclosure. The priest came out with doña Alba, said something to her quietly then left. She went back into the bedroom to sit beside don Guillermo. A few minutes later, her voice broke through the silence. "*Memo, Memo. No te me vayas.*"

"Santiago! Santiago!" Alba cried urgently. "Come quickly."

He excused himself and ran to her. I took my dishes to the *pila* and rinsed them.

Even from the kitchen, I could hear doña Alba crying. "No, Memo, my love."

Santiago came back a few minutes later, his face ashen.

"What happened?"

"He's gone."

I turned and embraced Santiago. "I'm so sorry." Then I moved to don Guillermo's room. "Doña Alba?" She looked up from where she sat at the bedside still holding his hand.

"He's passed."

"I know. *Mis condolencias.*" She stood up and I put my arms around her. "He isn't suffering anymore."

The door burst open, "*Mami?*" Ana had arrived. "I told Oscar to hurry, but there was so much traffic." She looked at our faces then glanced at her father. "No!"

I reached out to her, but she pushed me aside and went to the bed. "*Papi? Papi? Ya vine.*"

"It just happened, Ana. I'm sorry." The room was heavy with death and sadness. The family needed privacy.

I went back to my room to make my phone call; now it had a second, sadder purpose. "Mom, you'd better come over."

"What happened?"

"Don Guillermo just died. Tell María Celia and have her spread the word."

"I'll be right there."

—

After the body was prepared, I helped Santiago and Ana slide him into a shiny mahogany casket. "He's at peace," I said to no one in particular.

Alba straightened his collar and lovingly brushed her hands over his face one last time. "He smoked for twenty years. I always told him he should stop."

Santiago, Oscar, and two neighbors carried the casket upstairs to a large room where wakes were often held. It was placed on wooden slats at waist level near an altar where a crucifix hung. Women began arriving with flower arrangements and wreaths.

Someone summoned the priest again to lead the mourners in prayer. He came up the steep stairs and stopped in front of the casket. "He was a good man. We'll pray for him but I know his soul will rest with God and the Virgin."

"Thank you," doña Alba said, eyes brimming with tears.

I arranged chairs for the visitors and made phone calls. I called Juan José and told him about don Guillermo. "It happened just after I got back."

"I'll be over as soon as I can."

I did what I could, then went to the kitchen to help the women prepare refreshments. Mom came in a moment later. "I can't believe he's gone."

"He was an upright man," doña Conchita said. "They are always the first to go."

Juan José came in a few minutes later with Mayor Jaime just behind him. Already dozens of townsfolk had come to pay their respects. Juan José and Jaime greeted people who were at the door, then began working their way back to us. The women in the kitchen stiffened as they saw the mayor approach. I heard whispers and voices behind me.

"Why would Juan José bring that man into this house?"

"Just because they're related doesn't make it okay for a villain to enter the home of an honorable citizen."

"He's been threatening Veronica. What nerve of him to come here."

"Not only that, but look where he comes from. He puts on airs, yet his mother was a house servant and his father a thief. What can anyone expect from someone like that?"

"I can't believe Juan José would bring that man here. He should have more respect. He's don Quique's son."

Anger filled me at their spiteful words. Even though I'd have thought the same thing only days earlier, I found myself siding with my brother and his uncle. Who were these townspeople to judge? I knew Mayor Jaime was trying to do the right thing now. What did they know?

"Juan José, Mayor Jaime," I said, moving forward to greet them. "Thank you for coming to pay your respects."

# CHAPTER TWENTY-NINE

THE STRAIGHT-BACKED WOODEN CHAIR HELPED KEEP ME AWAKE THAT night, surrounded as I was by grief, Ana on one side, Santiago on the other. A wood-framed photograph of Guillermo from earlier years was balanced on the coffin in front of us. Flowers and wreaths filled the room. Lit candles nestled among flower vases on the floor; their pooled wax dripped and hardened into colored puddles on the tiles.

Memories of don Guillermo brought tears to my eyes. My best friend's father. Our families spent a lot of time together when we were young. He was the one who called me after Dad was murdered, and comforted me during those agonizing days. He was no longer here to offer fatherly advice. I had loved him like family.

The Godoys grieved, but I couldn't help thinking that at least they had known it was coming. None of us had been prepared for the horror of my father's death. I had started crying for Guillermo, but I continued for myself. I grieved again for my father, for all the things left unsaid. The sopping tissues balled up in my pocket were witnesses.

"Vero, get some sleep," Ana said. "You've been up most of the night. Oscar and I slept some earlier." I looked at my watch. Four in the morning. My brain was so thick with exhaustion, it barely registered.

I nodded and left. I needed to be alert for Jaime's plan and had promised to be at his house by eleven.

The alarm on my cell phone woke me at half past nine. I dragged myself back upstairs to check on the wake.

Mom was there, freshly showered and smelling like soap. "Vero, how late were you up? You look like hell."

"Thanks, Mom. Your honesty overwhelms me."

She grabbed my arm and escorted me to a quiet corner. "Juan José told me about today. Shall I come with you?"

"Can you? I'd appreciate it."

"That's why I'm here. Find me when you're ready."

I took a chair in the back of the room, crossed myself, and said a quick prayer. I glanced around. María Celia was whispering to doña Conchita and doña Meches. Don Fila dozed on the other side of his wife, mouth agape, a tempting invitation to flying insects. On the far side of the room, Tio Carlos sat alone, looking downcast and ashamed. He sneaked occasional glances at María Celia, which she ignored.

The Godoys didn't have a pumped water storage tank, so I took a quick Moyuta-style shower, scooping water out of large tubs and pouring it over my body. Shivering, I wrapped myself in a towel and dressed hastily.

In the kitchen, a serving girl filled Styrofoam cups from a large percolator, another added milk and sugar, and two others took filled trays to mourners. Three women prepared tamales for later, wrapping banana leaves around the mixture of lard-treated *masa* with cooked pork inside. Two others fixed ham-and-cheese sandwiches on sliced white bread. Another woman sat at the table with a plate of food in front of her.

"*Buenos dias.* I'm just looking for coffee and a quick snack." I helped myself to a cup of coffee from the offered tray and grabbed two bananas from a large bunch on the shelf. I peeked into a basket on the table, took out a roll, slathered it with black bean paste from the stove, and went outside to eat in the garden.

Sunlight filtered through the tree branches, where birds were singing. From the other side of the yard I heard the green parrot. "*Albita, Albita,*" he cried in distress.

A blanket still covered his cage. I put down my food and freed him from the dark. He flapped his wings, settled down, looked at me with round dark eyes and greeted me, "*Qué tal, mi vida? Cómo estás?*"

"*Pepito lindo,*" I cooed back at him. I put my finger through the cage wires. Rage filled the little parrot's eyes. He hopped over, opened his beak wide, and clamped down on air, just missing my finger.

I went to look for Mom.

Mom and I followed Juan José's directions to Jaime's recently built three-story house, located in a new section of town. When we arrived, we walked through an open garage and up the steps in the back. Several Americans and a group of Guatemalans, all dressed in army fatigues, moved out of the way as we approached. The leader asked me, "Are you Veronica Villagrán?"

I identified myself.

"You're the only one allowed to pass."

"This is my mother."

He looked at her, then back at me, and decided. "Go ahead, ma'am."

We went down a hallway and into the living room. Juan José was looking out the window. He turned when we came in. "It's begun."

Despite large windows, the room was dim. It resembled a mountain lodge in Canada or Alaska with trophies hanging on the walls: Dall sheep, moose, and elk. A flattened bear hide with bared teeth and shiny eyes stared at me from in front of the stone fireplace, its cinnamon-colored fur warming the granite floor. Stuffed creatures with glassy eyes stood against a wall. A taxidermist's dream. For me, the stuff of nightmares.

"Wow, this is some living room," I said with raised eyebrows.

"He likes to hunt," Juan José explained unnecessarily.

Mom crossed the room to inspect the bookshelves which were filled with books—a set of encyclopedias, a dictionary, and a large collection of literature. I wondered if any of the books had been opened, or if they were only for show, like the high school certificate in his office.

Next to me, a balding man fiddled with a recording machine, completely absorbed in his task. Satisfied, he made the final click and the recording began. He looked up, then offered his hand. "We haven't officially met. I'm Jake, Jake Stern, with the U.S. Drug Enforcement Agency. You must be Veronica." His handshake was firm and dry.

Jaime and Juan José's plan would get rid of Chico and Montaña for good. After all, they were the ones doing the actual moving of drugs. Jaime just allowed it to happen in his territory. Left unsaid was the fact that only Jaime had the brains to mastermind the criminal activity. His motivation? The profits.

The DEA had agreed to the plan since Jaime's connection to the president made him an impossible target. In exchange for turning in Chico and Montaña and testifying against them, Jaime would be free to pursue his political career. He had signed an affidavit earlier that morning stating he would never again be involved in the illegal drug trade. The other two would be held in prison in Guatemala, later to be extradited to the United States on drug trafficking charges. The U.S. had a long arm when it came to the war on drugs. If all went as planned, they would likely spend the remainder of their days behind bars.

We heard cracks and pops from the recording machine. A car door slammed shut. Jake gestured for silence while we listened.

"Hey, *compadre*, you got everything settled?" The voice sounded distant. Jake fiddled with the dials again.

"She'll be at my house at one. My nephew's there to let her in. He finally convinced her to sell. Stubborn *gringa*."

"Very sexy stubborn *gringa*." There was a moment's hesitation. "You sure your nephew ain't playing the fence?"

"Why would you think that?"

"Rumors. I heard she didn't want to sell after all. A bunch of ladies were up at *Las Marías* cleaning. Why would they be doing that if she's planning to sell?"

"He convinced her, okay? I'm giving him a cut. The least I could do."

Silence. That must have satisfied him, I thought. Money talks.

Seat belts clicked and the engine rumbled.

"Let's pick up Montaña, and then get movin'."

"The sooner, the better. This has dragged out way too long."

Music blared from the speakers, and Mr. Stern readjusted the knobs. "Turn that down, Chico. I can't hear myself think."

"I thought you liked it loud."

"Not today."

A few minutes later the car door opened and shut. "You got ammo, Montaña?"

"Enough for a fucking army," he drawled. "*You* probably have even more."

Conversation was scarce for the next half hour. I got up, restless. So much was at stake.

Through a large window facing the Pacific Ocean I imagined I could see the three men on the road, driving to the coast to pick up the money. Jaime arranged for the Sunday pickup on the grounds that it was safer than

a weekday to move the large sum of cash. He promised the bank manager
a nice tip.

What was going through Jaime's mind? Was he having second thoughts?

When crackling and static started, I raced back to the couch, taking Mom
with me. We waited quietly, holding hands, straining to hear every word.

"Good idea doing this on Sunday, *compadre*."

"Sometimes I get inspired," Jaime said.

"Does Jorge know we're coming?"

"That's a dumb question. Give me a break. Why do you think we're
doing this today? You think we'd be able to get the money out during the
week? It's a shitload of cash."

"You nervous or something?"

"Why would I be? I got my *compadres* armed to the teeth. Anybody'd
be crazy to try and mess with us."

The interchange stopped for a while, followed by a series of hisses and
pops. With each sound, Jake fumbled with switches.

The car stopped and the music turned low. The bank manager's voice,
timid and nerdy, came in. He sounded frightened. "Hurry please. Do you
have everything?"

"Do we *look* like we're missing something, asshole? You're the one with
the keys. Lead the fuckin' way," Chico said in his distinct growl.

The car doors closed and muffled footfalls echoed through the speaker.
A few minutes later they came to a halt.

"Jesus. Finally."

"Is this them? How many suitcases are there?"

"Four. I tried to get only large denominations, but in the end I settled
for what I could get," Jorge apologized. "Your two million dollars are here."

"I thought you kept ours separate, asshole. Lemme count it," Chico's
voice said roughly. "Open the bags."

*Click, click.* Papers shuffled.

It was so quiet in Jaime's living room that I could almost hear the fish
swimming in the corner tank. We waited forty minutes as they counted the
money. I looked up at the walls. Cheap framed paintings, the kind available
in drugstore racks, hung among the trophy heads. I stood up and wandered
over to his CD collection. Ranchera music and mariachi bands dominated
the selection, Madonna and Shakira seasoned it, and Led Zeppelin capped
it. I kept looking for clues. *Who is the real Mayor Jaime?*

"Let's go," a voice said from the speaker. I hurried back to my place on the sofa.

Car doors opened and closed. The radio music began again.

"How much will we get from the next drop?" Jaime asked.

"You should know more than me, *compadre*. It's always two hundred kilos—a million bucks a shipment. Five thousand dollars a kilo, split fifty-fifty." There was a pause. "What the fuck, Jaime? It was your idea to offer two shipment's worth for the farms."

"Right. Just checking."

"You got your head stuck up your ass?" The men chuckled.

"Bet you wish it were stuck up Veronica's," Montaña drawled.

"When's the next gig, guys?"

"Why the questions? I got the guys set and ready in Las Lisas for Thursday night."

"I thought we was goin' to El Chapetón," Montaña muttered.

"See, that's why I asked. You guys are in charge of the activity. Make sure you know what you're doing."

"Is the *licenciado* ready in Moyuta with the paperwork? I don't want this legal shit to drag out," Chico said.

"He'll be waiting for us at the house with Veronica and my nephew when we arrive."

"Let me call. You can't trust lawyers."

"No need. I took care of it."

Hissing and buzzing came over the speaker. "I took care of it," Jaime repeated loudly. "What the hell's wrong with you guys?"

"This is Chico. You got the paperwork ready? ...He didn't let you know it was today? ...No, at his house." Silence reigned for a few minutes.

"What the fuck, Jaime? Why're you lying to us?" There was a moment's pause, then it occurred to him. "Oh fuck, Montaña. I was right. This is a trap."

"Wait, what are you talkin' about? I wouldn't double-cross you guys. We go way back. I talked to a different lawyer this time. Didn't trust that last one," Jaime protested.

"It's the gal, ain't it? You always did have a thing for her."

"Stop the car," Chico demanded. A minute later, he repeated. "I said, stop the fuckin' car."

"I got you covered, Chico," Montaña said. Thumping noises came over the speaker. A struggle?

Bile rose in my throat. I felt ill. Things were going terribly wrong. Mom held my hand tightly.

"Stop! You're making a mistake. Listen to me."

"We don't need to hear nothin'. The money's here anyway. We don't need you anymore."

Gunshots sounded through the speakers. I felt the bullets in my gut.

We only heard static after that. The DEA agent adjusted the knobs as if nothing had happened. Juan José's face was ashen.

My heart raced and my hands trembled as I raised them to my face to push back my hair. The static filtered out, we heard the car radio playing softly.

*It wasn't supposed to be like this.*

We heard voices again. "Push him out, Montaña. Damn it, I should have taken him outside. Now the fuckin' car's all bloody."

Rustling noises came through. "He's wired."

"Leave him. Let's get the hell out of here." The trunk opened and closed. The last words we heard were distant. "No, you idiot. Leave the car. We'll flag down another, cross the border, and be gone in no time."

Overcome with nausea, I raced to the bathroom and vomited into the bowl. Of the three deaths that had touched my life recently, I could stand Jaime's the least, because his blood was on my hands.

# EPILOGUE

*One Week Later*

"Sorry I have to leave before your party ends," Jake said as I accompanied him outside.

"I didn't expect you to come all the way from the city for my housewarming."

"I still had evidence to collect. It gave me a good excuse. To be honest, Veronica, I wouldn't have missed it for the world. Before I leave, I want you to know that we will find them. International borders don't bother us. We have extradition treaties with most countries in Latin America. These are well-known criminals. Now that they're wanted for murder, it isn't only the DEA after them; Interpol is on their trail, too. It's just a matter of time. And when we do get them, we'll make sure they're extradited for drug trafficking."

"Thanks, Jake. I appreciate your help. I'll sleep better at night when I know they are put away for life."

He nodded and strode to his white Jeep, where two burly bodyguards stood watch.

Inside the house, several dozen people mingled in the newly cleaned living room. Two uniformed serving girls offered platters of *boquitas* along with wine and beer. As I stepped back into the gathering, Aunt Antonia silenced everyone and turned to me. "Veronica, why don't you say a few words?"

The guests moved back to give me room. I cleared my throat, not really prepared for a speech. "Thank you all for coming. This has been an eventful three weeks for me. In this short time, I attended three funerals, witnessed two murders, was shot at, threatened, and betrayed. I'm starting to get the hang of being in Guatemala once again."

My guests chuckled.

"Of course, you all know I've decided to stay. I couldn't help blabbing to the whole world way ahead of time.

"What you don't know is that my boss in San Francisco has agreed to let me do contract work while I live here. I'll travel back to the Bay Area occasionally, but with reliable Internet service now in town, I should be able to do my work from the comfort of my house."

"We're delighted to have you home. It's time for a new start. And that goes for many of us," María Celia said. "With all the treachery, tragedy, and violence behind us, this celebration was in order."

She raised her wine glass in a toast. The others followed. "To Veronica. May her future be bright and her days peaceful."

"To Moyuta, may a safer future be ahead for all of us," doña Conchita said.

"To friends and relatives," I countered.

"To family," Juan José said, lifting his glass again.

Ita smiled shyly. "To our new family!" She pointed down at her middle.

"Congratulations!" Aunt Antonia hugged them both. "I'm so happy for you. I'm sorry to have been judgmental, Juan-Jo. You excel as a brother, and as a nephew."

Ita nudged her way close to Juan José. "And as a husband."

I accompanied people to their cars. I embraced family members as they got ready to leave and thanked them for coming.

"*De nada*, Vero," my cousin Mario said. "We'd love to come and visit you occasionally. We don't want our kids to forget their roots."

"All of you are welcome, both here and at the beach house."

"Vero, where's your mother?" doña Meches asked as she and don Fila headed for their car.

"She left for San Diego the day before yesterday. She had to get back to work. She said to tell everyone goodbye. I think you'll be seeing more of her now that I'm settled in."

Doña Conchita's parting words were, "Remember me in the next election."

"You can count on it," I said.

María Celia came next. "You always have a friend with me."

"I know. Likewise."

Ana and Oscar lingered. They approached as I returned to the house. "Veronica, I could hardly wait to share this with you," Ana said, then looked over at her husband. "We're so thrilled."

I tilted my head with a question on my face.

"Touch." She grabbed my hand and placed it on her swollen belly. I felt a small kick.

"Oh, Ana. He moved!"

"We want you to be his godmother."

"I'd be honored," I said. "What will you name him?"

"James."

I knew it had two distinct translations into Spanish. "Will you call him Santiago or Jaime?"

"Just James."

Santiago was the last to leave. "Vero? I've done a lot of thinking this past week." He shifted his weight and looked down. "I'm so impressed by you. You were so brave to take a stand like you did."

"I was lucky. It could have turned out differently."

"I'm glad it didn't." He put his arms around me. I was stiff at first. He tilted my chin up with his hand and I looked into his eyes. "I don't know what I would have done if something had happened to you. I didn't realize until now how much I care."

I felt myself softening. He closed his eyes and kissed me. "*Te quiero.*"

His words warmed me, but I wasn't ready to make a commitment just yet. "Let's take it one day at a time," I said. "It's been a long few weeks."

"Whatever you say. I'll be waiting for you when you're ready."

When all the guests were gone, I closed the door and went back to the living room. Yesterday's cleansing rains had washed the sky. In the distance, the surf met the sand in a thin white line. Beyond, the Pacific lapped at the Central American coast, that tiny isthmus separating two major oceans. Outside, the coffee trees were flowering; a blanket of white blossoms covered the fields, and in the breeze their blossoms moved like butterflies, beautiful and fleeting. The intoxicating perfume of the coffee flowers filled the house. I was home.

# ACKNOWLEDGMENTS

This story is a quilt of happenings and events pulled from the lives of many people in Guatemala, patched and sewn together as the life of Veronica. Nearly every event recorded happened to someone here, and many of the characters are fictionalized versions of flesh and blood. I have so many Guatemalans to thank for sharing themselves and their stories with me. Some will recognize their story and others might not.

From a technical point of view, many people helped with *The Coffee Diary*. I often say it takes a whole village of people to write a novel. Many thanks to my mother, Ann Gates, for encouraging me and helping all through the editing process; we learned the art of writing together. I'd like to thank my book club here in Guatemala who didn't say anything negative, even after reading my awful first draft. Special thanks to Kate Dunnigan-Atlee who pointed out where improvements were needed. Many thanks to my uncle, Phelps Gates, who also read this story in its initial draft and only gave me encouragement.

I'd also like to thank Julio Martinez, Mitsubishi Corporation's Central American import/export coffee representative, who faithfully sent me the Coffee Diaries every year, which were also part of this book's inspiration.

I had many reviewers in thenextbigwriter.com workshop who coaxed me along and pointed out blatant flaws: Marc Delalangue, Sharon Thatcher, R.A. Keenan, Alan Sugano, Archie Hooton, Charles Dumond, John DeBoer, J.L. Campell, James Knight, Ann Elle Altman, Tom Endyke,

Patti Anne Yaeger, Chris Delyani, Lisa Leibow, Ben Duiverman, Rudy Termini, Tina D.C. Hayes, Zack Rodriguez, and John Malone to name a few.

I can't forget Rosemary James and everyone at the Faulkner Society in New Orleans. If this story hadn't been selected as a finalist for novel-in-progress, it would have been much more difficult to find a publisher.

Thanks to everyone at MacAdam/Cage Publishing: Pat Walsh for initial interest in the manuscript, Dorothy Carico Smith for picking it up and reading it, not to mention her great artwork, Michelle Dotter for great editing and, of course, David Poindexter for making it happen. Many thanks to my agent, Deborah Grosvenor, for her infinite patience and support of me during this long process.

Most of all I'd like to thank my family who stuck by me when I was completely absorbed in this project: my two daughters, Andrea and Caroline, who continue to inspire me and were themselves the inspiration for Veronica's character; my husband, Eduardo Godoy, who can probably see himself reflected in parts of Quique's character and, amazingly enough, still loves me.